VIVID

a novel

JANA JONES

Cover Design: Lance Buckley

Identifiers:
ISBN (hardcover) 9781736688410
ISBN (paperback) 9781736688403
ISBN (e-Pub) 9781736688427

Library of Congress Control Number: 2021903182

"We are each other's harvest;
we are each other's business;
we are each other's magnitude and bond."

- Gwendolyn Brooks

CHAPTER 1

2016

Sheri Calloway pulled her faded terry cloth bathrobe tighter as she wearily eyed the late-summer darkening skies. An ominous mass of storm clouds formed over the pleasant three-bedroom rambler the Calloway family had called home for nearly twenty years. There was a weather warning for Greenville and the surrounding areas as Hurricane Donovan made its way up the eastern seaboard. But Sheri had smelled the rain long before the National Weather Service started sending out those annoying emergency broadcast shrieks which always got her Pekingese, Lady, worked up so badly.

She took a deep breath and massaged her temples, the red light on her phone steadily blinking in her peripheral vision. She hadn't checked her voicemail, but the Caller ID let her know Yolanda was the one who had called. The two good girlfriends had stayed in touch after Sheri returned home to North Carolina. Sheri could only imagine what new news Yolanda had managed to come across.

Her gaze bounced back and forth between the encroaching storm clouds and the persistent blinking coming from her telephone.

Sheri had already worked a ten-hour shift the previous day at RightMart, and she wasn't expected in until six that evening. As assistant manager, Sheri's workdays weren't nearly as strenuous as they used to be back when RightMart was Ambrose and Sons. When the RightMart people had come around, Lester Ambrose decided to close both of his stores and make his way down to Florida with a suitcase full of big bills, leaving Pitt County in his dust.

The smell of honeysuckle wrapped itself around Sheri's nostrils as she continued to watch the sky. It always seemed that the smells of nature got stronger as storms approached. Roses, gardenias, paperwhites, lilacs—all vying for dominance. The honeysuckle bushes had always been Peach's favorite. The little girl would snip the tip off the flower with surgical precision, pulling out the stem and enjoying the sweet nectar. Between those and the blackberry bushes, Sheri had regularly found herself pleading with her daughter to come inside to eat her real dinner.

"I need to call Yo back," Sheri mumbled to herself as she reached over to press the pound sign to start her voicemail.

"SHER, YOU NEED TO ANSWER THIS PHONE! Girl, I've got some major news!" Yolanda Johnson's voice shot out like a cannonball blast. "Sher, this lady's been trying to contact everybody from the Parent Crew. Our story is getting some new attention because of what's going on up there in Flint. It's a damn shame what's happening to those people! Anyway, I think it's going to be a real article, too. Not one of those fluff 'We really didn't mean any harm' pieces the paper likes to run from time to time about Sloane-Douglas."

Sheri was well aware of the articles that had come out over the years. Especially after the settlement. Glowing accounts of community service work done throughout the city as well as weak, vaguely worded mea culpas for negligent research practices.

Yolanda's voicemail message continued: "The lady's name is Alicia Allen. She's a reporter for an 'online investigative journal'—her words, not mine. Anyway, CALL ME! Remind me to tell you what Tater told me the other day. Call me!"

The force of Yolanda's voice made Lady yelp.

"Oh, be quiet, you know her voice. You hungry?" Sheri looked over at the dog as if waiting for a response. Lady was getting up there in years, and Sheri didn't know how much longer the girl had left; she was thankful for her company.

Besides the usual check-ins from family, Sheri didn't remember any other calls coming in. She reached into her drawer to pull out her reading glasses. Now with clearer vision, she pulled the phone closer for a more thorough inspection of her Caller ID. Champ. Popsee. Skeeter. Champ. Gloria. Popsee. Popsee. Sheri read off the names under her breath.

After one more push of the back-arrow button, a new name and number flashed across the screen: Baltimore City Monitor. The call had come about a week ago. Sheri took a deep breath as she found the voicemail.

A poised young voice spoke back to her. "Yes, hello, my name is Alicia Allen and I'm with the Baltimore City Monitor. I'm trying to reach Ms. Sheri Calloway. I'm working on a piece about the families involved in the CEC/Sloane-Douglas lawsuit. We have noticed a renewed interest in the case, which we attribute to the water crisis currently taking place in Flint, Michigan. I can be reached—" Sheri stopped the replay.

"Shit."

In the corner of the room, Lady barked.

Sheri got up with a slap of her thigh. "Hungry?" She made her way to the kitchen to refresh Lady's water bowl and food dish.

Walking through her home, the faces of Sheri's children smiled back at her. School pictures, pictures with Santa, pictures with the Easter Bunny, pictures from family reunions, prom photos. Champ, Popsee and Peach had to be the most photographed children east of the Mississippi, Sheri used to laugh to herself. She would have it no other way.

Sheri's mother and grandmother hated having their pictures taken, so images of the two of them were precious to Sheri because of their rarity. Titi's aversion to picture-taking was why there weren't many photos of Sheri growing up. A tattered school picture here, a faded Polaroid from a family barbeque there, but nothing more than that. Almost as if Sheri had jumped over childhood altogether.

"You need some food in your belly, Miss Ma'am." Sheri reached down to lightly scratch Lady, who had managed to curl around her left ankle. "Do you want your food, or do you want the leftovers Champ brought over yesterday?"

Sheri's eldest son, Kareem, known in the family as Champ, was the manager at the high-end steakhouse over by the convention center, Porter 42. Sheri was so proud of her boy. From a young age, Champ had always been a focused leader. The boy took himself seriously and expected others to do so as well. It was as if the creator had given him an innate sense of direction and purpose.

Undeterred by the learning challenges he'd faced in grade school, Champ had worked his way through college and graduated last May from Eastern Carolina. Weather permitting, he had an interview at the medical center later in the week with their tech support department. Sheri had made sure to light a candle for him, and she'd told Cousin Eunice to add his name to the prayer list First Emmanuel emailed to the saints every week.

Sheri cut a tiny piece of strip steak for Lady and placed it next to her silver food bowl, which she filled with Kibbles 'n Bits. She picked up the second silver bowl and ran it under the tap to fill it with water.

"You should be okay for a little bit." Sheri watched Lady begin her morning feast.

With Lady taken care of, Sheri went over to her kitchen phone to return some calls. Popsee, her middle child and youngest son, was the first up. While Champ was the sober leader, Popsee was part enforcer and part charismatic showman. It hadn't surprised Sheri that Popsee was the child who had made her a grandmother. Despite having a place of his own, Popsee usually split his time between Sheri's house and his girlfriend, Lenida's, townhouse a few miles further into town.

Sheri heard two rings before music came crashing into her eardrum.

"Pop! Pop, please turn that mess down!"

A mock British accent came over the line, "Well, good day to you, too, dear mother."

Sheri could hear him smirking over the phone. Keyon "Popsee" Calloway was every bit of his father.

"Glad to hear you're finally calling folks back. Acting like you don't want to talk to people. Looks like the storm is coming; you gonna be okay over there?" Popsee asked.

"You know me, I'm hanging in there. Supposed to be working later this evening, then I'm off the next two days. Where's Kayla and KJ?"

Although he and Lenida were both known to become oddly skittish at the mention of marriage, Popsee had been an active presence in his children's lives since day one. Kayla and Keyon Jr. rarely went without. Both of Lenida's parents were ministers, so her getting pregnant not once but twice outside of marriage rattled the church folks something serious. Sheri tried not to pass judgment on how the young couple lived their lives. She made it clear that, as parents, their priority should always be the well-being of the children.

"KJ and Kayla are with Lenida's family right now. They're over in Farmville for a family reunion."

"You didn't want to go?"

"No, Mama, you know they don't like me."

"Lenida went with them?"

"Yeah." There was a tinge of embarrassment in Popsee's voice. "She's been calling me, though. Both of us are watching this storm, trying to see how the weather is gonna go. They're supposed to be back tonight."

Sheri wanted to talk a little longer but could tell Popsee had other matters to attend to. "Well, I'm not going to keep you longer than necessary. Take care of yourself and call me if you need me."

"Aight, Ma. Love you."

Sheri let out a slow sigh and shook her head. Lady, napping in her doggie bed, made satisfied gurgling sounds.

"Don't pee in that bed, girl. Let me know if I need to walk you." Sheri shifted her weight in the chair as she dialed Yolanda's number.

"Aye girl, you call that reporter yet?" Yolanda cut right to the chase.

Despite the terrible circumstances that had brought them together, Sheri was glad for Yolanda's friendship. She was good people, through and through. A genuine woman who loved her children and wanted the best for them.

9

Sheri shifted in her chair and rubbed her knee. "Was going to call her after I talked to you. What did she want exactly? What did she say to you?"

"She's doing some type of investigative article about our lives and what happened to us. Interest seems to be picking up again because of all of that madness happening in Flint. I've been calling everyone from the crew, tryin' to give 'em a heads-up."

"To be honest, Yo, I haven't talked to too many people about that part of my life, other than you and some family. People need to know what happened to us, but reliving it just gets me frustrated all over again. I get furious just thinking about it all."

"Sis, who you tellin'? If there's a hell below, they're all gonna have first-class tickets. Every single one." Yolanda let out a low, bitter laugh. "They stole from our babies, Sher. We can't let these folks forget."

"Girl, didn't you say Tater said something? What's he up to?" Sheri asked with extra enthusiasm, trying to shift the conversation.

"That boy made Employee of the Month!" Yolanda boasted triumphantly. "He told me—get this—he told me, 'Mom, in a few months, I'm going to own this place!' Sher, he set me straight!" Yolanda let out a loud cackle, and Sheri knew her friend was doubled over with laughter.

Charles Lamont Johnson, affectionately known by everyone as Tater, was Yolanda's pride and joy. One would think he was her only child, but he was the third of Yolanda's four children. Yolanda's knee baby. His was a very difficult birth; Yolanda often recounted how she had been in a bad place during much of her pregnancy with him.

"Chile, I was sad the whole damn time," she'd say.

Despite protests to the contrary, there would always be a still, small voice within the hard-working mother that told her it was all her fault. Everything. All of it. She had dropped the ball. It was a common sentiment among all the parents. Quiet guilt mercilessly gnawed at them. Their penalty for trying to do right and having everything implode in their faces.

"And I believe him," Sheri replied with a nod. "Charles 'Tater' Johnson Enterprises coming right up!"

"Sis, so how the babies doing?" Yolanda asked.

"We're maintaining down here. Champ's got a big interview coming up, so pray for him. Popsee's doing his thing. I told you he's an electrician, so all the construction around here is keeping him pretty busy. Peach is fine. She's in a good head space right now. She's bettering herself." Sheri ran down the updates of her brood.

"Miss Maya Peach Calloway, the grand diva herself!" The smile on Yolanda's face was evident over the phone line. "With them pretty dimples. Tell everyone I said Auntie Yo loves them."

"I will, girl. I love you. We've got to 'Stay Up,' like the young folks say." Sheri smiled.

"Sheri?"

"Yeah?"

"Call her."

"I will, Yo. I promise I will."

Sheri hung up the phone and stared out the kitchen window that faced the backyard. Talking with Yolanda always took Sheri on a trip back through time, whether Sheri wanted to go or not. Sheri tried to remember only in doses now. She remembered what she needed to remember. Her children served as living reminders of the lies, the deceit, the cruelty. How their futures had been handled with casual disregard. In the eyes of the powerful, they did not matter.

They stole from our babies, Sher.

Sheri got up to make a cup of tea. Champ and Peach had bought her a cute tea kettle for Christmas some years back. It was lemon yellow, the same color as her kitchen. She recalled how her cousins Gloria and Skeeter used to always joke about her tea habit. "Where the hell you get that from?" Skeeter would ask every time she saw Sheri make a cup. "Bet never made us no hot tea."

Sheri took her fresh cup of black tea and stood in the living room, scanning the space as if it hadn't been her living room for fifteen years. Lady had fallen asleep, which left Sheri alone with her thoughts. She looked up at the pictures, taking in every beaming smile, furrowed brow and missing tooth.

They stole from our babies, Sher.

Sheri turned and made her way back to the kitchen table. She thumbed over the Caller ID one last time.

"Hello? Baltimore City Monitor, Alicia speaking," a measured, relatively pleasant voice answered.

"Hello, this is Sheri Calloway. I'm returning your call. You wanted to speak to me."

"Ms. Calloway! Yes, thank you. Thank you for returning my call," Alicia replied. "Ms. Calloway, if you have time, I would really like to interview you. I've already spoken with Ms. Johnson, Mr. Gamble and Ms. Neal. I'm working on a piece about the families involved in the lawsuit against the New Horizons housing program. Are you available for a quick interview?"

"Sure, I'll speak."

"Thank you so much. I sincerely appreciate this," Alicia sighed with relief. "I've read all of the articles that ran in the Baltimore Sentinel. I know how much you and the other parents fought. Can you give me your backstory? I have in my notes that you're from North Carolina. What led you to bring your family to Baltimore during that time?"

They stole from our babies, Sher.

"I had dreams. Dreams for myself and even bigger dreams for my children," Sheri said softly. "I guess I just had the belief that if you try to do right, the road will open for you."

"Just so you're aware, Ms. Calloway, you can remain anonymous if you—"

"Absolutely not. No, I want everyone to know that we are still here."

"Yes, ma'am."

With that being made clear, Sheri leaned in her chair, took a sip from her cup, and transported.

CHAPTER 2

1992

"Champ, we're going to need to move on to a quieter activity in a few." Sheri whispered her words, but her eyes let her eldest son know that it was time to wind down.

"But Mommy, you said it's good for me to keep learning my words," the little boy countered, still looking down at the screen of his Talking Whiz Kid toy laptop with his younger brother.

This boy is going to have my hair pure white before it was all over. How did he get to be so sharp, so fast? Sheri wondered in amazement.

Sheri had always been a good student, but she never counted herself for much. But this one, this oldest boy of hers? He absolutely fascinated her. He was her little genius. Six years old and smart as a tack. His teacher, Ms. Collins, said Champ was able to spell second grade-level sight words.

"It's not just us on this train, Kareem," Sheri reminded her son. "You know I love that you want to learn, but we can't forget our manners."

The young boy sat up in his seat, stretched his neck as far as it could go, and did a quick scan to survey the Amtrak train car bound for Baltimore. While he saw a few people, the boy noticed that it was mostly empty seats. He gave his mother a slightly quizzical glance. "Ten more minutes?"

"Fifteen!" Popsee yelled out, the middle and index fingers of his right hand still stuffed in his mouth.

"Twelve," Sheri countered. "Twelve minutes, and then we can move on to coloring."

"Coloring is for girls." Popsee gave the suggestion a quick dismissal.

"Coloring is for everyone! You love to color. When did you stop liking to color?" Sheri was genuinely shocked. She thought she had a little more time before Popsee reached the stage where boys did one thing and girls did another. With him, every day came with a new surprise, and she was tired already.

"Shhhh!" Champ furrowed his brows at his little brother. "Manners."

Sheri looked down at Peach resting contentedly in her lap, totally oblivious to her brothers' negotiating. She kissed the baby girl atop a head covered in thick, chestnut-brown curls.

"Peach Cheeks always sleep," Popsee observed, two fingers still hanging from his mouth. While Popsee was a finger sucker, Peach was faithful to her trusty thumb for self-soothing needs. Champ had skipped that stage altogether.

Sheri wondered. She looked across the boys and out the window as the sun began to set on the horizon. She wondered what type of new world she was bringing her babies into. She had prayed about this move for months.

Back home, there had been whispers for years. Then the lay-offs came, then the firings with no due process. When it was all said and done, what had originally been a hundred employees was down to a crew of about twenty. The day they finally closed the Robinson Brothers Furniture Factory felt like the end of a winding, anxiety-filled carnival ride, and Sheri had been there through every twist and turn.

When the strange men with the cold, empty eyes came around the factory wearing sharp suits and hard hats, Mr. Jonathan warned everyone to tighten up, both in their work performance and in their personal spending. He suspected things were about to get messy. In his nearly forty years at the factory, Mr. Jonathan had seen it all, and he knew when a takeover was brewing. In times past, when other larger companies bought the factory, the workers had been allowed to stay. Generally, the supervisors changed but, thankfully, not much else.

These men were different. Everyone suspected that they weren't Carolina men—or even Southern men. There was no trace of familiarity, something the workers could identify with. One could only imagine what the new iteration of Robinson Brothers would look like.

Sheri stayed close to the elders at the factory and followed their lead. It helped her as the waves of lay-offs and firings came. If worst came to worst, she could always work at Buddy's Diner with her cousins Eunice and Pauline. Sheri also had the option of working at the Sea Star plant, where so many of her relatives worked. But Robinson Brothers felt like home. She enjoyed the company of her work family, many of whom had been her coworkers since she was in high school.

Every now and again, Sheri would make quick trips upstairs to the factory's assistant foreman's office.

"Calloway, I can only tell you what I know," was Mr. Simms's standard response, although, as time went on, his tone got softer, almost apologetic.

Last Christmas, Mr. Simms and two of his nephews came over to Titi's house wearing Santa hats and bearing gifts. Champ's toy laptop and Sheri's Walkman came from that holiday haul, which also included an assortment of books and other gadgets. Sheri suspected Mr. Simms had known what was coming back at the factory but likely was only able to say so much. When closing day finally arrived in April, the air was somber and resigned. The workers exchanged hugs and shared beers in the parking lot.

Sheri had never intended to work at Robinson Brothers for as long as she did. It was supposed to have been her steppingstone to college. The plan had been to save up money and go to school, someplace far from Sheri's hometown of Spruce Junction. Sheri had dreams of majoring in business management. She typed pretty well and her teachers always told her she had a way with words. Sheri figured she would be right at home in an office.

Though her life had not gone as planned, Sheri was determined that her three would have a clear path to school, scholarships and all. They wouldn't have to deal with their lives being redirected and having to start over again. "Write your own ticket," Sheri would frequently reiterate to her brood. "Once it's in your brain, no one can snatch it from you."

Sheri adjusted Peach on her lap and checked to see if she was wet. The two-year-old was just coming around with getting comfortable going to the potty, but since this was a long trip, Sheri had put a diaper on her to be on the safe side. She reached up to smooth the edges of her copper-colored hair, currently wrapped up and secure under a faded pink-and-yellow scarf. She wanted a fresh start, and what better way to show a reset than with a new look?

The train ride seemed endless. The family had been traveling since three that morning, when Uncle Syl drove them to Raleigh to catch the train. He must have asked about thirty times when Sheri and the children were coming back. "We already don't see Glo and Skeet as it is now," the man lamented. "We losing y'all, too?"

Sheri's eyelids were beginning to grow heavy with the weight of the day when she looked out to see a sign with 'Welcome to Baltimore – The City That Reads' in bold black-and-gold lettering quickly flash past the window. A smile tugged along the sides of her mouth. The Calloways had arrived.

Sheri had been on the phone with Gloria for much of the previous day, so she knew her cousin would be at work when the train came. That meant Jimmy Budd and Skeeter would be the ones to pick them up from the station. Sheri checked her watch and saw that they had arrived on the dot. She took it as a good omen. Things were already working out.

"We here." Sheri nudged her boys awake. "Y'all, we here. Wake up. We here. Champ! Popsee! Boys, we here, get up now."

Sheri nuzzled Peach's neck to wake her up. Champ was the first to let out an annoyed whimper while wiping his eyes. Popsee opened his eyes but quickly closed them. Sheri reached between the boys to get Champ's computer and stuffed it in her duffle bag. "C'mon, we here."

Other passengers had started stirring, and she wanted to make sure the kids were alert. It was time to move. Peach let out a big yawn and looked out the window. "Mom-Mom?" the little girl called out for her grandmother as she turned to watch the passengers begin to get up from their seats.

Sheri shook her head. "No, baby. Mom-Mom is back home, Peach. She's in Spruce Junction. We're in Baltimore now. This is our new place. We're here with Cousin Gloria and Cousin Skeeter and Mister Jimmy. Can you say it? Gloria. Skeeter. Jimmy."

Peach gave her mother a look of determination as she formed her mouth to get the words out properly. "Ora. Keeta. Yimmy."

"You got it, girl! That's good." Sheri smiled. My baby is so smart. "That's real good." She gave Peach a tight squeeze and covered the baby's face in kisses.

Now fully awake, Champ shot up in his seat to watch the passengers file out onto the platform. "Where they at? They here to get us? Can they see us?"

"We've got to get inside the train station first, son. We're still on the train." Sheri laughed. "Look around." She clapped her hands. "Make sure you have everything. Once we get up, we're out of here."

Champ and Popsee checked under their seat and in the corners. All clear. Champ and Popsee put their bookbags on their backs, and the family made their way out of their seats and down the aisle to exit the train. They huddled together on the escalator as the mechanical stairs pushed them further up toward the station's main waiting area. The bright overhead lights were the first thing that hit their eyes. Sheri tried her best to keep the children from sensing her sudden feeling of disorientation.

"Alright, y'all, we're going to take a seat near these doors, okay?" Sheri sounded like a tour guide.

Champ, Popsee and Peach, who had since gotten down and decided to walk a bit, huddled around their mother and moved with her to the tall, cherrywood benches.

"Peach, I know you need to be changed," Sheri noted, more to herself than her daughter. She checked the bottom of the baby's pants. Still dry. Plus, she wasn't crying, which meant she wasn't uncomfortable. Things were still working out.

"Ma, I'm hoooongry." Champ let out an uncharacteristic wail.

"Me too!" Popsee seconded.

"Can we eat something? When can we eat?" Champ continued, his face covered in sleepy frustration.

Sheri ruffled through her duffle bag to see if there were any more snacks. "Alright, we're in business. Here ya go." She stuffed

17

a pack of cheese crackers in each of the boys' hands, first taking a cracker out of Popsee's pack to give to Peach. The little boy looked up at his mother.

"I'll pay you back," Sheri said with a quick wink. Popsee looked back down without a word and enjoyed his treat in silence.

As the children were eating their snacks, Sheri looked through her bag for her camera. Now was as good a time as any to take some pictures to commemorate the moment. The Calloways were officially in their new city, and Sheri needed to keep her hands busy to fight off the nervousness and the doubts that were slowly starting to creep in.

God, is this the right move? Am I doing this right? Should I have stayed? What about my children? Is this a good place for them? I want them to have opportunities. I hope this is right.

"I need a damn Newport," Sheri muttered under her breath while smoothing down her already smooth hair. The cravings would still come from time to time, even though she had quit after she'd found out she was pregnant with Peach.

"Peanut?"

Sheri turned her head to get a good look at the woman standing at the end of the bench. She had one hand on her hip and was wearing a red polo shirt, khaki slacks and a pair of tan Sebagos. A straw fedora with a red band covered the woman's liquid black curls.

"Peanut!"

"Skeeter?" Sheri hesitated, then slowly stood up to take her cousin in. It had been a little over six years since the pair had seen each other.

"You did it again, huh? Just went on and chopped it clean, huh?" Sheri's face was covered in disbelief. "Well, it looks nice. Looks good on you. Oh, chile, this is too much."

"Who's Peanut?" Popsee was intrigued. "Ma, you Peanut?"

"I'm Mama to you," Sheri responded as she walked over to give Skeeter a big hug.

"Girl, it's just hair," Skeeter laughed as she shook her head, embracing Sheri in a deep bear hug. "Nothing but dead skin cells. Life goes on. These the babies! Hey there!" Skeeter greeted all three children with a booming voice that didn't seem to fit with her petite frame. "I'm your Cousin Skeeter. Y'all have a good trip? I'm glad to see you."

"Now say hi to your cousin." Sheri swatted at the children. "Open your mouths. None of y'all are shy. Come on now."

The three siblings mumbled "hi" in unison while cracker crumbs covered their mouths.

"It's been a long day, girl. We're hungry, and we all could use a good soak." Sheri looked over at Skeeter apologetically.

Beaming smile still in place, Skeeter laughed and clasped her hands together. "We gotta pick up the luggage, right? Jimmy's out in front in the car. How much stuff y'all got? Do I need to go get him?"

Sheri assured her cousin that they didn't bring too much from home and, between the five of them in the station, there would be enough hands. After getting the luggage, four gently used blue suitcases which came courtesy of Great Aunt Helen, the family walked out into the mild, late-spring evening.

"Where he go that quick?" Skeeter grumbled under her breath, carrying two suitcases and scanning the area for Jimmy and his car.

They walked further up past the main entrance and rounded the corner onto St. Paul Street, where Jimmy sat parked on the opposite side of the street. Skeeter let out a shrill whistle, and Jimmy's face shot up from the newspaper he was reading. After doing a quick check for oncoming traffic, Jimmy steered his green '79 Monte Carlo from one side of St. Paul to the other. Thankfully the traffic was light, so Jimmy had time to park the car and get situated.

"I thought you was going to try to stay in front?" Skeeter asked, slightly annoyed.

"The station people told me I had to move. They said the front is for taxis only." Jimmy hustled out of the car and began gathering the suitcases. "I ain't want no hassle. Nobody on these streets too heavy right now anyway, so we okay."

"Y'all, this is Mister Jimmy Budd!" Sheri smiled as she handed over her suitcase to Jimmy then greeted the man with a one-armed hug. As they had done with Skeeter, the three mumbled hello, but in this case, Popsee at least managed a half-hearted wave. Jimmy smiled, showing off his wide-gapped teeth, just one of the many features about him that drove Gloria wild.

"Anybody hungry?" Jimmy asked as he closed the trunk.

"Yes!" the trio cried out. It was quite possibly the loudest Sheri had ever heard her children. Peach's "yes" nearly blew out Sheri's left eardrum.

"Good, cuz I'm hungry too. How 'bout we do Wendy's? Everybody jump in." The group piled into the sturdy vehicle and Jimmy drove off.

Jimmy, Skeeter and Sheri made small talk on the drive to Wendy's and then later on the drive back to the house. Every so often, Sheri would shake her head in amazement at Skeeter's short coif. Skeeter's behind-length braid had been the talk of Spruce Junction for as long as Sheri could remember. The same Skeeter who had received the worst whupping Sheri had ever witnessed the day Grandma Bet took an extension cord to the back of her legs after Skeeter hacked her braid off using Uncle Syl's garden shears. The memory still rattled Sheri, even though now she suspected that the reason behind the beating went far deeper than some cut hair.

Skeeter turned around to face the children. "What y'all say we have a fun day this weekend? We can go to the movies." She turned to Sheri. "Y'all do movies? You know Punchy and his family don't believe in movies anymore. They got saved, so I've heard." Skeeter gave her cousin an inquisitive glance.

"We do movies, but you don't have to do all that, Skeeter. They a handful and—"

"Which is why you're coming with me," Skeeter interrupted her cousin with a big, toothy smile.

"Who car you takin'?" Jimmy narrowed his eyes.

"C'mon now, Jimmy, you already know the answer to that question." Skeeter flashed a full-toothed, dimpled smile in Jimmy's direction.

"Better fill up my damn tank," he muttered, eyes still on the road.

"Alright then, it's settled! A family fun day set for this weekend." Skeeter pumped her fist at no one in particular and turned back to face the front.

The car pulled onto East Preston Street and finally stopped in front of a neat, red-brick rowhome with marble steps. Gloria's place. Sheri remembered the day everyone down in Spruce Junction found out Gloria had been willed a house by her late father. It was the talk of the town for months. It seemed as if everyone was whispering, including some family. Jealousy was all it was, Sheri reasoned. Sheri had been so happy for her cousin when she found out. At least someone was getting a break.

Bet and some of the family turned their noses up about the news of Gloria's acquisition. Gloria's daddy was a Shaw, and everyone in town knew those Shaws were stuck-up and sneaky. Bet used to declare this as if it were an actual fact written in the Bible. Of course, none of this was ever said directly to Gloria, but she could sense the displeasure and resentment that surrounded her.

Everyone filed out of the car and made their way to the front door. Jimmy handled the luggage while Sheri and Skeeter herded the groggy children inside. Skeeter took the family upstairs to show them their new living space while Jimmy grabbed a quick smoke outside. With a flick of a switch, an extremely bright fluorescent light illuminated the bedroom. The children groaned and covered their eyes. Sherri nodded her head; she liked what she saw. The room had wood floors, a high ceiling, and a window that faced a park. This is good. A perfect place to make a fresh start.

The children had already huddled onto one of the twin beds and tangled themselves up into one large sleeping knot.

"Got something for you." Sheri flashed a mischievous smile at her cousin. She reached into her duffle bag, pulled out a small stack of Polaroids covered in a napkin, and handed them to her cousin.

Skeeter gently unwrapped the napkin as if she were handling the most precious of jewels. Her face went warm and soft as she smiled down at the photos of a little boy around the same age as Champ.

"He's getting big," Skeeter whispered as she smiled proudly at the Polaroids.

"Ooh, Skeet, he's so tall now and he's oh so smart. You know they got him taking piano lessons? He's so bright, cousin. You should be proud. You already know he's in great hands."

"Thank you, Peanut. This means a lot to me." Skeeter took a deep breath. "You didn't have to do this."

Sheri grabbed Skeeter's free hand and held it tightly. The cousins exchanged knowing smiles.

"I'm happy you're here, Sheri." Tears had started to form in the wells of Skeeter's dark, almond-shaped eyes.

"I'm glad to be here. We needed a new start."

As the night began to fall over the city, Sheri and her babies were now clean, fed and ready to spend their first full night in their new space. Sheri was used to the sounds of nature putting her to sleep, and although Gloria lived across the street from a park, she knew it likely wouldn't be the same. Sheri saw it as a minor adjustment that she would just have to get used to.

"Mom?" Champ's voice broke the silence in the room. "Is Cousin Skeeter a man?"

"Your cousin is a woman." Sheri turned and looked over at the second twin bed where Champ and Popsee were lying. "All girls don't look the same. Everybody got different looks. Doesn't change anything. Your Cousin Skeeter is your Cousin Patrick's mama."

This new bit of information made Champ's ears perk up. "I thought Aunt Ja—"

"Champ, baby. Please, no more questions," Sheri sighed. "It's bedtime."

"But why does—"

"No more questions."

Silence fell over the room as the Calloways' first day in their new city came to a close.

CHAPTER 3

The smell of bacon and fried eggs wafted through the halls and up the stairs of Gloria's rowhome, teasing and enticing noses and taste buds in the process. Gloria Shaw stood in the kitchen wearing a worn, yellow nightgown that gently hugged the ample curves of her six-foot frame. Even in house clothes, Gloria's magnetism couldn't be denied. Whenever Gloria came around, time stopped. Gloria knew the effect she had on people, but she had always been rather casual about her allure. The woman got it honest, courtesy of her mother, Juniper. It was the same cool, seductive pull that had drawn Gregory Shaw into Juniper Jeter's orbit all those years ago down in Spruce Junction.

Bet had warned her daughter to stay away from those Shaws. In Bet's eyes, the Shaws were a family of stuck-up Negroes who weren't worth their weight in cow dung. They looked down on the ones who put in an honest day's work out in the sun tending to land, which made them useless in Bet's eyes. It was a sentiment she had carried since she was a young girl.

"But he keeps following me, Mama," an overwhelmed Juniper would say.

Juniper knew Gregory in passing, but she mostly spent time with his younger sister, Arlene. All of the Shaws were good-looking people. Big and sturdy folks with glowing, honey-brown skin and striking bone structure. Juniper had been happy when Arlene told her she was leaving for school. Bennett College, she said. Arlene's plan was to become a teacher just like her mother and her grandmother before her. Juniper always enjoyed it when Arlene talked about her plans for the future. All Juniper had was a job at Sea Star. She refused to complain, though. It was good work, and it beat picking tobacco.

It was at Arlene's goodbye party where Gregory was able to get a good, long look at his little sister's friend. She radiated sensuality, but her meek, downcast smiles let him know she hadn't stepped into her full power yet. She had skin the color of deep mahogany, and the yellow dress she wore gave her the look of a sunflower in full bloom. Juniper's signature look, the final touch, was the white dogwood petals she would place in her halo of dark hair that she usually wore in a neat bun or two French braids. It wasn't extravagant, but it always seemed to set the men in town afire something serious, and Gregory Shaw was no exception.

Despite the fact that she was much younger than him, he wanted her. Despite the fact that he lived in Baltimore with his lawfully and faithfully wedded wife, he wanted her. Despite the fact that he claimed membership at two churches, one in Wilson and one in Baltimore, he wanted her. Gregory Shaw was used to getting what he wanted, and Juniper Jeter would be no different.

Every time Gregory was back in Spruce Junction, he would bring gifts for Bet and make small talk with Juniper's father, Franklin. He came around Buddy's Diner, where he knew she could often be found laughing and gossiping with her cousins. He would drive over to the Sea Star plant on the days she worked.

Juniper noticed Arlene's brother sniffing around her, but she didn't know what to do. This was a full-grown man pursuing her, and she wasn't used to attention like this. Bet would stay in Juniper's ear, telling her the men in town were always watching her, but Juniper had never noticed their stares. Eventually, however, the young woman grew to like the attention, so she allowed Gregory to continue his chase.

Gregory brought her fresh blossoms for her hair and jewelry that accentuated her long neck and glowing skin. He brought her fudge candies and took her on drives out in the country, where they would fish and pick blackberries. Their favorite place to talk was down by Sharps Creek, where they would have conversations about everything and nothing at all as they sat under the willow trees. It would be under one of those willow trees at Sharps Creek where Gloria was conceived.

Juniper hid her growing belly for as long as she could. During one of his trips down from Baltimore, she finally told Gregory. He stood there, tall and quiet, then nodded his head slightly in acceptance. Juniper's mother, Bet, had the opposite reaction. It was as if a bomb had exploded inside the family's wood-framed house. Juniper's sisters jumped in to keep their mother from hurting the pregnant young woman. Bet hollered into the night about the sins and curses Juniper was letting in.

Right before fall turned into winter, Juniper gave birth to a big, pretty baby girl she named Gloria. Gregory was there at the birth, and the two argued about last names. Juniper was adamant that her baby was a Jeter and not a Shaw. Gregory rolled his eyes at the new mother, but he softened and cooed at the gorgeous, chocolate-brown baby with a head full of thick black curls as she squirmed in his powerful arms. Gregory saw Juniper all over her face, but he knew he was in there somewhere, too.

Soon after her second birthday, Gloria began splitting her time between Spruce Junction and east Baltimore, where her father lived with his wife she affectionately called Ms. Hazel. From the start, Juniper was unsettled about her child living in the same house as Gregory's wife, although Gloria always assured her mother that she was being treated well. Nevermind the cold and hostile stares the girl received any time one of Ms. Hazel's relatives came by. Nevermind Ms. Hazel casually saying Gloria was her punishment for not being able to fulfill her natural duties as a wife. Ms. Hazel never spoke those words from a place of anger or malice. For her, it was just another accepted fact, as if one had said the sky was blue.

Living between her mother's and father's homes would be Gloria's routine until it was time to start senior high school. Gloria and Ms. Hazel petitioned hard for Gregory to allow the teenager to live in the city during the school year. Ms. Hazel wanted Gloria to attend Paul Laurence Dunbar Senior High School. Dunbar was Ms. Hazel's alma mater, and she stressed to her husband how important it would be for Gloria to attend a school with such a strong academic reputation.

Gloria had always felt as much East Baltimore as she did Spruce Junction. She considered herself one of the lucky ones in the family. She had grown up in the city and out in the country, so, in her eyes, Gloria felt that she had received the best of both worlds.

Gloria hummed and took a long drag of her Newport while she plated the food for breakfast. Jimmy Budd was already in the kitchen reading the morning paper, as was his usual practice. Gloria heard some movement on the stairs and looked up as Skeeter walked into the dining area, rubbing her eyes.

"Just the woman I want to see." Gloria took another drag from her cigarette as she arranged the plates on the table.

"What I do now?" Skeeter slumped into the seat like a troubled student waiting to talk to the school principal.

"Patricia Ann Jeter, I told you about sneaking your lil' evening friends into my home." Gloria threw a disapproving glance her cousin's way as she walked over to get the bacon from the counter. "We got kids 'round here now, we all gotta do things differently."

"But Glo, we didn't even—"

"Ain't no 'but' nothin,' Skeeter. If you can't afford a motel room or something, then just go to their place. But you gonna stop bringing strange ni—"

"Corn has ears, y'all," Jimmy Budd said while still looking at his morning paper.

In her peripheral vision, Gloria saw Popsee peering around the entrance to the kitchen, taking in the entire conversation.

"We don't sneak in on grown folk's conversations around here." Gloria spoke to the wall that divided the kitchen and the main hallway. "Go get your mama and the rest of them churren and tell 'em it's time for breakfast."

Popsee quickly scampered up the stairs to relay Gloria's message.

Skeeter rolled her eyes while Gloria shook her pin curl-covered head and laughed. "Chile, it's gonna be a whole new ballgame with these babies in the house."

Skeeter got up to pour orange juice into the cups for the children as the kids came down the steps toward the dining room.

"Igarettes!" Peach yelled as she toddled her way downstairs with the help of her brother. "Igarettes! Camp, I 'mell igarettes!"

Jimmy Budd let out a deep chuckle as Gloria ran her cigarette under the faucet, then turned to open the back door to let the smell out. Heavier footsteps were heard slowly coming down the steps behind the children.

Sheri was still adjusting to life in her new city. Skeeter had put in a good word for her over at the paper factory, and she was fortunate to have landed a job there as soon as she arrived. Skeeter had worked at the factory going on two years, and as was her usual custom, her charismatic charm made her everyone's favorite.

"Here she go!" Jimmy Budd smiled at Sheri as he folded his paper and wedged it behind the napkin holder on the table for quick access.

Sheri gave a round of morning greetings as she double-checked to make sure Peach was properly situated at the table. Champ, being his usual dependable self, had already made sure Peach was pushed all the way up to the table and secured in her seat. After Gloria said grace, the room stirred with the hum of morning conversations while Gloria's favorite station (forever known as WEBB despite the call letter change) filled in the gaps with Sam Cooke, the Five Stairsteps, Ruth Brown and other soul music offerings.

Popsee loved listening to old-time music. He and Mom-Mom could usually be found dancing and singing in the living room to all of her Aretha Franklin and Motown albums. The young boy looked up from his plate and took a long, thorough scan of everyone at the dining table. He then closed his eyes and rocked his head from side to side, letting the music take over him.

"This your song, Pop?" Skeeter laughed as she looked over her glass of orange juice at her little cousin.

"Knows good music when he hears it." Gloria nodded as she raised her glass of juice toward Popsee before taking a long sip.

Popsee opened his eyes and smiled a smile that Sheri knew had come from a place of genuine happiness. It was the first time Popsee had really opened up in the weeks that they had been in Baltimore. Seeing her child smile filled Sheri with both gratitude and relief.

"So what's the paper talking 'bout today?" Gloria asked Jimmy Budd as she lovingly traced his lower jaw with her fingertips. It was as if the couple had the table all to themselves.

"Just the usual. Crime. There was a fire or something up at Hagerstown." Jimmy Budd shrugged as he picked through his eggs. "That ol' Billups in the paper say he's thinking about running for Congress."

"That man is a damn clown," Gloria snapped. "He can think all he wants to. Only thing he cares about are the cameras. Man would be at the opening of a damn alley trash can if there were cameras around somewhere."

"Just like his daddy and his no-good uncle." Jimmy Budd gave a dismissive wave as he got up from the table.

"Baby, get my work bag for me, please?" Gloria called out to Jimmy Budd's retreating back. "Should be next to the shelf by the door."

Jimmy grunted to show acknowledgment as Gloria turned to come face-to-face with Sheri.

"Got something for you." Gloria smiled and did a happy bounce, which caused her curves to ripple under the housedress. "Remember you told me that you wanted to go to school for business? Didn't forget! Went down to the community college to get you some brochures and registration forms."

"Girl, Peanut, that's a lot." Skeeter seemed genuinely stunned by her cousin's potentially full schedule. "I mean, you got the babies, got work and now school? I'll help as much as I can, you know that."

"Another thing," Gloria remembered. "That ol' Ms. Nancy finally got outta there, so now the front desk folks are going to be hiring. So I need for you to pick out the nicest outfit you brought up with you, because we're meeting with Mr. Heath this Thursday."

Sheri had to catch herself. So much was happening in such a small window of time. Champ, Popsee and Peach all looked at their mother with faces that showed both happiness and concern. Sheri reached her arms over the table to grab hold of Gloria. The two women gave each other full, all-teeth smiles. Then Sheri grabbed Skeeter's hand. "I appreciate this," Sheri said. "I brought us up here to restart our lives, and I'm grateful for you both. I don't take any of it for granted." Sheri squeezed both of their hands.

Jimmy Budd came back to the table with Gloria's bag in tow. Gloria fished through her black-and-gold work tote and finally pulled up a stack of glossy papers. "For you, Miss Ma'am." The rich tone of Gloria's voice made her words bounce off the walls of the rowhome.

Sheri took the brochures from Gloria and began showing them to the children. She lifted Peach out of her seat and placed the little girl on her hip. "Look at this. You see this, Miss Peach?" Sheri gave Peach her own brochure to examine.

"Mommy is going to school again. To college. What I say before we left?" Sheri quizzed her trio. "C'mon now, I know y'all remember what we said."

"Making better moves." Champ continued to closely examine the glossy paper his mother had given him.

"Exactly." Sheri nodded and lightly ran her hands over Champ's brown curls. "We're making better moves this year."

CHAPTER 4

Although she missed home dearly, Thomasina was truly thankful to be away from Spruce Junction. She loved how Newark made her feel. People sitting on their fire escape playing instruments, nearly every corner hosting a harmonizing group of teenagers whose melodies kissed the air. The constant movement and activity made it a wonderland come to life.

Thomasina was one of the favored children in her mother Bethel's large brood. Bethel was often overworked and overwhelmed. It was Thomasina's duty to make sure Bet's life was as peaceful as possible. Through strategic and perhaps divine intervention, she managed to escape much of the frustration her mother regularly unleashed on just about anyone in her way.

One uneventful April morning, Thomasina had gotten up to feed the chickens and the hogs. She washed the little ones and herself, got dressed, then calmly returned to her bedroom. There she sat down and unleashed a thunderous scream that rocked the Jeter house like a flash flood.

Thomasina didn't notice her father, her uncle and his wife running into the room to shake her back to herself. Thomasina didn't see her mother frozen in the corner of the bedroom, staring at her daughter in complete horror. Thomasina didn't know her piercing screams had sliced through the air and landed as if shards of glass. Thomasina didn't hear the whispers of the people who said you could hear the screaming all the way down by the Bibbys' place.

With shot nerves, Bethel sent a telegram to the only person she knew who could bring her child back. Before leaving for New Jersey, Bethel's older sister, Myrtle, had been the person everyone in town visited for their special spiritual needs. Bethel highly doubted Myrtle was getting the same business up north that she'd gotten around Spruce Junction. The woman's expertise was coveted all throughout Wilson County.

When Myrtle came down to Spruce Junction to check in on her niece, it felt as if no time had passed. The regal woman, petite and pecan-colored with searing hazel eyes, gave subdued greetings to her sister before proceeding to walk quietly around the house four times, lightly sprinkling salt from a small, black pouch she pulled from her dress pocket. Once she was finished, a young boy holding a jar of water met the woman outside the front door. With the water jar firmly in her grasp, Myrtle stepped over the threshold of the house and made her way to the room which held her niece. She softly shut the door behind her.

As the sun rose the following morning, Myrtle exited the room as quietly as she had entered it. She found her sister huddled at the dining table, fighting sleep.

"Nothin' holding her, she's going to be fine." Myrtle placed a hand on her weary sister's shoulder. "Sometimes a mind just falls inside itself." It was a sentiment Bethel understood all too well.

By the end of her visit, Myrtle had successfully convinced her sister to allow Thomasina to stay with her in Newark.

"For just a little while, Bethel."

Thomasina was happy to help her aunt run numbers for Big Charlie and his men. Aunt Myrtle also worked as a laundress and sold dinners out of her apartment. The third floor walk-up always smelled of amber resin, a fragrance Thomasina loved from the first time she smelled it.

About six months after moving to Newark, Thomasina got a job at Louise's Cafeteria over on Central and Norfolk. After receiving her first paycheck, Thomasina ran to buy Aretha Franklin's album to hear her favorite song, "Skylark." When there was no work to be done and the house was settled and quiet, Thomasina would drift away as Aretha's ethereal voice carried her far beyond the heavens.

Major Calloway was the smallest of Lionel and Doris Calloway's five sons. He was the runt of the pack, and the feeling of having to prove himself followed him wherever he went, which encouraged his love for fighting. For a while, the young man had been able to channel his rage in the boxing ring, which led him to a 24-2 record in his weight class. One day, while taking a smoke during his work break at Fleming's Grocery, Major was awestruck at the sight of the pretty, red, doe-eyed girl who lived in the apartment building on the corner. She looked just as sturdy as she looked soft, which fascinated Major. He could also tell that the girl with the full, pretty lips probably didn't take much shit off people.

Four days a week, Thomasina rode the bus up to Central and Orange and walked the rest of the way. It gave her a reason to walk past the Cumberland fish market where he worked. He was a man's height, with the broadest shoulders Thomasina had ever seen. He would have been perfect for farm work. On a good day, she would catch him flashing a confident smile that showed off his pretty, white teeth. He had eyes that snatched you up and held you close, almost as if he could see right through a person. Thomasina often daydreamed about losing herself to him.

Major had taken to observing the girl as she ventured in and out of her building. He knew her schedule, and he had already rehearsed his lines for the day they finally crossed paths. Major had always been fairly confident when dealing with the ladies, but she made him nervous for some reason. He finally got his shot one evening as she was coming down the block from the bus stop. Always good for a joke or two, he was able to get a laugh out of her. Making her smile was as big a win as any of his fights.

One morning, he asked Thomasina what her name was, and she thought she would melt right there on the sidewalk. She wasn't fully prepared for the trance his warm brown eyes put her in. She learned his name was Michael. A simple name, yet so beautiful. Michael and Thomasina laughed and talked like they had been buddies the whole while. He joked about her accent, which made her roll her eyes in feigned disgust. Thomasina blushed a color not yet discovered when he admitted that it was all in fun, that her accent was so beautiful it made even the simplest words sound like music.

Major squirmed a little in his pressed shirt and slacks as he walked up the steps to Thomasina's apartment. He was taking her to the movies, their first real, official date. Aunt Myrtle opened the door and looked him over one good time. Myrtle's stoic, poker face was not an uncommon sight for Thomasina, but Major seemed to shrink a little beneath it. Myrtle bid the couple safe travels and returned to her favorite seat in the living room. When Thomasina came home later that night, her aunt gave a word of caution: "There are fangs hiding behind that boy's silly grin. Got a good amount of mean in him."

While Thomasina enjoyed going out with Major, her heart yearned for more. She would drift and daydream about Michael as she listened to her albums. Michael made her feel pretty and warm. Major was by far more persistent, but Michael had her heart—if he wanted it. One day, while walking past the fish market, Thomasina watched Michael hold everyone's rapt attention as he stood by the large scale recounting some epic story about God-knows-what. The audience laughed loudly at some parts while growing stark silent during others. Thomasina could have stood next to the market window all day just to watch him hold court.

Major had started back training to get ready for a bout coming up on Valentine's Day. The purse was two hundred dollars. On the night of the fight, Major got into the ring ready to conquer the world. He looked out into the audience and saw Thomasina sitting in the stands wearing the prettiest royal blue dress and a string of pearls. Sleek pin curls framed the left side of her heart-shaped face. Thankfully, Major was able to harness enough composure to win the fight that night, but the money wasn't the prize the young man craved after his win.

Thomasina worked to function normally despite the swelling and nausea. She still walked by the fish market, but it had been weeks since she had seen Michael's face. Aunt Myrtle saw Thomasina's condition and asked the young girl how she planned to handle it. Thomasina thought about her mother and how she had turned into a ball of fury after what happened with Juniper. She took a deep breath, reached out for her aunt's extended hands, and held them tightly.

Thomasina and Major awkwardly walked hand in hand into his parents' home. Thomasina had carefully arranged her outfit so that her condition wouldn't be too noticeable. As if on cue, Doris Calloway's hard, green eyes narrowed in on the girl's midsection. Major formally introduced his girlfriend to his parents and three of his brothers as Doris walked back into the kitchen to bring out the rest of the dinner to the dining room table. Thomasina's offers to help had been immediately shot down. As the family continued to wait for dinner to be served, the sound of footsteps came from the main hallway. Thomasina lifted her eyes from her growing belly and saw him standing there in the flesh.

Michael.

"Michael, Thomasina. Thomasina, Michael." Major gave a rushed introduction and waved dismissively as his brother walked over to kiss Thomasina's hand.

Major stared fireballs into his brother's back as Michael stood up from his bow to Thomasina. Irritation covered Major's face, and he tried his best to not cause a commotion. It would be the last thing he needed, since the family always rushed to side with Michael about everything anyway. When Doris returned to the table, Lionel said grace and everyone quietly ate dinner. Thomasina had no appetite, both embarrassment and nausea taking turns gnawing at her. The young woman wanted to disappear.

The wedding day came exactly one month later. Thomasina oiled herself with a special mixture Aunt Myrtle made for her. She slowly began to get dressed, taking breaks between each piece of clothing to catch her breath. Myrtle and Thomasina arrived at the Calloways' home in a chauffeured Cadillac driven by one of Big Charlie's guys. This time as in the last, Thomasina was greeted by critical eyes when she rang the Calloways' bell. Two middle-aged women met the bride-to-be at the door. Neither tried to hide their judgment.

The ceremony was emotionless. The minister talked about the importance of being rooted in the word of God. Major grunted his vows. Thomasina said hers in a whisper. The reception consisted of punch and a yellow cake Major's aunt had made. Thankfully, someone had the heart to turn the radio on, and music provided cover for the awkward silences.

Later, Major got hold of some Wild Turkey, which instantly loosened up the newlywed. With the whiskey in his system guiding the way, Major stepped to Michael.

"If you try to make any moves on my wife, you won't have to worry about the bullets in Vietnam killing you."

◆ ◆ ◆

Sheri remembered how the air felt strange that entire week. A heavy, foreboding presence hovered over the Jeter house, and Sheri couldn't shake it as much as she tried. Thomasina and her daughter had long since returned to Spruce Junction, but the terror of Major Calloway lingered like a specter. For some reason, it did not come as a shock when he showed up in the Jeters' front yard, wearing all white and screaming for his bride. The house, usually filled to the brim with bodies, noises and movement, was empty and silent save for Titi and Sheri.

"Thomasina Calloway, your knight has arrived!" Major did an overly exaggerated bow at the bottom of the front steps. "I heard you've been taking visitors down here! I guess your ass forgot you had a husband!"

Sheri frantically tore through the house looking for Uncle Syl's shotgun. Although she had no recollection of her father, Sheri remembered the few stories Titi doled out like breadcrumbs. Stories of violence and manic rage that eventually sent the young mother back to North Carolina with an infant in tow.

Sheri shook her head, wondering what the odds were that Major would come to Spruce Junction at the exact moment when only she and Titi were around. A cruel, unfair twist of fate. As her daughter flew around in a panic, Titi sat in a daze, almost as if she had made peace with the fact that this would be how her story ended.

The yells quickly turned into growls as Major made his way up the front steps. "What! You ain't taking visitors no more? I thought you liked visitors!" Major screamed from the other side of the wall. "You knew it was only a matter of time, right? Jail wasn't going to keep me away forever."

With a force that made the entire house rock, Major kicked in the door and came face-to-face with his wife and daughter, who left Newark under the cover of darkness so long ago. Sheri reflexively jumped and hurled one of Bet's rusted cast irons at her father. She then found some old bricks and began to toss them just as Major pulled out a .38 from his waistband and snatched Titi by her throat.

Titi let out a garbled cry as Major dragged her out of the house, through the yard and toward the car, with Sheri loudly screaming and hanging on to Titi by her lower legs. Sheri's eyes darted back and forth between Major and Titi—both of them seemed to be physically present but mentally gone. Save for Major's occasional grunts, Titi's whimpers and Sheri's yelling, all around the Jeter house remained quiet. The stillness of that day would forever haunt Sheri's memory. It was as if God wanted Major to kill them.

"Let's go, bitch." Major yanked open the passenger side door and used the last few ounces of his boxing-developed upper body strength to throw his wife into the car. He fired off one shot into the air, which made Sheri fall back at the recoil. Major jumped into the driver's seat, and the '81 Pontiac Bonneville roared to life as Sheri stumbled to her feet, weakly giving chase to the quickly disappearing vehicle.

Sheri had never tried drugs before, but the rest of the day, the young girl felt as if she no longer had control of her body and mind. Some said she made it down to the Bibbys' place to get help, while others maintain that it was one of the Bibby brothers who found the girl not too far from her house in a haze of delirium.

Sheri remembered speaking words, but she couldn't give an account of what she said. Sheri remembered seeing the men in uniforms, but then they would disappear. Sheri saw Bet, Uncle Syl and Aunt Juniper as well as her cousins Skeeter, Punchy and Fox sitting around her bed, but soon, like mirages, everyone evaporated. Day turned into night as both cold and hot tremors racked Sheri's body.

Sheri remained tethered to the world by the faintest of threads as word slowly got back to Spruce Junction that their beloved Titi was indeed alive. Three young boys happened to see a car careen off a bridge, flip in the air and eventually land upside down in the Toisnot Swamp. As her daughter continued to float through time and space, Titi was recovering in the hospital, grateful that Aunt Myrtle saw fit to come back home and save her one last time.

There would be an entire block of missing time in Sheri's head from when her mother was kidnapped to the day she gingerly walked up the front porch steps with the help of Uncle Syl. Sheri and Titi didn't speak about it between themselves and were slow to give any recounts to curious family members, many of whom had read the small article in the East Carolina Chronicle about the grisly car wreck that left one person dead.

As for Major Calloway, Sheri had never been able to make heads nor tails of his relationship with her mother as well as his place in her life as a father. Besides her mother's brothers, the only other male figure in her life was her Uncle Mike. Sheri received gifts and cards filled with money faithfully on every birthday and special occasion. Major had always been a figure relegated to the shadows. Since she was technically his next of kin, Titi made the decision to cremate Major's body and mail the ashes back up to Newark along with a copy of the news article about the crash.

Not wanting to leave Titi behind was a big reason Sheri had always been reluctant to leave Spruce Junction. It wasn't as if Titi ever encouraged her daughter to find herself and see what else was out there. In Titi's eyes, they were both content and everything was perfectly fine as is. It would take three tiny arrivals for Sheri to finally make an attempt to break free from Spruce Junction's suffocating grip. It was her duty to want more for herself because her children deserved the best of her.

Sheri didn't expect Baltimore to have all the answers, but she needed this move to be the compass point that would lead her and her babies to something better. 'Make better moves' had become Sheri's main affirmation for both herself and her children. The college brochures Gloria had given her were just the beginning. Sheri was motivated to go out for everything she felt her family deserved.

CHAPTER 5

"**W**here's Jimmy with them damn crabs!" Gloria stood at the top of the front stoop staring down the street as if she could will her boyfriend to arrive quicker.

"Told ya you should have called them in," Skeeter yelled from the kitchen. "They would've had them ready. He's probably waiting in line with the rest of the damn city."

Just then, Skeeter went over to the stereo and slipped in a cassette tape. The bass from the song seemed to shake the entire house, and Champ, Popsee and Peach came running from the backyard to get a better listen.

"A guy at my job sells these tapes, and every—"

"Skeeter, turn that mess off, please," Gloria snapped as she waved her manicured hand in annoyance.

"C'mon, Gloria. Everything can't be Smokey Robinson and the damn Miracles all the time."

"Don't trash Smokey!"

Sheri shook her head at her two cousins and laughed. Popsee started rocking in rhythm to the music, and Peach joined in. Champ still looked skeptical.

"This is cussin' music." Gloria stood with her arms folded, facing the living room. "Plus, I thought gospel was supposed to be your thing."

"I love all kinds of music." Skeeter flashed her dimples and bopped along with Popsee and Peach. "I can listen to DJ Boobie and The Mighty Clouds of Joy. I don't limit myself."

"This doesn't sound like rap." Sheri moved in closer, wearing the same skeptical expression as Champ.

"That's because it's Club music." Skeeter continued nodding her head to the rhythm. "A guy who used to work at the factory sells these tapes. It's dancing music. You can tear a floor up with this."

Gloria waved her hands in exasperation and went upstairs to change clothes. By this point, Popsee and Peach were off in their own world, dancing to the beat.

Skeeter flashed a big smile as she pointed at the two little dancing machines. "If the babies like it, then I've won." She walked over to the folding chairs and started wiping them down with a soapy cloth. She looked to Sheri, who was sitting on the couch. "So how's the new job coming along? You miss us at the factory yet?"

"Ooh, girl." Sheri's eyes lit up just thinking about her new office space. "It's real fancy. Reminds me of those offices you see on the soaps."

"Yeah, that's Gloria, alright." Skeeter nodded. "Got her a real good gig, but it makes sense, being that she's a college woman and all. The people treat you decent?"

"They're nice enough." Sheri tilted her head and looked off into the distance, trying to come up with the right words to describe her new surroundings. "They seem okay. Mr. Heath is nice, and he seems to really like Gloria. The ladies in my office both seem pretty friendly. Listen, I'm just there to work, but if I get in cool with some of the people, then that's fine."

"Like the old people say: it's a living." Skeeter shrugged as she started taking the chairs outside to the backyard.

Champ ran over to help Skeeter with the chairs while Popsee and Peach continued to dance to the club music. Sheri felt relieved to see her babies loosening up and getting comfortable in their new city. She wanted them to have the best experiences possible. Any sign that she was doing things right was always appreciated.

"Thank you for the help, sir." Skeeter smiled while setting up the tables and chairs in preparation for the cookout.

"You're welcome," Champ said in his usual all-business, no-nonsense tone.

"You miss Spruce Junction?" Skeeter looked at the young boy. He already had a presence that was mature for his years.

"Yes. Popsee and Peach miss it, too. We miss Mom-Mom and all our cousins."

Skeeter stayed silent, listening. She understood the tugs of home too well.

Champ, deep in thought, furrowed his brows. "It's like... I'm happy to be here. It's something different, but I miss home, too. I'm in the middle, I guess."

"It's okay to have those feelings." Skeeter got on one knee to come face-to-face with her young cousin. "There's a lot happening. A whole new city. You're changing schools. A new group of friends to hang with. Take it at your own pace. It'll be okay."

Champ set his chair up and gave Skeeter a pensive glance. "Do you miss Spruce Junction?"

Skeeter briefly wondered if she should give him the honest answer or an answer that wouldn't shake him.

"Sometimes," she admitted.

"Are you ever going to go back?" Champ leaned forward slightly, awaiting a response.

"Maybe. Nothing is ever set in stone. Spruce Junction is my home, but so is Baltimore."

Champ took a minute to get a good look at his older cousin, a woman he didn't even know existed just two months ago. Her hair, usually worn slicked back into a ponytail, reminded him of baby doll hair. She had a friendly face and a happy smile. He could tell she smiled a lot, but a part of Champ wondered if she was sad, too. So far away from everything and everyone.

"IT'S ABOUT DAMN TIME!" Gloria's voice bounced off the walls like a ping pong ball as she stomped down the steps.

Jimmy Budd and his buddy Rico had finally returned lugging four bushels of crabs, two shopping bags full of sodas, a case of paper towels and two snowballs.

"That's what took y'all so long, those damn snowballs," Gloria admonished the men as they brought their haul into the house.

"Looks like you started the party without me," Jimmy muttered under his breath, flashing Gloria a suspicious look from over his shoulder.

"I ain't start shit." Gloria spat the words out while giving her man a firm stare that warned him not to try her.

Gloria followed behind Jimmy and Rico and swapped out the club tape for some Midnight Star. Skeeter was out of her mind if she thought they were going to listen to that wild bass for the entire night. Right as the music changed, Gloria and Jimmy's friend Lloyd walked into the house with his girlfriend, Joanne.

"Miss Sweet Stacks!" Lloyd's nickname for Gloria annoyed Jimmy to no end. She just knew they were going to fight about it one day.

"Oh shut up." Gloria cut her eyes at him, but her grin always told on her. Broad-shouldered with a defensive lineman's build, Lloyd reached down to hug his friend, letting his hand rest on the small of Gloria's back while lightly kissing her collarbone. Gloria turned to double-cheek kiss Joanna, who looked as if she were already riding her own personal rocket ship—completely oblivious to everything but still trying to function as coherently as possible.

Out in the backyard, Sheri, Skeeter, Jimmy Budd and Rico had just finished setting up. Sheri made a kids' table for her brood so they could enjoy themselves and not have to overhear any grown folks talk.

"Are any other kids coming?" Champ looked up at his mother.

"I don't know, baby." Sheri saw the disappointment in her son's eyes. From what she had seen so far, Gloria and Jimmy didn't seem to have friends who had young children. It was one of the reasons she was looking forward to school starting. It would give Champ and Popsee the chance to socialize.

George, another friend from the neighborhood, came up from the alley on his bicycle. The man greeted everyone and tossed Sheri a wink. He was a handsome enough man, but it was clear that he had been through a few things. Jimmy Budd handed him a cold beer as he found a seat at one of the tables. A few more friends of Gloria and Jimmy arrived through the front entrance, said their greetings to everyone and began helping themselves to crabs and beer.

Sheri and Skeeter helped the boys pick the meat out of the crabs while Peach sat contentedly eating the leg meat that Sheri had pulled out beforehand. Gloria, after making a second, considerably longer trip to her bedroom, returned to the backyard. The woman seemed to float across the grass as if she were the belle of the ball. She rolled her hips to the music while she joked with the guests. Sheri noticed the man who came with his girlfriend was absolutely eating Gloria up with his eyes.

Gloria soon came skipping over to the table where the children were eating and nuzzled the top of Peach's head with kisses. Peach seemed startled but quickly recovered when she realized it was just her cousin. Gloria squatted down and tried to pull out Peach's chair so the child faced her directly.

"Sheri, does this baby know how to do Miss Mary Mack?" Gloria asked, her eyes suddenly filled with concern.

"Umm, I don't think so. I haven't taught her yet." Sheri continued working with the crabs. "She doesn't have the coordination for it right now."

This revelation nearly knocked Gloria down on the ground. "COORDINATION?"

Both Sheri and Skeeter flashed startled looks at each other before turning to Gloria, trying to figure out why their cousin had gotten so loud all of a sudden.

"Miss Peach doesn't need coordination to play Miss Mary Mack! MISS MARY MACK, ALL DRESSED IN BLACK! That's just in our genes!" Gloria insisted as she feverishly rubbed Peach's small knee.

Lloyd came over and stood behind Gloria as she continued to squat by Peach's seat. Gloria looked up and smiled at the towering man with the broad shoulders and the brown eyes. "This here is my cousin Sheri. She just moved up from Spruce Junction."

"Uh-huh, I see the fine runs in the family." Lloyd nodded at Sheri, but his eyes went right back to feasting on Gloria.

Gloria strutted back to the table where Jimmy Budd was sitting, leaving Skeeter and Sheri to make sense of the strange exchange which had just taken place. Sheri wore an expression of genuine confusion, while Skeeter could no longer hide the irritation that had been tugging at her since the party began.

A Spades game soon convened, with Jimmy and Gloria on one team and Rico and George on another. Someone had turned off

Midnight Star, and the sound of blues music came wafting out from the living room.

"Y'all heard about that needle program? The one they startin' with the health department and Sloane-Douglas?" George asked eagerly.

"What type of needle program?" Jimmy Budd looked up from his cards. He didn't have a good hand this round but figured Gloria should get them over the hump.

"You can swap your old needles for clean, new ones. No questions asked." George nodded. "Doesn't sound too bad. These days you never know what you could be dealin' with out there. The Mayor already gave his blessing."

Gloria rolled her eyes and twisted her lips but didn't say a word. Jimmy scratched his chin with his cards.

"I don't know about that one, Georgie boy." Jimmy frowned. "Anything that Sloane-Douglas puts its name on is automatically suspect in my eyes. For all we know, they could have dipped those needles in cyanide. Passin' them out to the people like candy."

George shrugged and looked at his cards. "Who knows? Doesn't hurt is what I say."

"The word been around for years anyway. People walk into Sloane-Douglas for somethin' simple, and they don't walk back out." Rico stared down at his cards.

"Y'all, can we just play the game? I don't like this talk," Gloria pleaded.

Sheri looked over at the woman who had come with the tall man whose eyes had been locked onto Gloria all night. She was a pretty woman, and Sheri could see that she was relatively young. Her brown skin had an unnaturally dark cast to it, almost as if parts of her face had been scarred. She wore a coral linen midriff top and matching wide-legged pants. Her sandy-brown hair was brushed up in a loose topknot. She sat in a chair with her legs folded at her ankles and her hands resting in her lap.

Sheri noticed the woman hadn't eaten or drunk anything the entire time. She just sat and nodded off. When they first arrived, it seemed as if she was trying to stay alert and awake, but as time went on, it was clear that she had given herself over to whatever demons she had been fighting.

The humid summer air hung low, and Sheri began to round up her brood to go back in the house. Since everyone was outside, that meant they would have a little more time to take their evening baths before bed. Champ and Popsee both acted as if they were going to start whining, but one look from Sheri let them know she wasn't about to play that game. Especially not in front of company. All three children waved goodnight to the guests and Jimmy while Gloria and Skeeter both received goodnight hugs and kisses.

"That lady was sleeping real hard, Ma. She didn't even eat." Champ was completely stunned as they came in from the backyard and walked through the dark kitchen.

"She had a long day," Sheri said dryly as she ushered her children up the stairs.

Early the next morning, Popsee tossed and turned on his side of the narrow twin bed he shared with his brother.

"There is a cat crying outside the window or somethin'." Popsee let out a loud, annoyed sigh. "I keep hearing it. I'm trying to sleep and I can't."

Sheri heard it too, but she knew it wasn't a cat. She and her son were hearing moans. It had been going on for a while, and Sheri had hoped the children wouldn't notice. Thankfully, Champ and Peach were sleeping through it, but Popsee was liable to wake them both up if he got mad enough.

Eventually, the moans stopped. Sheri heard the sounds of a door shutting and then footsteps on the staircase. Since their window faced the street, Sheri quickly got up to see who had been causing the commotion. Although she couldn't see Gloria, she heard her voice rising up to the bedroom window. Sheri's eyes widened when she realized Gloria was talking to the man from the party. The one with the girlfriend who had been nodding off. He walked over to his car but soon turned around as if he planned to go back in the house with Gloria.

Sheri did a quick scan of the street and noticed Jimmy Budd's car was nowhere to be found. Besides Gloria and the guy, their block of Preston Street was empty. Sheri heard shrieks and giggles as Gloria's friend lifted her up and twirled her around as if she only weighed two pounds. Sheri quickly spun her head over toward Champ and Popsee, praying her youngest boy wasn't eavesdropping with her. Thankfully, Popsee was still lying down with his hands covering his ears.

Sheri tip-toed back to bed and pulled Peach close while the baby slept, lost somewhere in her own blissful dream world. A million questions ran through Sheri's bemused mind: What's going on in this house? Did Gloria even introduce that guy? Where the hell is Jimmy Budd? Does he know what's happening?

Sheri heard a car start and drive off. She then heard the front door shut and footsteps slowly coming upstairs. Sheri looked over at the boys; Popsee had thankfully drifted back to sleep. She kissed Peach's forehead and stared up at the ceiling. Sheri could only imagine what type of foolishness her cousin was trying to keep under wraps. No one truly ever knew what the next person had going on in their lives, and real life often wasn't what it appeared to be.

CHAPTER 6

The September dawn found Skeeter sitting on the edge of her bed, wiping her eyes to shake off the last few tugs of sleep. Skeeter was usually the first one up, even on days when she didn't have to be at work until late afternoon. After showering and getting dressed, she made her way downstairs to prepare breakfast.

Heaven 600 was Skeeter's trusty morning companion as she adjusted the dial to get the clearest signal. The voices of Bebe and Cece Winans came drifting out of the speakers as Skeeter swayed to the music. Skeeter was a fan of all the gospel voices, from the big-voiced choirs to the backwater quartets. She even loved the gospel singers that had more of an R&B sound. She never understood why the church folks got so mad about so-called secular music, since it all came from the church anyway.

Skeeter's love for the Good News came honest. Her father, Joe Richard, had been a singer with the Carolina Soul Disciples, a gospel quintet that performed all throughout eastern North Carolina. Joe Richard, known in the family as JR, had only one goal in life: to get as far away from Spruce Junction as humanly possible. Everyone already swooned over JR's looks, and for him to have a voice that could bring down any house? It was unfair who received all the favor.

What would end up being the highlight of the young man's singing career was when his group had an opportunity to open a few shows down in Charlotte for the Caravans. Friendship Missionary Baptist was packed to the rafters to hear the powerhouse gospel group and get a glimpse of the dynamic young woman out of Durham who sang the roof down so hard the Caravans had to sing "I Won't Be Back" five times before the audience allowed them to leave the stage.

Over time, alcohol became the crutch that got JR through his day. His groupmates pleaded with him to get it together. The last thing they needed was for churches to stop booking them. The Carolina Soul Disciples was supposed to be their ticket out.

Life became a blur to the singer. Days ran into each other, and JR often didn't know if he was coming or going. During one of these blurs in time, JR crossed paths with a young, studious Indigenous woman from the Haliwa tribe who managed to attend every performance whenever the Soul Disciples were in the Rocky Mount area.

On a cool late-September afternoon, a tall, lanky man wearing a wide-brimmed Stetson hat with an elaborate, beaded band arrived at the Jeter home. He walked up the front steps holding the hand of a little girl who was no older than two. The toddler had small, curious eyes, skin the color of coffee with heavy cream and tousled coal-black hair. She wore a brown dress that looked to be about three sizes too big. The man knocked on the door and was greeted by two women who looked as if they had not been expecting visitors.

"This is Joe Jeter's child," was all the man was rumored to have said as he handed the little girl over to the taller of the two women. He then turned and walked back to his car. The now startled women were yelling out questions, but the man didn't bother to acknowledge them. His work was done.

JR finally returned home six days after the little girl had been unceremoniously handed off. His mother, Bet, and his sisters, Jackie and Juniper, were waiting for him like police officers waiting to interrogate a criminal.

"You wasn't gon' tell us you had a baby, Joe?" JR's oldest sister, Jackie, spoke first. Disgust covered her face.

"Is this your baby, JR?" Juniper asked. Her eyes filled with disappointment.

The little girl stared at the man with no spark of recognition passing between the two. She yawned and buried her small, heart-shaped face in Jackie's full bosom as she tried to fight off sleep.

"IS THIS YOUR BABY, JOE?" Jackie asked at full volume. This made the child stare up at her newfound auntie in confusion and fear. Jackie planted kisses atop the girl's head as an apology for making her jump.

JR mumbled something indecipherable, but it was no use—the man was obviously drunk. All three women rolled their eyes.

"Do you know her name, Joe? Does she have a name? We've been calling her little girl," Juniper pleaded with her lost brother.

Again, JR slurred incoherently, causing Juniper to shake her head and stare down at the floor, wondering where everything had gone wrong with her younger brother. Out of all of Bet's children, he was the one who had it all: charisma, looks, talent. Yet there he was, just another country-ass wino.

"Patricia Ann Jeter." Jackie spoke the name in solemn reverence.

Bet looked up at the ceiling, and Juniper smiled at her sister as tears formed in her eyes. Patricia Ann had been the name of their young, free-spirited sister, who the family had lost too soon.

Jackie looked down at her niece and softly lifted the little girl's face to meet hers. "Patricia Ann." She smiled lovingly at the child. "We're your people. This is your home."

The girl gave a dimpled smile to the gorgeous, brown-skinned woman with the round face and the sophisticated, bouffant-style up-do. She lifted her finger to touch Jackie's chin.

"I ain't raising her." Bet finally broke her silence.

"Mama!" Jackie and Juniper gasped and stared at their mother in disbelief.

"Don't 'Mama' me. That ain't my child and I ain't raising her. Don't know where she come from. Just showed up. Man dropped her off and we supposed to do the heavy lifting? She look like one of them Halifax County people anyway. Send her back to them."

Juniper stared across the table at her sister with a look of disbelief. Jackie hugged the little girl tighter and came to the realization that she was going to have to keep this baby girl as far away from her mother as possible.

Patricia Ann received the nickname of Skeeter, and everywhere Jackie went, Skeeter was right there with her. Skeeter got popular around Spruce Junction due to her having hair so long she could sit on it. As she got older, though, Skeeter began to despise her lengthy tresses. She couldn't climb trees nor swim the way she really wanted to because her hair always got in the way. She didn't have enough fingers to count the ways her mane got on her last good nerve.

Skeeter was ten years old when she finally acknowledged to herself that she was different than the other girls. That year, during the annual carnival, Skeeter nearly fell over her feet trying to keep up with Rose Perry. Rose was nice to everyone in school, and Skeeter would often daydream in class about her, wondering what foods she liked and what music she listened to.

The cycle of Skeeter innocently navigating through taboo waters all while the boys in town made loud overtures of love toward her would be the hallmark of Skeeter's teen years. She was scared to say anything to Ma Jackie, but she suspected Ma already knew. Bet was the one Skeeter had to keep away from.

One day, completely fed up, Skeeter took Uncle Syl's shears that he used to cut the rich white folks' bushes and began hacking off her long, black strands. Her cousins gasped in horror when they discovered what Skeeter was doing. Right as Skeeter was cutting the last section of her mane, Bet showed up in the doorway of the woodshed with an old, dusty extension cord. The older woman's eyes were filled with hate. Skeeter was genuinely convinced she was going to die that day in the shed. A whoosh sound buzzed quickly through the air as Bet began striking the girl with laser precision, concentrating on Skeeter's exposed legs.

"Tomboys ain't in the Bible," Bet mumbled more to herself than to the girl she was brutally beating.

Despite her granddaughter's screams of pain and the screams from the other grandchildren, Bet, in a trance, continued beating. She'd had enough of the rumors. Enough of the whispers of Skeeter kissing girls behind Buddy's Diner. Bet saw the sneers and the cold, nasty stares from the other women around Spruce Junction, and she was tired of it all. Hell, Bet didn't even know if this thing was really her son's biological child.

"Tomboys ain't in the Bible."

Bet only stopped after her arms got sore. Skeeter was a heap of bleeding, crying flesh slumped in the corner of the shed. She screamed so loud and for so long she lost her voice. Her skin was torn open and she could no longer walk. The other grandchildren, with tear-stained faces, quietly stepped into the shed to carry their cousin back to the house to recuperate. Ma Jackie had been too late to save her girl.

When word finally got to Jackie, she stormed into the Jeter house with the fury of a lioness. She was fully prepared to send her mother to God on that day. Skeeter slipped in and out of consciousness as her family diligently tended to her bloody legs. Bet had left the house without a care for what she had done.

"She's been through so much, Father. Shine on her, please. She is your child." Jackie's tears fell on Skeeter's face as she prayed and pleaded to God to save her sweet girl.

After the whipping, Skeeter completely lost herself in church. She was there when church opened. She was there when church closed. She was there to teach the babies in Sunday School, and she was one of the first ones there every Wednesday for Bible study. She wanted to be made right. To be made whole. A young, traveling minister saw the teenager's zeal to truly understand the Word and decided to take advantage. Skeeter was six months pregnant before she could finally admit to herself and tell Ma Jackie that she was having a baby.

Skeeter reached out to Gloria a few weeks before her due date. Over time, Gloria's house had emerged as the safe harbor for both family and friends to pass through. The telephone conversation was full of surface pleasantries, but Gloria was perceptive enough to know her younger cousin was likely facing trouble back home.

Angry spring winds swept through Wilson County the day Patricia Ann "Skeeter" Jeter decided she was finally done with Spruce Junction. She had come to terms with the fact that it would never be her home. She loved Ma Jackie with all of her heart, but she knew she would never be able to live free there.

The cherubic baby boy playfully kicked in Ma Jackie's bracelet-covered arms. From the passenger side of Uncle Syl's truck, Skeeter blew kisses and waved goodbye as she departed to the bus station.

♦ ♦ ♦

Sheri hustled down the stairs to throw together breakfast for Popsee and Champ's first day at their new school. She had submitted a leave form for two hours because she wanted to spend a few minutes with each of her sons' teachers. Sheri threw on an old, faded shirt over her work clothes to make sure her outfit stayed clean.

The music coming from the kitchen made Sheri pause. She hadn't heard anyone else moving around that morning when she was getting the children ready, but there was Skeeter, gliding across the kitchen floor wearing an oversized t-shirt and some basketball shorts. She was twirling and humming as she plated the scrambled eggs with cheese, bacon and grits. There were already half-filled glasses of orange juice waiting on the table.

"Where the kids?" Skeeter asked.

"Umm." Sheri stood, completely stunned. When did her cousin do all this? What time did she wake up? "They're coming down behind me. Let me go check real quick."

Sheri ran back up the stairs to move her brood along. She had already gotten them dressed and ready. She hoped they hadn't gone back to bed.

"Champ! Popsee! Peach!" Sheri clapped her hands as she marched back up the steps. She heard the whimpers coming from the hallway, but today was definitely not the day.

"Can we have ten—"

"No!" Sheri was not in the mood for Champ's negotiations. "C'mon, y'all. It's the first day of school. We're scholars in this house. You should have beat me down the steps."

The three children groaned and sulked down the steps with their heads down.

"'mel good." Peach did a little dance as they got closer to the kitchen.

"Everyone thank your Cousin Skeeter! She made us this delicious breakfast!" Sheri's eyes widened as the children found seats at the table.

"Thank you, Cousin Skeeter," the three said in unison. It was a much warmer reception than when they had first met at the train station.

Skeeter smiled proudly as all three children eagerly wolfed down their breakfast.

"New city, new school. Gotta start off with a hearty breakfast. I hope you all have a wonderful day today." Skeeter clapped her hands and smiled at the babies as she began cleaning up and putting things away.

"Thank you, Cousin. This is really good." Champ looked up from his plate and gave Skeeter an appreciative smile.

"Thank you, Cousin!" Popsee echoed his brother.

"Yank you," Peach said, making sure to let her thanks be known as well.

Sheri mouthed thank you to her cousin and blew her an air kiss.

The melodic voice of Deniece Williams came over the radio as Skeeter ran to the windowsill to turn the volume up. "THIS IS MY SONG!"

Skeeter put the dishrag down to glide and twirl to "God Is Amazing." She floated with each note and moved around the kitchen, lost in her world. It was as if everything had stopped, and the spotlight was on Skeeter. The children had finished inhaling breakfast and, although they wanted seconds, no one wanted to be the one to disturb their cousin. Skeeter was glowing, and Sheri didn't know if she had ever seen her cousin so happy and content. It comforted Sheri to know Skeeter had finally found peace.

After all of the years of feeling out of place, used and discarded, Patricia Jeter had found a home within herself. She was who she was and she was free. Sheri hoped to one day get to such a place. She was trying with all her might to find her sanctuary. Sanctuary for both her and her children. All four of them could have stayed there and watched Skeeter twirl all day. Some people lived their entire lives never knowing the feeling that covered Skeeter as she danced in the kitchen that morning.

Sheri briefly thought about Bet and what she had done to her cousin. After that day in the shed, Sheri never felt safe around her grandmother again. Titi was Bet's favorite, so Sheri managed to escape much of her grandmother's wrath. Despite this, Sheri saw

Bet as someone to avoid at all cost. Skeeter still wore the scars of that beating. Deep-red scars crisscrossed both her legs. The hate that had scarred her no longer had her bound, though, because, as Niecy sang, God is truly amazing. Skeeter was freer than Bet had ever been in life. All was truly well with her soul.

Sheri quietly clapped her hands to get her children's attention. Time was ticking, and they had a full day ahead. She wanted to give Skeeter a hug and kiss goodbye, but she didn't want to disturb her cousin's joy. Sheri quickly cleaned up the dining table and backed out toward the hallway to gather bookbags and jackets. She took her cousin's joy as a good sign for the new school year.

CHAPTER 7

A cacophony of sirens, car horns and other miscellaneous rush hour noises filled the air as Sheri and Gloria walked into the downtown office building. Sheri was still getting used to working in such a buttoned-up environment. It was obvious the days of Robinson Brothers were long gone. She was thankful Gloria had been able to pull some strings in order for her to get the job. Sheri had a better start than most moving to a new city, and she didn't take it for granted.

Gloria wore a navy-blue St. Johns Knit suit with gold buttons, sheer stockings and navy-blue pumps. Sheri laughed to herself, thinking about how Bet would flip out if she could see her citified businesswoman of a granddaughter. Even in a fairly conservative style of dress, Gloria's curves still were able to poke through. Sheri wore a dark, slate-grey suit and a cream blouse. Black flats and a string of pearls finished the look.

"We're still on for this afternoon?" Sheri asked as they waited for the next elevator up. Today was the day Sheri was finally going to register for spring classes at CCB. She had pored over the brochures Gloria had given her just about every night. She had enough money set aside to register for two classes.

"Of course! I think I'm probably more excited about all this than you are, honestly." Gloria smiled at her. "You brought your determined self right up here from Spruce Junction. Just a hittin' the ground running. You're a real stick of dynamite, girl."

Sheri looked down at her shoes and could feel herself blush.

"You know" — Gloria leaned closer to her cousin as if she were about to tell the biggest piece of gossip — "he keeps asking about you."

Sheri pursed her lips and gave Gloria an uncomfortable stare just as the elevator arrived.

"I think I'm going to invite him over for Thanksgiving." Gloria leaned against the elevator wall, picking at invisible specks of lint on her jacket sleeve.

"Please don't."

"He's fine, he's got a good job and his nose is wide open," Gloria rattled off the qualifications of the delivery driver who had his eyes on Sheri. "Maybe not Thanksgiving, but I can put together a card party. Something informal. I'll send him an invite."

"Gloria, I just got settled." Sheri shook her head, frustrated. "I'm not trying to deal with that just yet. I already told you my plan is –"

"I know, I know. You're going to go to school so you can do better for your babies. I know." Gloria rolled her eyes as the elevator lurched upwards. "I'm not telling you to marry the damn man, God."

Thankfully for Sheri, they had an elevator to themselves. She wasn't in the mood to deal with her cousin, and there would be no one to witness her annoyance.

"He fine, Sheri. You gotta at least admit that."

"And how is he even asking about me?" Sheri gave Gloria an accusatory glance just as the door opened up to her floor. "Are you bringing me up to him? Does he know we're related?"

"Yes." Gloria gave a defiant neck roll. "Yes, he does. I told him you and I were people."

"I don't need you playing matchmaker for me."

"First of all, I'm doing no such thing. The way I see it, you were going to catch his eye whether I was around or not." Gloria shrugged as the elevator doors closed, separating the cousins.

It had been a good while since Sheri had been on a date. Back in Spruce Junction, her cousin Angie matched her up with a mechanic friend, but he got weird once Sheri said she had children. Then there was the guy from Eunice's church whose mother really didn't take to Sheri, so that was over before it even began.

For a while, Sheri had been platonic friends with Randall, a former Robinson Brothers co-worker of hers before he got laid off. Sheri sincerely enjoyed Randall's company. They had outings with the children where they taught the boys how to fish. Randall was her comfort after Kenneth suddenly turned cold once Peach was born. He would cut the boys' hair and teach them how to dap.

Everything was going so well until Randall made it known that he wanted to take things to another level with Sheri. Why can't we just stay friends? I just need a friend right now. I love you, the children look up to you. Why can't that be okay? Sheri remembered pleading to him. What they had was light and sweet. It felt genuine. She was heartbroken when everything fell apart.

Later, Sheri learned some guys at work and some of Randall's family members had given him a real hard time about his place in her life. They said he was weak and a sucker being used by a single mother. They said Randall was no better than a flunky and that Sheri was making a joke out of his manhood. Once Sheri learned this, she felt as if she had been stabbed right straight in the heart. Was a relationship only valid if sex was involved? She vowed to teach her children that there were many ways to show love.

Sheri's mind quickly went back to her biggest task of the day. She had talked with Titi a week or so ago about her plans to start college. Titi didn't sound too moved, but she made Sheri promise to call Uncle Mike with the news. Generally, it was Uncle Mike who got excited about her life announcements anyway. Sheri made a mental note to give him a call.

Tuna fish sandwiches with Utz plain chips on the side fueled the second half of Sheri's day as she sorted and filed patient invoices. It always astounded her how much people paid in medical costs. Everything had a price. Sheri felt there was a cruel irony for a person to get well only to be buried in medical bills for the rest of their life. Sheri continued her work while R&B quietly played in the back corner of her cubicle. She didn't notice the delivery man with the gleaming smile standing there holding a package and a clipboard.

"Anita fan?" His skin tone was about the same shade of tan as his work uniform. He was a hair taller than average height, and he had baseball mitts for hands. His dark-brown hair was cut in a low fade, which added to the youthfulness of his face, and he had a small dimple in his chin and the prettiest, whitest teeth Sheri had ever seen. There was a sparkle in his eyes. If life had been hard for him, it definitely didn't show.

"Yes, I like Anita," was all Sheri could manage to say. She could only shake her head at her awkwardness. Sheri looked into his dark-brown eyes and then down at his work shirt where his name was stitched. Harold. Such a sensible name. She already knew Gloria had sent him over here.

Harold softly cleared his throat. "I just needed to drop this off for Ms. Shell." He lifted the box slightly.

"Yes! I'm sorry. I was trying to get these invoices together. Let me sign for this." Sheri took the clipboard off the top of the box and signed. Harold placed the box on Sheri's desk.

"I'm Harold, but my name is stitched on my shirt, so you probably already knew that." Harold laughed.

Sheri nodded and pointed at his chest. "Yup, saw it right there."

There was a brief pause between the two as electricity began to slowly form in the air.

"I'm Sheri, but you probably know that already. Thanks to Gloria."

Harold looked down at his work boots and smiled while looking as if Sheri had caught him red-handed. He continued to linger around Sheri's cubicle opening a little while longer as if trying to find a way to lengthen the conversation.

"So, how are you liking it here?" he asked.

"I like it. The pace is a little different than what I'm used to back home, but change is good. I like not having to be on my feet all the time." A look of embarrassment flashed across Sheri's face when she realized what she'd said. She didn't want her words to be seen as an insult to the man who made his living constantly on his feet.

Harold didn't seem to notice Sheri's faux pas. "Look..." He glanced down at the top of the file cabinet in Sheri's cubicle. "I don't want to make things awkward since we're both on the clock right now. I think you're absolutely beautiful, and I would like to have a way to talk to you, outside of just this work situation."

Sheri decided to cut right to the chase: "You seem really nice, but I have children and I'm signing up for school today." Her schedule was already tight, and the last thing she needed was a man trying to compete for time that she didn't have to give.

"That's great to hear. You're focused and you've got a lot on your plate. I can definitely respect it." Harold leaned forward and looked Sheri square in her eyes. "It doesn't have to be today or tomorrow. Until then, I guess we'll just continue seeing each other when we see each other. I needed you to know, directly from me, how I felt."

Harold flashed Sheri one last smile. Gloria's cousin had him intrigued right out of the gate. He knew there would be some work involved getting to know this one, but he was willing to put in the effort.

CHAPTER 8

1993

It was a relatively pleasant winter evening as Sheri stepped through the red-painted double doors of Lexington Square Elementary School for the first Parents' Night of the new year. Sheri tightened her cranberry-and-gold scarf and filed in with the rest of the parents. Gloria had volunteered to pick up Peach from the daycare, which meant Sheri would be able to devote this evening to just her boys.

Sheri walked through the sand-colored hallways. She smiled at the large, plastic boards that displayed random 'Did You Know?' facts along with affirmative quotes and pictures of notable African-American trailblazers such as Mae Jamison, Ben Carson and Oprah Winfrey. She made her way towards the school cafeteria and saw Champ and Popsee waiting in the doorway. Their eyes lit up when they saw their mother coming their way. Sheri did a little jog to her sons and greeted them with a hug and kiss.

"MA! WE MADE SOME STUFF IN AFTERSCHOOL!" Popsee's eyes were big with anticipation as he led her to a long bench towards the back of the cafeteria covered in various art projects. Popsee lifted up a collage he'd made from different magazine clippings.

"Can I take it home tonight?" Sheri asked.

"Yup. Mr. Keith said today is the day everything is going home," Popsee explained.

Sheri turned toward her eldest, who had been fairly quiet. "Where's yours, sir?"

Champ walked up further to another cafeteria bench and pointed out his own collage. Sheri tilted her head and looked at the magazine clippings Champ had pasted to his poster board. There were pictures of smiling men at work. Happy firefighters, construction workers, doctors and truckers stared back up at Sheri. She put her arm around Popsee's shoulder and looked over at Champ.

"What was the theme?"

"My future," Champ replied, wearing his usual serious expression. "But I didn't see what I really wanted, and that was a man on a computer. I want to work with computers when I grow up."

Sheri leaned down to kiss her steadily growing son on top of his head. "Your time is coming. I see it already. My own little computer wizard." Sheri took both pieces of art with her and lovingly placed them in her work tote bag. She planned to put them on their bedroom wall once they got back to the house.

Parents and their children were finding places to sit around the front of the cafeteria as Principal Stanley Morton walked into the large room. Mr. Morton was a rather short man with a bald head, full beard and penchant for tailored suits. The peanut butter-brown man had a voice just like one of those Quiet Storm radio DJs. Sheri observed him moving about, trying to get the microphone set up. According to the flyer, there was supposed to be a full schedule of speakers, and there was no time to waste.

Eventually, the parents' night started and the presentations began. Mr. Morton spoke first. After him was Ms. Dobbins, the vice-principal, then Ms. Sullivan, who supervised Lexington Square's afterschool program. After the school staff portion of the night was over, representatives from various community partners lined up to speak.

A woman with shoulder-length black hair, a narrow face and piercing grey eyes came up to the microphone and gave the crowd a stiff wave and an uneasy smile. Sheri folded her arms as she waited for the woman to speak. She introduced herself as Irene Gibbs from the Community Empowerment Center, an agency devoted to helping families reach their goals in life. She held up a flyer for the New Horizons Housing Program, which provided affordable housing to select families around the city.

Sheri leaned forward to get a better listen. Although she felt that she was in a good place over with Gloria, it never hurt to see what her options were. Sheri knew eventually she would have to move. The plan had always been to have space for her children to grow and stretch out. The woman noted that the selection process was competitive, and all applications would be thoroughly screened. Every approved family would get their own house—not an apartment—and the rent would be at a discounted rate.

After the speakers, Sheri attended the community fair in the cafeteria. Not surprisingly, a long line had formed alongside Ms. Gibbs's table. She made small talk with each of the parents as they reached to get a flyer, a CEC ink pin and a little squeeze toy with CEC stamped on it. Sheri brought the boys to a bench closer to the table and went to go stand in line and wait her turn.

"Well, hello there!" The woman seemed far less nervous at her table than she had been at the microphone.

"Hi, I'm very interested in your program." Sheri nodded.

"Wonderful! Please, take a flyer and check us out. As I said, it's a very selective program, but it is definitely worth it. We believe every family deserves their own home. A place to grow and thrive." Ms. Gibbs flashed a plastic smile at Sheri. "We look forward to receiving your application!"

Once the January chill hit them, Sheri and the boys quickened their pace on the way back to Gloria's house. Champ and Popsee seemed to have gotten a second wind, and both complained about being hungry. Sheri crossed her fingers in hopes that Gloria or Skeeter had something left over.

Sheri was greeted by the sound of a church organ when she opened the door. Skeeter and Peach, both in their own gospel trance, were dancing around talking about how they were expecting a miracle. Sheri and the boys were able to walk in fairly unnoticed.

"Ma, we hungry!" Popsee yelled over the music.

Skeeter snapped out of her holy reverie and pointed toward the kitchen. "There's food in the fridge. I cooked."

Sheri warmed up plates of chicken Alfredo for her and the boys. Afterward, she made sure to put up the collages from school.

As small as it might have seemed, the pieces made the space feel like home. Once everyone was washed and sleeping, Sheri took out the flyer to look it over once more. She patted the glossy sheet of paper and slid it back into her tote bag. For now, everything was good.

◆ ◆ ◆

Gloria turned off the burner, sliced open the aluminum foil and poured the popcorn into a large bowl. She poured a generous amount of melted butter over the fluffy, white kernels. Jimmy Budd decided to stretch out his long limbs and sit on the floor while Skeeter and the children got comfortable on the sofa. Gloria's floor model television gave the living room a hazy glow.

"Sheri, it's about to come on," Gloria called up the stairs to her cousin. She took the large bowl of popcorn and sat on the couch directly behind Jimmy Budd, who rested his arm on her thigh.

Sheri came down the steps and found a seat next to the sofa. A can of grape soda was shared amongst the siblings, passing sips until the sweet syrup was gone. Sheri rolled her eyes, wondering how late her babies were going to be up that night.

"I missed this the first time it came on TV, the live broadcast. I read about it in the magazines afterward, though. Michael Jackson doing the moonwalk. It was everywhere." Gloria softly massaged Jimmy Budd's temples as they waited for the show to start.

"Yeah, I don't even know what I was busy doing in 1983." Jimmy Budd lazily scratched his chin.

"Well, that was before you met me, so whatever you were doing, it wasn't anything worthwhile."

Jimmy Budd yelled out a laugh and playfully buried his face in the softness of Gloria's thigh.

Skeeter ran to turn the volume up on the TV just as the announcer began reciting the names of attendees.

"Shhhhh!" Gloria yelled out to no one in particular. "Y'all don't know this, but the Shaw home was a bonified Motown household. Okay?"

The sound of young Detroit pulsated all through the house as everyone rocked and danced to the rhythm. Peach's eyes lit up, watching the people dancing and singing on stage. Champ sat munching fistfuls of popcorn, jamming to the music. Popsee ran over and began two-stepping next to the television. Laughter filled the room as the family erupted into cheers for both Michael Jackson and Popsee.

"I remember when all of 'em were on the Ed Sullivan show and Michael came out with that purple hat." Gloria nodded. "Yup, I was sitting right here in this very living room. Me and Ms. Hazel."

Skeeter got up and began cleaning up with the help of Champ and Popsee. Sheri stayed seated and pulled out a folded piece of paper that had been in her pocket.

"Whatcha got?" Gloria looked over at Sheri.

"It's a flyer for an affordable housing program. Got it the other week at the boys' school." Sheri continued to thumb over the sheet of paper.

Gloria gave Sheri a curious look. "We ain't rushing you out, Sheri. I mean, you practically just got here."

"I know, and I appreciate you." Sheri shifted in the chair. "I just wanted to see what the city had to offer. It's a program run by the Community Empowerment Center and Sloane-Douglas."

Both Gloria's and Jimmy Budd's heads snapped in Sheri's direction. "Sloane-Douglas?!"

"Do you even know about that place? People walk in there and they don't come out right, Sheri." Gloria rolled her eyes at her cousin's naiveté.

"It's just bad history. You have to watch yourself around those folks," Jimmy echoed Gloria's sentiment.

The couple must have talked for about two hours nonstop, trying their hardest to convince Sheri that this was a deal with the devil. They detailed how there had always been a history of mistrust when it came to Sloane-Douglas Hospital, especially in Baltimore's Black community.

"Just be careful, Sheri, that's all," Jimmy warned in a voice that sounded even more tired than usual. "Always keep a close eye on them. Always."

CHAPTER 9

Sheri gazed into the April night sky, trying to see if there were any visible stars. Watching the stars illuminate the deep Carolina sky was always one of her favorite pastimes back in Spruce Junction. Lightning bugs would shine around her as she meditated on what, exactly, lay beyond the cover of darkness.

She waited for Harold to bring his car around to the front of the movie theatre. The pair were on their first date night and, so far, everything had been wonderful. After Sheri initially denied him her telephone number, Harold continued to quietly pursue her. He wasn't overbearing, which Sheri sincerely appreciated. On one occasion, when Harold was off, he came by the office and the two had grabbed lunch. Sheri ate her usual chicken salad sandwich and plain chips while Harold bought something from the canteen. They people-watched, compared Anita Baker songs and joked about how aggressive the pigeons were that particular day. Sheri was crushed when her break was over and she had to return to work.

Harold pulled his white Mazda around to the front of the movie theater and flashed a grin from the passenger side window that sent a quick tingle throughout Sheri's body. He opened Sheri's door with an exaggerated bow. She giggled as she slid into the passenger seat and made herself comfortable. The dial turned to V-103 as Gerald and Eddie Levert's voices filled the air, singing "Baby Hold On To Me." Sheri wondered if the song was a sign. She quickly shook her head and smiled to herself, reminding herself not to ruin her good time by overthinking.

"I don't know about you, but my mind is still on that steak," Harold laughed as he put the car in drive.

The pair decided to try the new steakhouse that opened just outside the city lines. It was Sheri's first time in the "county" that she always heard people talking about. Over dinner, Harold talked about his plans to eventually become an independent driver and secure contracts with businesses handling their delivery needs.

"There really is room for everyone, whether people want to acknowledge it or not," Harold observed during their dinner at the steakhouse. "The key is finding your lane."

He also mentioned that his brother had a home remodeling business that he helped with on the weekends. Sheri asked him when he found time to rest, and he gave her a humble shrug.

"I'm still looking for my lane, but I'm excited that I'm back in school again." Sheri took a sip of the red wine that Harold had selected for the table.

"Honestly, I'm still learning about these different types of wines," Harold had whispered to Sheri conspiratorially after he placed the order. "My older sister and her husband go to vineyards, so I'm just going on her word."

Piano music played quietly in the background as Sheri talked about how well the children were adjusting to life in their new city and how much she appreciated their patience. The move had been a big adjustment for everyone.

"You know you glow whenever you talk about them." Harold gazed at Sheri over the candlelight.

"Well," Sheri began, laughing self-consciously as she felt herself blush, "they're really pretty cool kids. I'm not just saying that because they're mine, either."

Over rib eyes and sautéed asparagus, the two discussed family life, living in Baltimore and the dating scene. Harold admitted that his schedule made it difficult for him to find time to mingle and hang out. He and his cousin had gone to the Five Mile House a few months back, and it had made him realize that he wanted to connect with women in a different type of setting. Sheri told how Gloria and Skeeter wanted to take her out to the club when she first arrived, but she had ruled that out quick and early. Skeeter had shrugged it off, but Gloria moved around the house for the rest of the evening as if her feelings had been genuinely hurt.

Sheri reclined her seat and let the night breeze caress her face as Harold made the drive back into the city. Baltimore had a sultry beauty that really stood out at night. The corner lamps and lit buildings gave everything a haunting, film noir glow. Harold drove through downtown as people coming out of the Baltimore Arena filled the streets. Sheri pulled her seat up slightly to gaze upon the moonlit waters of the harbor.

"Can we stop? I mean… to see the water. I haven't had a chance to really see this part of the city yet." Sheri looked over at Harold.

"Of course. It's your night. No curfews over here." Harold found a parking space, and the two got out to walk around the water and see the sights of Harbor Place.

"I remember when they were building this area up. It was a pretty big deal. Everyone came out, and this really has become the place to be," Harold reminisced as he surveyed the glammed-up shopping areas and eateries. It seemed a far cry from the downtown of his childhood.

"I love this place, but then again, I love just being around water, period. It calms me. I would love a house on the beach one day." The thought of waking up and going to sleep around water felt like a dream to Sheri. Maybe one day.

"You're deceptively understated. I feel like there are so many layers to you." Harold took in the woman who stood just over five feet, but had a presence far bigger than her body. Her energy lured people in, and he wondered if she realized that about herself. "A person could be with you for years, and they'd still be finding out new things about you every day."

Sheri shook her head, her eyes staying locked on the dark water. "Well, God knows I'm not trying to be the mysterious type."

"I really enjoyed myself tonight."

Sheri felt herself go into full blush. She looked at Harold and gave him a wide smile. "Me too. This was nice. All of it." She gently grabbed his baseball mitt of a hand and held it in hers. Harold responded with a slight squeeze, and hand-in-hand, they walked back to the car.

The active downtown area quickly gave way to empty residential streets. Despite it being a Saturday night in April, Gloria's block was quiet from end to end. Harold found a space behind

Gloria and Jimmy Budd's cars. Ever the gentleman, he got out to open Sheri's door for her.

"Thank you, Harold."

Sheri leaned up to give Harold a quick peck on the cheek. Then, as she walked toward the marble steps of Gloria's rowhome, she stopped to turn back to give her date a full kiss on the lips. Harold wrapped his arms around Sheri's waist to pull her closer. His full lips felt like soft pillows as they brushed against hers. Sheri breathed in his cologne, which had mercilessly teased her nose the entire night. As if it dared her to inhale him inch by inch.

Sheri laughed and pulled back to say good night again as she made a second attempt to walk up the steps. She felt giddy and dizzy. She had put finding romantic love on the back burner when she made the move to Baltimore, and now here she was, floating around like an infatuated schoolgirl.

The door opened, and Sheri immediately noticed how quiet everything was in the house. The air was heavy and a strange smell hung in the air. A knot began to form in Sheri's stomach, and she knew something was wrong. She walked further into the house, but something told her to leave the front door open. At first she didn't notice them, but after her eyes adjusted, Sheri could see Gloria and Jimmy Budd passed out on the sofa.

"Hey!" Sheri called out to the two large blobs. Gloria and Jimmy didn't even look like themselves. Sheri took a deep breath and counted backward from three.

"Hey!" This time Sheri clapped her hands, trying to get the sleeping couple's attention. Sheri walked over to the front door to see if Harold was still outside. Thankfully, he hadn't pulled off.

"I think everything is okay, but could you wait here for a few minutes longer?" Sheri asked.

"I'll leave when I know you're okay," he called out to her. "Don't worry."

The sound of Harold's voice caused Gloria to stir. "What the fuck is going on?" she called out as she tried to fight through the haze. She wasn't wearing a bra, and her breasts were desperately trying to free themselves from her champagne-colored full slip.

Sheri whirled to face the living room. "Gloria, where the fuck are my kids? Where's Skeeter and what's that smell?"

Sheri no longer had the patience to use gentle words. She was fighting hard not to panic, but she felt as if she were walking through an acid trip-fueled dream.

Gloria mumbled something but went back to lying on Jimmy Budd, who had made no movements. Sheri honestly wondered if the man was still alive.

"Gloria!" Sheri hauled off and gave Gloria's chest a hard smack. "Where are my kids!"

By this time, Harold had moved from his car and stood at the bottom of the steps. He didn't know exactly what was happening, but he heard Sheri's yells and wanted to be closer just in case he had to run in.

"Kim got 'em, shit," Gloria spat while looking at Sheri as if they were two complete strangers.

"WHO THE FUCK IS KIM, GLORIA? WHERE ARE MY KIDS? WHAT'S WRONG WITH YOU?!"

"KIM LIVES DOWN THE GAHDAMN STREET! FOUR DOORS DOWN!" Gloria roared back, only to collapse at Jimmy's side yet again.

It took all of Sheri's strength not to pick up a lamp, vase or something heavy and beat her cousin and her cousin's boyfriend about the head. She could have easily taken them to meet Jesus that night, and the thought of having rage this raw actually scared Sheri. She quickly walked back out of the house, leaving the front door wide open. Fuck 'em.

Sheri thanked Harold again for waiting and told him that her children were down the street. Gloria had said they were four doors down, so that's where they went, but Sheri was fully prepared to kick in every door on Preston Street if need be. Thankfully, at the fourth house, a girl who looked to be around eighteen opened the door. Sheri could see all three of her babies sitting on the couch watching a Bugs Bunny cartoon.

"Hi, I'm Sheri, and those are my kids. I'm here to get them. Did my cousin promise you any money?" Sheri talked at a rapid speed as Champ, Popsee and Peach ran over and hugged her around her hips.

"Oh, don't worry, ma'am. Ms. Gloria already paid me. They've been really good. We were just watching some tapes. She told me you would be coming to get them."

"Oh, she did, huh?" Sheri couldn't believe Gloria. Aunt Juniper was probably rolling in her grave because of her daughter's mess.

Sheri kissed her babies and they walked back up the block alongside Harold.

"This is Mr. Harold, y'all. He's my friend." This was definitely not the way she wanted to introduce Harold to her children.

"Nice meeting you guys and lady." Harold smiled at all three of the children as he continued to walk up the street.

"Ma, we're hungry," Champ deadpanned.

"Miss Kim was nice but she only gave us chips!" Popsee's dissatisfaction couldn't be denied.

Harold looked over at Sheri, who was clearly consumed by her own rage-filled thoughts of what she planned to do to Gloria and Jimmy Budd.

"Hey. Do y'all like burgers and fries?"

"Yes." The three siblings cautiously eyed the new man who was clearly in love with their mother.

"We can go up to the Hollywood Diner. It's twenty-four hours and they have real good food. The best fries in Baltimore."

"Harold, it's late and we—"

"I'm not sleepy. Are you all sleepy?" Harold had tapped into a second wind, and he would have stayed with Sheri all night and through the morning if she needed him to.

"Not sheepy. Hungry," Peach whimpered and buried her face in Sheri's leg.

Sheri took a deep breath and looked at the children, who were staring at her with pleading eyes. She looked over at Harold, who had his own set of pleading eyes. She shook her head yes, and they turned from Gloria's steps to Harold's car. Harold made sure the trio were snapped in tight in the backseat while Sheri went back to Gloria's to shut the front door—but she didn't lock it.

It was past midnight when the group finally returned to the scene of the madness. The children were laid out in the backseat, full and asleep, while Sheri looked like she was still fighting to keep her composure.

"This was a wild night, and not in a good way." She spoke softly to Harold as a jazz instrumental quietly played to fill in the silence.

"It's nothing. I'm serious. I'm glad they took to me." Harold looked over at Sheri, then reached down to squeeze her hand. "I can help bring the kids up if you want. Since they're sleeping."

Sheri hesitated. She didn't know how the house would look or if Gloria would still be laid out in her full-breasted glory. She remembered Bet used to hate it whenever strangers would try to come into her house. 'Let them negroes sit right there on the damn porch!' she would always yell.

"If you could help me get them out this car and up the steps to the door, I'd really appreciate it."

Harold pulled up to the house, and Sheri saw that Jimmy Budd's car was gone. She highly doubted that he could fully operate a vehicle in the state she had seen him in on the sofa a few hours ago, but she was too burned out to even care.

"We're back," Sheri called over her shoulder, but she knew her babies were likely stone asleep. Today had been two days in one. Harold and Sheri both jumped out of the car and began corralling the sleeping siblings. Sheri got Popsee and Champ while Harold picked up Peach. They walked up the marble steps and Sheri pushed the door, thinking it was still unlocked. But the door didn't open. Someone had locked it.

Skeeter's probably back, Sheri thought as she fished for her keys and unlocked the door.

Harold handed Peach over to Sheri as Champ and Popsee stumbled through the doorway and up the steps. The kitchen light was on, so it wasn't as dark as it had been before.

"I keep saying it, but thank you so much. I appreciate it."

"No worries at all. Are you sure you don't want me to help you walk them up?"

Sheri shook her head, reiterating that she could handle the rest.

"I want to see you again." Harold stood at the top of the steps, looking as if he was fully prepared to stand there all night if need be.

Sheri stretched her neck to look at Harold over Peach's slumbering body. "I want to see you, too."

Sheri heard someone stumble, and she knew she needed to get all the way in the house to make sure her bone-weary boys didn't have any issues on Gloria's steep staircase.

"I don't intend for this to be our only date by any means, Ms. Calloway. You've got layers to you. I want to see as much as I can."

"Just like one of those canned biscuits, I guess." Sheri didn't know where that came from. Clearly, she was just as tired as her children.

Harold burst out laughing, which made Peach jump a little, but also helped cut some of the heaviness in the air. Sheri started laughing herself.

"Good night, Harold."

"Good night, Sheri."

CHAPTER 10

Sheri took out the New Horizons Housing Program flyer and examined it inch by inch. There was an image of a smiling family being handed house keys. Another image had a little boy riding his bicycle on a bright, tree-lined street. Sheri turned to look at the park across the street from the house. Usually, she didn't have this view. Now, however, Sheri was sitting on the boys' bed. The night before had run pretty long, so they had fallen asleep on the bed closest to the wall, which Sheri usually shared with Peach.

She curled her knees up to her chest and leaned against the wall, still staring out the window. It was time for an exit plan. It had been four weeks since the incident with Gloria and Jimmy, but the memory was still very fresh in Sheri's mind. Sheri felt stuck, and she hated that.

She looked at the housing flyer again. "Quick Application Process! Start Your New Life Today!" the colorful flyer boasted. Monday. Sheri would call out sick and go down Monday. She made a mental note to get her paperwork together so she would be ready.

Champ, Popsee and Peach were still off in their respective dream worlds. Champ had his arm around his brother's shoulders. Peach was nestled alongside her mother. Sheri wanted them to stay this way forever. She thought about Spruce Junction every day, but, over time, she had grown more comfortable with her move to Baltimore. The stars in her eyes were long gone, but she still felt that they were moving in the right direction.

Sheri thought about Titi. She knew she needed to call her mother. They'd last talked around the holidays, but the conversation was nothing more than pleasantries and surface talk. Sheri suspected that her mother had hesitant feelings about the move, but, to Titi's credit, she didn't rain on Sheri's parade. Although

Sheri missed home, she had resented the fact that she and her children had to be constrained to one place. She wanted to see what else was out there.

A car blasting bass-heavy music drove down the otherwise quiet street. Sheri laid back down in the bed and stared at the ceiling. Monday. Monday will be the day. Sheri closed her eyes but quickly opened them again. She still had questions. Lots of them. She didn't want to live in a house where it was obvious that she was very much in the dark about things.

Sheri went to Skeeter's room and found her in bed listening to music on her yellow Walkman. Knowing her cousin, she could be listening to anything, but Sheri figured that it was likely a gospel tape. She sat down in the chair close to the door and leaned her head up against the wall, waiting to get Skeeter's attention.

"Thinking about giving that housing program a chance. Going to go by on Monday to apply."

"Aren't you concerned about what Jimmy Budd said? All that talk about the hospital?" Skeeter sat up on her bed and took off her headphones.

"No. Can't say that I am." Sheri shifted her weight in the chair and folded her arms.

Skeeter swung her legs over the bed and sat upright. "I mean… it's just that… he's from here, and he would know more—"

"Jimmy Budd is a drug addict, Skeeter. Gloria is one, too. I don't trust their judgment about anything anymore, and there's nothing they have to say that I need to hear."

"Sheri!" Skeeter let out a shocked gasp, wondering what had gotten into her cousin.

"What?" Sheri's face was twisted in an angry sneer.

"Yeah, they have their struggles, but they're people too. Most importantly, they're our people. We family. They opened their home to us."

"When were you going to tell me that they were up in this house doing drugs, Skeeter?" Sheri's eyes narrowed as she leaned forward in the chair that was much too small to accommodate her hips. She stared at the woman long and hard as if she didn't know her. As if they hadn't spent summers catching lightning bugs, searching for cicadas and drinking cold Cheerwine.

"Let me guess, you're dabbling in them too, right?" Sheri shook her head in disgust and let out a bitter laugh.

"No."

"You came all the way up here from Spruce Junction just to smoke some drugs."

"I ain't on drugs, Peanut. Shit." Skeeter let out an exasperated sigh and rubbed her forehead.

Sheri leaned back and gave her cousin a hard once-over, still unconvinced. "Listen, my children and I need our own space. This whole situation doesn't even feel right anymore, Skeeter. Not since that night."

"Jimmy and Gloria feel terrible about what happened. I know. I hear their talks. They think you hate them." Skeeter pleaded with Sheri, her liquid-black eyes the size of saucers.

"They put my children in danger."

"They were over Kim's house. She's good people. I know her. They were okay, Peanut."

Sheri was in complete disbelief. She felt her cousin was too damn casual about the whole situation.

"Skeeter, I don't know Kim like that. To make this even worse, had you come home before me that night, I would have been none the wiser. I don't know what to believe anymore."

Sheri thought back to Gloria and Jimmy's party that previous summer, her yelling about Miss Mary Mack and Gloria's rendezvous with the strange man that wasn't Jimmy later that same night.

"Sheri, they were safe. Kim is good people. Nothing was going to happen to them." Skeeter spoke as measured and calm as she could muster. It was apparent that Sheri could explode at any minute. She understood her cousin's frustration, but she also knew that Gloria was fighting a battle that was far beyond what anyone could imagine.

"Think about it this way," Skeeter reasoned, "would you have wanted them to be in the house while Glo and Jimmy were shooting up? At least they cared enough to send the babies somewhere safe. You were out with Harold. I was working. It was a long week, and things are happening with Gloria at the job. I'm not excusing them—"

"Sounds like it to me." Sheri continued to look at Skeeter as if it were their first time crossing paths.

Skeeter let out a defeated sigh. "They needed their fix, Peanut. They're addicts. That doesn't make them bad people. Addiction is a disease. I saw it on the *Oprah* show. Just give them a little bit of grace."

Sheri let her arms down just to refold them again. She didn't know what to do anymore. She felt trapped.

"Think of it this way. It's no different than when JR used to be out on Bet's porch drunk all the time." Skeeter tried to connect Gloria's battle with her father Joe Richard's alcoholism.

"That's different."

"How?"

"That's alcohol and it's just not the same." Sheri turned her nose up matter-of-factly.

"Just because the drug is legal doesn't mean it ain't a drug. Drugs are drugs, Peanut." Skeeter countered.

Sheri slowly got up and walked back to her room. She knew what she needed to do.

◆ ◆ ◆

Sheri and the children hustled off the bus and made the trek to Eutaw Street and the Beechfield building, where the Community Empowerment Center offices were located. The cold, concrete edifice almost looked out of place surrounded by bucolic rowhomes and fragrant rose bushes. Champ held Peach's hand as they walked in front of Sheri and Popsee. Sheri was trying to wean Peach from the stroller, her ultimate goal was to purchase a car for her family.

"Alright, y'all, real quick." Sheri took out her camera a few steps away from the front door. She shooed the siblings closer together and checked around to see if anyone was coming so she would know how much time she had to get a few good shots in.

75

"Ma?" Champ protested.

"C'mon, real quick. Just two." Sheri smiled at her children. She was immensely proud of them. They were a smart, considerate and pleasant bunch. She considered herself blessed.

Popsee and Champ gave each other quick embarrassed glances while their mother played photographer on the sidewalk.

"We don't have that much time now!" Sheri put Champ and Popsee against the wall and positioned Peach slightly out in front and between her brothers. She nodded in approval and took a few pictures. Today marked the beginning of big things, and Sheri wanted to commemorate it.

After the photo shoot, the family walked into the building and received a swift blast of cold air courtesy of the overactive air conditioning unit.

It's warm, but not warm enough for that just yet, Sheri thought as she squinched her nose at the frigid blast. She checked in with the front desk guard and made her way to office 301. Community Empowerment Center was stenciled in large, blue block lettering on the glass door.

Sheri signed herself in and found seats against the wall to wait for her name to be called. She pulled out Champ's computer and handed it to her son. Popsee and Peach surrounded their brother as the computer came to life, playing a trumpet-like tune. Sheri looked around the fairly busy waiting room. She saw parents there with their children while other people sat off to themselves. There were tables littered with brochures and flyers for the various programs that were offered by the agency.

A man in business attire wearing tortoiseshell glasses and a low, tapered fade walked into the waiting area from a side door. He held a metal clipboard in his hand.

"Ms. Sheri Calloway?"

Sheri quickly got up and started gathering her belongings. The children slid out of their seats and followed next to their mother. The man in the glasses flashed them all a warm smile and directed them to the office area.

The office had two desks and two computers. Although there were no windows, the space was brightly decorated, with pictures of smiling families and affirmation quotes everywhere. The man ran out to get another chair as Sheri got the children settled in. He jogged back into the office carrying a green plastic chair that he placed next to Champ. Popsee moved over from the seat he was sharing with Peach to the green chair.

"Ms. Calloway." The man shook Sheri's hand as he took a seat in his wide-backed office chair. "My name is Jamal Mendenhall, and I hear that you want to know more about our New Horizons Housing Program?"

Sheri explained how she had gotten a flyer during Parents' Night at the school. She took out her pay stubs as well as the birth certificates for Champ, Popsee and Peach. The man had the aura of a seasoned minister as he tented his fingers on his desk and nodded his head.

Mr. Mendenhall pulled out a folder from one of his desk drawers and handed it to Sheri. The front of the folder was exactly like the flyer Sheri had been staring at for over four months. The smiling family, the little boy riding his bicycle—only this time on heavier, glossier paper. Mr. Mendenhall told Sheri the program was geared toward working parents that were serious about bettering their lives. Anyone the CEC deemed not a good fit would be flat-out denied. There would be a case management component to the program that the CEC would oversee in partnership with Sloane-Douglas.

At the mention of Sloane-Douglas, Sheri leaned back in her chair with a worried expression. Mr. Mendenhall seemed to notice and reiterated that the New Horizons Housing Program was a CEC initiative through and through, and Sloane-Douglas only provided limited medical case management to the families. Sloane-Douglas, he further explained, provided much of the funding to the program, which allowed the accepted families to pay such a discounted price in rent.

"They give us the money, we give them a little shine," Mr. Mendenhall explained in basic terms.

Sheri figured this was what people meant when they used the word bureaucracy. She looked over at the children, who had been quiet and attentive, giving the man in the glasses their full attention. Champ and Peach even had their hands folded in their laps.

Mr. Mendenhall photocopied the papers Sheri had brought to go with her application. He handed back the originals and the copies, telling Sheri to just bring the completed application with the copies when she came back, and she would be good to go. If she brought the application back to them by that Saturday, they could process her the following Monday, and she would have the final decision within seven business days.

Sheri took a deep breath. This was really happening. She was coming up on her first full year of living in Baltimore, and so much had happened in a pretty short amount of time. She would soon have her own home.

Sheri felt as if she were floating on a cloud, grateful that a wonderful opportunity had opened up for her and her family. She thanked Mr. Mendenhall and put the glossy folder in her pocketbook.

The May sunshine felt like kisses on Sheri's face. She smiled down at her little gang as they stood on the sidewalk, watching the people go by. Baltimore appeared to be in full bloom, and she wasn't in a rush to go back indoors.

"We hungry?"

"Yes!" The children all jumped in unison.

"I'm hungry, too, and I'm in the mood for a sub. C'mon, let's march!"

The Calloways marched through the streets of their new city on the way to Lexington Market. The last time Sheri had been at the market, she had come with Gloria and there had been a man with a table set up selling body oils. She was going to treat herself if she saw him today. A nice, light fragrance to match her happy.

CHAPTER 11

S heri sat cross-legged on her bed with a sleeping Peach in her lap. She lightly traced the outline of Peach's round face with her index finger. While both Champ and Popsee were on the tan side, Peach had a deeper cinnamon complexion with the prettiest red undertones. She had Sheri's nose, but the rest of her face and facial expressions belonged to Kenneth's mother. She liked to get silly, but she also had a soberness about her, so in that respect she was a mix of both her brothers. Sheri could usually find Peach sucking on her thumb, deep in thought.

Champ and Popsee had gone with Gloria and Skeeter to get snowballs. June was just getting started and the heat was already out in full force. Sheri wasn't in the mood for the sticky weather, nor was she ready to sit in awkward silence around Gloria. She had been mindful to not be outright disrespectful to her cousin, since she was living in the house rent-free, but Sheri still couldn't wrap her head around that night. On top of being scared and at her wits' end, she was embarrassed all of that had happened in front of Harold.

Since their first date, Harold and Sheri had gone on a couple of family get-togethers with Sheri's children and Harold's niece and nephew. One of their outings was a trip to Shake & Bake. It had been years since Sheri had put on roller skates, and it was fun watching the children take their first uneasy steps on the wooden skating floor. Harold's ten-year-old nephew, Amir, was already a natural. Champ watched the young boy's skating moves with an intensity that Sheri had never seen before.

Sheri continued to trace Peach's face, this time concentrating on her full, chestnut-brown eyebrows. This child has the most perfect eyebrows, and she doesn't even need them. Some people are fortunate, and they're none the wiser. Sheri lightly nuzzled her nose in Peach's hair and kissed her forehead. She leaned her back against the wall and looked out the window. She had turned in her paperwork to Mr. Mendenhall a few days after their meeting, and the big day was due to come sometime during the week. If everything went as planned, she and her children would be spending the summer in their own place.

◆ ◆ ◆

Sheri sat in her cubicle looking over her grades from that previous semester: one A and one B plus. She reclined in her office chair and gave a sigh of relief. To say that Sheri had been nervous about her return to school would have been an understatement. Although she was ready for the challenge, a part of her had been completely terrified. Her grades served as a reminder that she was more than capable of achieving whatever she put her mind to.

A transferred call broke Sheri's daze. She checked her telephone's Caller ID screen and stopped breathing when she saw it was the Community Empowerment Center. Sheri grabbed the receiver and gave a breathless 'hello.' Ms. Gibbs, from the Parents' Night, was on the other end. She informed Sheri that her application had been approved, and there was a pair of house keys on her desk with Sheri's name on them. She told Sheri that there would be a mandatory orientation session coming up on Saturday for her to attend, then she congratulated Sheri again and said she looked forward to seeing her on Saturday.

Sheri didn't think she would be out of Gloria's so soon, but for her to be able to land a house at a discounted rate was a blessing. Sheri moved her chair closer to her desk and took long, deep breaths. She was excited—this was when real life would begin. Skeeter, Gloria and even Jimmy Budd had been her lifeline, and now she would have to do more on her own. Sheri hoped that Skeeter would still be able to help with the children, but she knew that she could no longer take her cousin's presence for granted.

Sheri was excited about meeting her new neighbors. What kind of people would they be? She crossed her fingers that she would be moving onto a block with a lot of children. Although her children were each other's best friends, having a neighborhood crew of other young children was important as well. She didn't want her children to feel isolated in any way.

◆ ◆ ◆

"Good news! I'm getting the keys to my new place today!" Sheri flashed a large, dramatic smile like the game show hosts on TV.

"That Sloane-Douglas house?" Jimmy asked with sad eyes.

Gloria sucked her teeth and continued eating her fruit salad.

Champ, Popsee and Peach exchanged confused glances. They were able to detect the tension in the air, but hadn't yet developed the language to articulate how strange everything had been for the last two months.

"Lord knows we didn't want you here against your will. Don't call the cops." Gloria continued picking at her fruit.

"I've appreciated everything, Gloria. You know I'm grateful."

"Are you really?" Gloria gave a scornful laugh and folded her arms. She got up from the dining table and went upstairs.

Jimmy picked at his grits. "I can give y'all a ride to the place. What time you gotta be there?"

"Eleven a.m. Thanks, Jimmy."

"Yeah… no problems. Who's helping you move?"

"Harold." Sheri hadn't asked him just yet, but his name immediately popped into her head. She would have to call him that night after she got her keys.

Jimmy nodded his head slowly and scratched the tip of his nose.

About two hours later, Sheri loaded up the children in Jimmy's car, and they made the quick drive to the Beechfield building. When Jimmy pulled up, Sheri noticed a tall woman wearing large, gold earrings and a dark-brown-and-burgundy bun that covered the entire top of her head. The woman appeared to be having an argument with a security guard who looked as if he wanted to be anywhere but in front of the woman who towered over him.

Sheri and the children jumped out of the car and Sheri blew Jimmy a kiss.

"Remember what I told you, Sher. Keep your eyes on these folks."

Sheri and the children walked through the doors of the building with no time to waste. There was a sign in the hallway that read 'Orientation,' and Sheri followed the arrows to a large conference room. There were already three families sitting quietly, waiting for everything to begin. Sheri hustled everyone towards the front of the room and took a deep breath. She had forgotten to pack Champ's computer. Her eldest was just going to need to find another way to busy himself.

Ms. Gibbs walked in carrying five tote bags. She flashed the same nervous smile from Parents' Night. She welcomed everyone and congratulated the group again for being selected for the New Horizons Housing Program, and explained that everyone would get their keys under the condition that they sign a program acknowledgment contract.

Ms. Gibbs admitted that the rental houses were remodeled units with microscopic levels of lead dust present. The lead levels in each house were so low that they could barely be measured. As a courtesy to all participants, the children would be tested every three months to ensure that there was no lead in their bloodstream. The testing would take place at Sloane-Douglas at no charge to the families. All of this information was detailed in the program acknowledgment contract.

"What if we don't sign the contract?" a voice shouted from the back.

"Well, the keys to the units can only be given under the condition that the contract is signed," Ms. Gibbs explained.

A silence fell over the conference room. Sheri began chewing her bottom lip.

Ms. Gibbs could tell the energy in the room was turning. She reminded everyone that Baltimore was a city of old homes. The majority of the homes in the city used lead-based paint. The CEC and Sloane-Douglas had made sure that the proper lead abatement methods were used. This was done to ensure that the rentals would be safe for children under six.

Sheri continued to chew her lip, deep in thought, as she rocked in her chair.

Ms. Gibbs again reminded the parents that even though the lead in the house was undetectable, Sloane-Douglas was offering free blood tests as a show of good faith. She sat back down in the hard, green seat and folded her hands. "How about we give out some keys, shall we?" Again, the plastic smile remained.

One by one, she read off names as if it were a school graduation. Finally, she called Sheri's name. Sheri was finally getting her first house. Honestly, she hadn't expected it to be this way, but they needed their own space. Champ, Popsee and Peach started clapping as their mother got up to sign the contract and take her keys. Everyone in the room laughed at the little cheering squad. Sheri gave Ms. Gibbs a thin-lipped smile, signed her contract and took her keys. It was done.

◆ ◆ ◆

That following Saturday, the Calloways moved from Preston Street. It had been nearly a year to the day since they had arrived in the city. So much had happened within that span of time. New discoveries. New questions. Unresolved feelings. Sheri went to visit the house the Sunday after she signed her contract and got her keys. She took some cleaning supplies with her and scrubbed each room. She had to admit the space was very clean, and she didn't see any dust or debris anywhere. The air didn't even have that old house smell. So far, it seemed as if Ms. Gibbs had been a woman of her word.

Harold and his brother Marcus came in and loaded up Sheri's boxes in Marcus's truck. She didn't have furniture because everything belonged to Gloria. Sheri took down Champ and Popsee's collages, placed them in a folder and put the folder in her bag. Gloria, Jimmy and Skeeter watched as the two men loaded up Sheri's belongings. It felt as if someone had died.

"My new address is 1813 East Chase Street. I'm not that far. The telephone company is supposed to be coming later today, so I'll call you with my number once I get it."

Skeeter stepped up, gave Sheri a big hug and kissed her on her cheek. She stopped at each of the children, giving them tight hugs and kisses on the tops of their heads.

Gloria sat on the couch with her arms and legs crossed, staring daggers at Sheri, Harold and Marcus. Jimmy Budd stood off to the side with his shoulders slumped, watching the move.

"Once I get set up, I want us to have a cookout over at the house." Sheri shifted her weight on her feet and tried to figure out why she felt so bad. She hadn't done anything wrong. She wasn't the one who had been high out of her mind. She hadn't given the children over to a stranger. She couldn't figure out why the hard looks were being directed her way.

"Sher, we're all set." Harold peeked his head through the front door.

Sheri smiled at Harold and ushered the children into Harold's car. Marcus had already started up his truck. Skeeter and Jimmy stood at the top of the marble steps and watched as the caravan pulled off. Sheri and the children waved goodbye.

After the car was a little ways down the block, Sheri turned around and saw that Gloria had joined Skeeter and Jimmy on the steps.

CHAPTER 12

Sheri leaned against the brick wall of Lexington Square Elementary, sneaking a quick smoke before Champ's spelling bee. The street was awash in deep greens, warm golds and crisp reds. Fall had always been Sheri's favorite season; she saw it as the time when Mother Nature showed off all of her fanciest outfits. She could have easily stood outside in the brisk October air for the rest of the day.

The "emergency Newport" had tossed around in Sheri's purse for about a month. She'd had her first smoke in over three years a few weeks after she moved into the house. She bought the pack of Newports during her lunch break and stuffed them in her bag like contraband. Sheri was still angry about the way things had gone down the day she moved from Gloria's house. Also, the words of Jimmy Budd still ran through her mind about keeping an eye on Sloane-Douglas.

Champ's spelling bee started at ten a.m., so Sheri fanned herself in an attempt to get the smoke smell off her coat. All she could do was laugh, as she doubted the frantic hand movements actually did anything. But at least it made her feel better. She vowed to throw the rest of the pack away when she got home.

Champ had been over the moon when his teacher selected him to represent his class in the spelling bee to commemorate School Works! week. Every fall, Lexington Square Elementary went all out to show their school pride in events that were one part pep rally and one part educational showcase. Sheri knew the boys were in the big leagues now. Their school back home was very nice, but this new one had an entirely different level of polish.

Sheri walked down the hall toward the auditorium. A sea of brown faces of all shades wearing neat, blue uniforms filed into the cavernous hall, each child excitedly whispering despite the one finger on their lips. School staff methodically counted classes off and directed them to assigned rows. Sheri slipped in and found a seat in the second row from the back. This would be the first of two spelling bees. The first bee was for students in first and second grade, while the second was for the third, fourth and fifth graders.

Principal Morton got up to say a few remarks and to give the rules of the bee. There was a corresponding spelling word sheet for each grade. If a contestant successfully spelled all of the words from their grade's spelling word sheet, they would then move on to spelling words for the next grade. Once Mr. Morton sat down, six students walked onto the stage in a single-file line. Sheri gushed with pride when she saw her son, who was fourth in line. The auditorium broke out into thunderous applause once the contestants sat down.

One by one, the students carefully spelled out their words. The young audience was clearly engrossed with what was taking place on stage, watching with a seriousness that would rival a playoff basketball game. Champ's name was called. He was given the word 'pudding,' which he successfully spelled, then sat back down to loud applause. When a student spelled a word incorrectly, the ding of a table bell signaled that their time in the bee was over.

Sheri checked her watch; she had told her job she would be in that afternoon, but now she was having second thoughts about coming in at all. She hadn't thought an elementary school spelling bee would be this intense, but there she was. Three students remained on stage, and Champ was still standing tall. The moderator gave him the word 'suddenly.' Champ had been on a roll for the bulk of the tournament, but it looked as if that particular word had stopped him cold in his tracks. Sheri turned her head and narrowed her eyes. She knew her son knew this word. He spelled it all the time on his Whiz Kid computer.

The moderator reminded Champ that he had ten seconds remaining.

"Suddenly." Champ swallowed and took a deep breath. Right as he began to speak, the timer went off—he had no more time left. He had to spell the word now. "Suddenly. S-U-D-I..." Champ closed his eyes and squinched his nose. "S-U-D-I-N-L-Y."

Champ stared down at the stage dejectedly before the elimination bell even sounded. Sheri wanted to run down the aisle and carry her boy away. Sheri knew Champ could spell that word; she knew it was his nerves messing with him. She was so proud of her son. He would always be her Champion above all else.

Champ lifted his chin as he quietly took the steps to exit the stage.

Before Sheri knew what she was doing, she got up and scuttled down the side aisle toward the front. Champ saw his mother coming, and 'don't embarrass me, please' flashed across his face. Sheri stopped in her tracks and blew him a kiss from the aisle. He gave her an appreciative smile and nod. He may have been knocked down, but he wasn't out. It just hadn't been his day.

The October chill helped calm Sheri's adrenaline rush, which had come courtesy of a spelling bee that proved to be far more agonizing than expected. She was able to get a hack that dropped her off a block up from her job. With her mind still with Champ at Lafayette Square, Sheri didn't notice Gloria standing right by the stairwell.

"When are you going to stop acting like we don't work together?" Mouth twisted, Gloria had never looked more like Bet than she did right then. Usually, she was a taller version of Juniper, but all Sheri could see was an angry Bethel Jeter.

"What do you want me to say?" Sheri folded her arms. If a standoff was what her cousin wanted, then a standoff she was going to get—even in their good work clothes. Sheri thought Gloria had a lot of nerve coming at her as if everything had been her fault. "You got high out of your mind and you gave my children to someone I didn't even know—"

"But Kim—"

"I. Don't. Give. A. Damn. About. Kim." Sheri gritted her teeth. Now she was mad. "You and your boyfriend are addicts. And ya need some damn help. In my face like you're the one who has the right to be offended. You were wrong, Gloria! You've been wrong. You ARE wrong."

Gloria turned her nose up in defiance. "We're still people, too. You can't just throw us in the trash. No one's perfect, Sheri. It was a bad day, but that doesn't make us bad people."

Sheri shook her head and headed toward the elevator. Although she loved her cousin dearly, Sheri had enough on her plate, and this wasn't her fight. Gloria would need to sort this out on her own.

Back at the house, after dinner, Sheri clapped her hands and did a type of dance-scoot towards the refrigerator. She came back to the table with an ice cream cake, which she placed directly in front of Champ, then turned to pull out a package from the kitchen drawer.

"Kareem Calloway, this is a token of appreciation for your stellar showing at the spelling bee today," Sheri proudly announced as she handed the gift to her son.

"Ma, I lost." Champ shook his head at his mother's oversight.

"Regardless of the outcome," Sheri defiantly sniffed, "you had a good showing and stood tall till the end. I saw how much you practiced your words, Champ. You put so much thought into everything you do. Keep that up, Son. You're going to go so far."

"Thanks, Ma." Champ smiled and looked over the gift and cake contemplatively.

Sheri got up and put slices of ice cream cake into four bowls. She knew sugar so close to the bedtime cutoff was playing things close, but Champ had shown so much heart that day. What type of parent would she have been if she didn't acknowledge it?

Later that night, after the last of the baths were taken, the last tooth brushed and the last bladder emptied, Champ lay on his bed, eyeing his gifts in the moonlight. The card had cut-out pictures that reminded Champ of when they made collages in afterschool. On the front of the card was a cut-out of a black man getting ready to run a race. Champ examined the card and the pictures that covered it. There was a message inside from his mother written in delicate, cursive writing.

Champ looked over the books she had given him. A book about notable African-American scientists and a book about notable African-American writers. Amongst other things, Champ was becoming a budding history buff, so the books were a perfect gift. Sometimes Champ went back and forth over whether he wanted to be a computer person or a teacher. Some days he wanted to be an explorer like Matthew Henson, who he had learned about two weeks earlier.

Champ let out a deep sigh and dropped his arms along his sides. Out the window, beyond the window bars, there was a world, and Kareem Calloway's wheels were already turning, trying to figure out ways in which to see it. He thought about all of the computer games the class played on Friday fun day. In some games, they were climbing mountains. In other games, they were traversing through jungles. Although he thought he would have fared better, Champ refused to let the spelling bee get him down. It only showed him that he was going to need to work even harder to get to wherever he wanted to go.

CHAPTER 13

1994

The frigid cold cut through Sheri's wool coat as if it were made of tissue paper. The sharp, clacking sound of her heels reverberated all the way down the block as she made her way to her children's school.

"Ms. Calloway, it is urgent that you meet with us," the nasal voice dripping in barely concealed disdain had spoken from Sheri's answering machine earlier that week. "This is in regards to Keyon's ongoing misbehavior during the school day. He has become a significant distraction to his teachers, and we believe that it may be time to make other arrangements for him during the school day."

Sheri fumed as she got buzzed into the school. What other arrangements was she supposed to make for a damn first-grader? She fought hard to remain calm and measured, but she had had enough. Between this and the headaches that seemed to rack both her boys for days on end, Sheri slowly felt herself coming undone. Make better moves, girl, she reminded herself.

As she stepped into the lobby, Sheri removed her gold-and-hunter-green scarf to smooth down the few stray strands that lifted from her freshly styled French roll hairdo. Normally Sheri cringed at the thought of winter and cold days in general, but this time the chill in the air was exactly what she needed to stay sane. She had taken off for the rest of the workday since she didn't know how long this meeting would be, and she wanted to give herself some time.

A woman with a drawn face and cold eyes escorted Sheri into the conference room where Popsee, Mr. Morton, Ms. Dennis and some other man sat awaiting her arrival. Sheri's eyes zoomed right to her son to make sure he was fine. He had a distant look, as if he were sitting with them in body but not in mind. The faraway look in Popsee's eyes unnerved Sheri, but she knew not to let that show around these people who probably didn't have her child's best interests at heart anyway.

Mr. Morton, the bespectacled school principal with the shiny bald head, rose to shake Sheri's hand. "Ms. Calloway, we are very glad you could be here today." He nodded at the other adults sitting around the table. "We believe this conversation is necessary because we are at a critical juncture in regards to Keyon's behavior, and it is our hope to devise a solution." Sheri sighed and nodded as she tried to no avail to make herself comfortable in the rough and outdated conference room chair.

Ms. Dennis shot a quick, timid look in Mr. Morton's direction before she began. "Ms. Calloway, for the last three months, Keyon has been having extremely disruptive outbursts in class. He's been having difficulty concentrating, and he regularly complains of his head hurting. Some of his classmates seem to find his behavior amusing; however, I am deeply concerned that these occurrences belie an emotional—"

"Keyon, sit in the waiting area for me, baby." Sheri made sure to make direct eye contact with Popsee. The boy seemed to come back into himself as he slowly rose from the conference room seat.

Ms. Dennis spoke again, "Oh, I feel that it is important that Keyon—"

"I make that determination," Sheri countered, giving Ms. Dennis a glare that could have easily melted ice.

Ms. Dennis swallowed hard, shot the two men in the room annoyed glances and began shuffling through her papers. Mr. Morton took off his glasses to rub his temples as Popsee quietly got up, grabbed his bookbag and walked out of the conference room.

"Now, continue." Sheri looked over at the three adults remaining in the room. Ms. Dennis's eyes shifted from Mr. Morton to the other man, who sat a few seats down from her.

Mr. Morton spoke in a measured tone. "Ms. Calloway, we really are trying hard to come up with strategies that will help

Keyon. As you know, our motto here is 'Every student can learn,' and we stand by that statement. We just need to know that you are working with us on this. Parents sometimes feel that it's the school's responsibility to set their children straight. Please know, Ms. Calloway, that this is not the case. There must be a partnership."

"While I have faith that you all have good intentions toward my son, I believe this could have been handled differently." Sheri sat back in her seat. "This shouldn't be the first time that I'm hearing about these class disruptions. Keyon is not an angry child. He's not a destructive child. That is not him. He's confident. He's curious. He will challenge you if he has questions, and that's because he is intelligent." If this is what her son had to deal with every day, Sheri could see why he would be frustrated.

"Well, Ms. Calloway," Mr. Morton said, nodding soberly, "I have Mr. Jonathan Lerner joining us today. Mr. Lerner is with the Institute of Urban Children and Families, and I believe that he may be the missing piece that we have been looking for." Mr. Morton gestured to Mr. Lerner.

Sheri gave him a dismissive once-over. The man's checkerboard shirt looked a size too small, and his strawberry-blonde hair was oily and limp. He reminded her of the screaming preachers that used to come on after all of the real TV shows went off.

"Yes, Ms. Calloway," the man began, "the IUCF provides many services to children and families living in the city of Baltimore. In the case of Keyon, we are gladly offering a full medical screening as well as monthly behavioral diagnostic assessments at no cost to you." He smiled as if he had just offered Sheri the deal of a lifetime.

Pangs of unease shot through Sheri as she shifted in her seat. Mr. Lerner continued, "We believe that establishing a schedule of consistent monitoring will allow us to tackle the barriers keeping Keyon from doing his best in the classroom. Also, our renowned staff will provide case management for you as well, as you continue to work with Keyon." Mr. Learner pulled a business card out of his leather billfold and handed it to Sheri.

Mr. Morton cleared his throat and solemnly looked at Sheri. "Ms. Calloway, if Keyon does not get a full assessment from the IUCF, we will have no other choice than to suspend him the next time there is an incident in class."

Sheri's chest tightened, and she quickly gripped the chair handles to keep herself steady. *These bastards. They're really trying to kick my son out. What is all this? What is happening?* Sheri's mind raced as she reached to take the business card.

Mr. Lerner smiled. "And we're open on Saturdays from ten to three, so it should be no problem getting Keyon on the schedule."

"Thank you for this; I'll get right on it." Sheri gave a quick nod to Mr. Learner as she rose from her seat, then leaned over to give everyone a quick handshake. It was as if she were moving in a dream. Mr. Morton spoke some more, but Sheri could no longer hear him. She had drifted too far. She exited the conference room and had the office page Champ. When Champ came downstairs, his face was covered in confusion. He wanted to stay in school—the class was about to watch a science video. But Sheri was done with Lafayette Square Elementary for the day. With her two sons in tow, the trio stepped out into the frigid winter air.

Every so often, Champ and Popsee would grimace or blink their eyes hard as they slowly ate their Happy Meals, a cheeseburger for Champ and chicken nuggets for Popsee. "Headaches coming back?" Sheri asked the boys as she picked at her fries. It had been an unexpectantly long day, but something in Sheri suspected that the ride was just beginning.

"They never went away," Champ said flatly as he opened his toy.

"It happens all the time in Ms. Dennis's class," Popsee sighed in frustration. "The lights hurt my head. I told her, Mom, I really did. I told her about the lights."

Sheri took a small bite of her Filet-O-Fish sandwich, but she didn't have much of an appetite. "What happens," she asked, looking at her sons, "when the headaches come while you're in school?"

Champ and Popsee exchanged quick glances. Champ spoke first. "Mr. Sykes lets me lay my head down on the desk. We have a chill-out corner where the bad kids go, but sometimes he lets me sit there if my head hurts really bad."

"It's the lights." Popsee pointed his finger up at the weathered fluorescent light fixtures on the ceiling of the McDonald's. "And the noise. When the other kids talk loud, it just makes it hard."

"Makes what hard?" Sheri asked.

"Makes school hard." Popsee let out an exasperated huff of air and slunk down in his seat.

"My head was hurting when I was in the spelling bee." Champ's brown eyes were downcast as if he were talking to the smiling Ronald McDonald dining tray cover. "Ma, I knew those words. All of them. I practiced. I just couldn't…" The young boy's voice drifted off. "It felt like somebody took a pencil and erased my brain."

◆ ◆ ◆

Saturday found the city awash in bright winter sunshine as Sheri and the children made their way to the first of Popsee's IUCF appointments. The urge for a Newport was extra strong that morning as Champ and Popsee galloped down Fayette Street, with Sheri following closely behind, pushing Peach in her stroller. The family of four stepped through the doors and entered a space that looked like a Dr. Seuss book come to life. Peach squealed and cheered at the brightly colored walls covered in cartoon characters and scenes from children's books. Champ and Popsee jetted straight to the puppet show station in the corner of the room before Sheri could even get the stroller all the way through the door.

"Don't cut up," Sheri whispered loudly to the backs of her sons' heads. Peach whimpered as she watched her brothers make a beeline toward the toys. "You're gonna have to wait until I get us signed in, and then you can play."

"The toys get 'em every time," the red-haired woman laughed from behind the desk. With her glittery glasses and jewel-covered glasses chain, the woman reminded Sheri of a jazzy Mrs. Claus. According to the receptionist's badge, her name was Debbie.

"Hi, good morning. We're here for Keyon Calloway's eleven a.m. appointment," Sheri said as she signed into the visitor's log.

"Aww, yes." Debbie glided in her rolling office chair to the other side of her relatively small front desk space. She held up a folder to show Sheri. "Got him ready right here. He'll be seen by Dr. Rooney. Just have a seat, and she'll be out shortly."

Sheri nodded and swallowed a lump that had risen in her throat. The thought of Popsee having to get screened and tested made her nauseous. It was already enough her babies had to submit blood work, thanks to their new house. Now this. Sheri made up in her mind that this particular stint with IUCF would be a short one—even if it meant changing schools. After talking to Harold's sister, Sheri was convinced that the schools in the northwest part of the city were the way to go.

Peach walked over to meet up with her brothers, who had since moved on to the Lego station. Sheri looked around at the other parents there with their children. She wondered if they had been forced to come here like she had been. Soon, worst-case scenarios began to scratch along the corners of her mind. What if these people put Popsee on some type of medication? What if they made him transfer to a different school, away from his brother? Sheri looked over at her babies lost in their own worlds, playing with the building blocks. She would have been fully content to sit there and watch them play forever.

"Keyon Calloway?" an older woman with a chic, feathered blond haircut called from the doorway leading to the examination rooms. Sheri hated to end playtime, but it was time to get down to the business at hand. The four made their way towards the back, with Popsee leading the way.

"Are you Mr. Keyon?" the woman smiled. The young boy nodded as the woman reached to shake his hand. "I'm Dr. Rooney, so pleased to meet you."

Sheri checked the woman over. She didn't appear to have cold eyes, unlike the men who had come through and turned Robinson Brothers upside down. She was tall and had a lean build, which made Sheri wonder if the woman had been an athlete when she was in school. Then again, Gloria was pretty tall, and she hadn't been an athlete. So who's to say?

"Ms. Calloway." The woman extended her hand to Sheri. "Kathy Rooney. It's so good to have you all here today. This will likely be the longest of the appointments for Keyon, only because we'll be running a few additional tests in addition to the behavioral assessments."

"Like what?" Sheri asked as they settled in examination room four.

"Hearing, vision, as well as a blood test."

"Blood? We got that done already about four months ago. All of my children. They tested them over at Sloane-Douglas."

The woman bit the end of her ink pen and nodded at Sheri. "I hear you, and I understand. As part of his first visit with us here at IUCF, the blood test is required before we are allowed to continue with any additional assessments. I know it may be an inconvenience, but it would only be a one-time test. We want to eliminate the possibility of lead poisoning."

This made Champ and Popsee look up at the woman with wide eyes. Sheri highly doubted they knew what lead poisoning was specifically, but the two boys may have been aware of what it meant for someone to be poisoned.

Sheri took a deep breath. "If that is a part of the procedure, then it's fine." She just wanted it all to be over. She could only imagine how Popsee felt.

The medical technician, a young man with an easy smile who looked to be a few years younger than Sheri, came in to take Popsee to the next examination room for his vitals and screenings. After that, he brought Popsee back to draw his blood, using some type of cartoon dog puppet to disguise his hand. Sheri laughed to herself, watching Popsee look more offended than amused at the puppet hand disguise. But while the puppet dog fell flat with Popsee, Peach sat wide-eyed and absolutely riveted.

The young med tech with the easy smile waved goodbye to everyone as Dr. Rooney returned. "Well, the ucky part is out of the way, huh? Thank goodness for that." She smiled and shook her hands in mock exasperation.

Sheri handed Champ a brand-new Fun Pad activity book along with a pack of crayons, which he then took to the opposite side of the examination room and quietly kept himself busy. Peach wiggled her way off Sheri's lap and went over to her brother. He carefully tore out a coloring sheet and handed it to her, then put the box of crayons within her reach.

Dr. Rooney explained to Sheri that all subsequent visits would consist of split sessions. The first session would be a one-on-one with Keyon and then a follow-up session with the three of them. The one-on-one discussions would be one hour, while the group meetings generally ran no more than thirty minutes. Sheri nodded and took mental notes, but she told Dr. Rooney that her main concern was whether or not they were going to put her son on medication.

"He's aware, he's alert and he's observant," she told Dr. Rooney, making sure to look the woman square in her eyes. Sheri had come to terms with the mandatory assessment sessions, but it would be a cold day in hell before she allowed them to turn her son into a zombie.

Dr. Rooney assured Sheri that the goal was not to medicate Keyon but to implement strategies that would make his time in the classroom more manageable. Also, Dr. Rooney noted, IUCF policy stated that the decision to medicate a child could only be approved after a panel decision.

"Checks and balances, and all," Dr. Rooney tried to reassure the wary mother.

After being quiet for most of the conversation, Popsee finally opened up about how he was adjusting to the new school, how he felt that Ms. Dennis didn't like him and how he sorely missed Spruce Junction and Mom-Mom. When Popsee mentioned Mom-Mom, Peach immediately stopped her coloring and focused her attention on what was being discussed on the other side of the room. Sheri wanted to disappear right there on the spot. She knew her babies were homesick—hell, she was homesick—but she had hoped that the yearnings for home weren't hitting them as hard as they actually were.

On the way out, Sheri scheduled the next appointment for Popsee. Debbie told Sheri that she should be receiving a call around Tuesday or Wednesday of the following week with Popsee's blood test results. Sheri nodded as she worked to unlatch Peach's stroller. The foursome stepped back out into the Baltimore winter chill, which had gotten a little stronger while they had been inside. Sheri wasn't in the mood to catch the bus this time around, so they walked up a block to get a hack.

97

Catching a hack was something that Skeeter had put Sheri on to. Sheri remembered all the tips Skeeter and Jimmy Budd had given her when she first moved to the city: Don't get into any cars you feel strange about. Negotiate a price up front. If a cab drives up instead of a hack, just wave them off; they already know what it is.

Sheri found a spot for Popsee and Champ on a bus stop bench, parked Peach's stroller, casually stuck her middle and index fingers out and waited. Not long after, a woman in a blue station wagon drove up. Sheri gave a silent prayer of thanks that it was a woman driving. She had noticed, in times past, that some of the male drivers would get a little too friendly, and she really wasn't in the mood, especially since she was with her children.

On the drive back to the house, Sheri learned that the woman's name was Phyllis. Her family had moved to Cherry Hill from Gastonia after her father got a job working down at the shipyard. Sheri admitted that she was still learning her way around the city, but she wanted to do as much as she could with the time she had. Phyllis lit up when Sheri told her she was taking classes over at CCB.

"Good for you, baby. Go as far as you can and don't let anything hold you back. Don't be too hard on yourself, either. We're all taking this thing one day at a time."

Sheri nodded and fought to hold back the tears. After the IUCF visit, Ms. Phyllis's words broke through like warm sunshine through the rain clouds.

CHAPTER 14

Wednesday moved like a whirlwind. An already frantic morning routine got even more hectic as Champ whimpered about stomach pains. Sheri felt terrible, since Champ rarely complained about anything, but she was in no position to call out and stay home. She didn't have much leave to spare, plus she had an exam that evening in her Business Management class. They stopped at the corner store on the way to school to pick up a bottle of ginger ale, which Sheri made Champ drink the rest of the way.

Being her usual godsend self, Skeeter had already told Sheri she would pick up the children from school that day, which would give Sheri extra time to study for her test. It wasn't as if she didn't know the material; she knew it backwards and forwards. It was a matter of nerves. Every day, Sheri worked to strengthen her confidence. She knew it was important to steadily affirm herself.

Sheri got to work a few minutes early, which gave her time to grab a cup of coffee and a muffin from the office canteen. She was in line to pay for her items when she heard the steady clack of pumps. She knew they belonged to Gloria even without looking toward the door. Sheri turned toward the exit and saw her cousin gliding across the vestibule floor. The two made eye contact, and each flashed a smile and gave a quick nod.

Just as Gloria moved beyond Sheri's view, she heard footsteps that sounded more like a marching stride than a casual pace. Sheri looked to see who was stomping across the floor and saw Linda, the human resources manager who had replaced Mr. Heath some months ago. *Why is she stomping like that?* Sheri twisted her face. *Wait. Is this heifer following Gloria?*

Sheri paid for her things and walked over to get a better look without being too obvious. Maybe she was overthinking things, but something looked off. Was this woman following her cousin?

Sheri thought back to what Skeeter had told her about the issues Gloria was having at work. Was Linda trying to make trouble for Gloria?

Sheri made a mental note to go up to Gloria's floor during her break. The cousins were slowly repairing their relationship. Despite what had happened, Gloria had done so much for her, and it wasn't in Sheri to hold grudges—especially against family.

Sheri was able to catch an open elevator and pressed the button for the tenth floor. She had notes to transcribe from the acquisitions meeting, and her plan was to hit the ground running early to squeeze some study time in at the end of the day.

One of Sheri's favorite things about her job, besides the steady check, was the beautiful views of the city. After spending years working in a windowless factory, having the chance to see scenery out of a magazine would make just about anyone stop to pinch themselves. When the days were shorter, Sheri would glance out the floor-to-ceiling picture windows and think the city looked like a gleaming sea of diamonds. She wondered if it ever got old, the mesmerizing feeling that came over her every time she the city in its full glory. She hoped it wouldn't.

"She's in here!"

Sheri knew it was her coworker before she looked up.

"They came into our office by mistake." Sandra flashed her usual Vanna White smile at Sheri. "Someone has a secret admirer, hmm?"

Sheri took off her transcriber's headset and came face-to-face with a delivery man holding a vase of long stem pink and white roses. "Miss Calloway?" he read off the card.

"Thank you." Sheri nodded and smiled at the delivery man. All of a sudden, a swarm of butterflies took flight in her belly. She hadn't expected flowers, and it had been a few days since she had last spoken with Harold. Sheri had wanted to call him over the weekend, but the IUCF visit with Popsee had drained her too badly. She had just enough energy for her three, and no more.

Sandra cleared her throat. Sheri had completely forgotten that she was there.

"Young love?"

"A thoughtful friend," Sheri demurred.

Sheri felt warm as she stared at her flowers. She absolutely refused to even think about how long it had been since she had indulged. Sheri liked Harold because, while clearly making his intentions known, he played it slow and he didn't overwhelm her. Usually, when a person helped you move, they felt like they had some rights to you, but not Harold. Also, the children really enjoyed the outings with Shayla and Amir.

Sheri had moved to Baltimore with a mile-long checklist, but maybe there was space to add one more thing.

Halfway through transcribing the meeting notes, Sheri decided to take a break a little early. She checked in with her supervisor before catching an elevator to Gloria's floor, which always seemed to be a hub of activity and movement. The energy between the two floors felt like night and day.

"Hey, lady." Gloria looked over at Sheri, who was standing in the doorway of her office. "Whatcha doing round these parts?"

"Checking in on you. I just wanted to see how you were doing." Sheri quickly slid into Gloria's office and found a seat in one of her blue-and-grey chairs.

"I'm holding on."

"What's happening with you? Is everything okay?" Sheri leaned over and lowered her voice to a whisper. "What was that with Linda this morning?"

Gloria let out a chuckle and pursed her full lips. "That ol' hard stompin' heifer? Nothing's going on with her that I can't handle. Sometimes people smell themselves and want to throw their newfound weight around, but you know what?" Gloria leaned over almost nose-to-nose with Sheri. "I'm a heavyweight my damn self."

Sheri knew all too well that her cousin could hold her own with no problem, but she wanted Gloria to know that she had her back, too.

"I'm here."

"I know." Gloria reached over to grab Sheri's hands. "So how are things at the house?"

"The house is good. Skeeter's over a lot, but you already know that. She's been a huge help with the kids now that school is back in session. Got an exam today, so wish me luck."

"Girl, you already know you've got that. Is there any doubt?"

Sheri smiled and squeezed Gloria's hands. "Let me get out of here and go on back downstairs. Girl, you know Harold sent me flowers this morning?"

This made Gloria's eyes light up, and she flashed Sheri a mischievous grin.

"We're friends, Glo," Sheri said matter-of-factly.

Gloria shrugged. "There's nothing wrong with having a visitor to the garden every once in a while."

"Gloria!" Sheri turned deep red.

"What?" Gloria shook her head. "Anyway, we're having a game night Saturday. I just got a new VCR, so I'll send Jimmy out to get some videos for the kids. We would love to see y'all."

Sheri nodded. "That sounds good. I know my crew is going to love that." She smiled as she headed down to her floor, then turned back to face her cousin. "Gloria, thank you."

Sheri called the house before she clocked out. Champ's stomachache was gone, but it looked like Popsee's headaches were back. Peach was okay for the most part, but Skeeter had noticed the girl seemed a bit irritated. Skeeter also said there was a new message on the answering machine. Sheri immediately got a feeling it was IUCF calling her back. She packed up her work tote and headed out into the evening air.

There was a light drizzle when Sheri got off work, but she didn't mind. The twenty-minute walk to the Lombard Street CCB building always helped clear her nerves before class. It allowed her to turn off work Sheri and activate student Sheri. She was still floating about the flowers from earlier today. It had been a while since she had been courted. *Hell, have I ever really been courted?* She had to stop and think hard. She and Kenneth had been schoolmates, and what they'd had would have been considered puppy love by some. However, looking back, it's not like he really went out of his way for her. Little gestures of affection that made her feel special had been rare during their time together.

Kenneth was nice enough, but the sparks were honestly never there. The best thing to come out of that situation was her babies, so she would never complain. Being with someone who thought of different ways to make her smile would be a nice change of pace.

Sheri shook her head to snap out of the haze. She waved at some of the other students as she walked into the school building, then took a deep breath and did a quick wiggle to get the jitters out one last time. She found her favorite seat towards the middle of the lecture hall and waited for class to start. Going back to school was one of the best decisions Sheri had made for herself, and she was thankful that she had pushed past the feelings of being past her "prime." Sometimes, Sheri had to remind herself that she was still a young woman, and she had a lifetime of chapters to fill. She had always planned to go to college, and now she was finally getting the chance to realize her dream.

Sheri's mind drifted back to the conversation with Gloria earlier that day. It had been brief, but it was definitely needed. Her cousin had been gracious enough to open her home to the four of them, no questions asked. No judgment. No lectures. No condescension. The night of the incident had angered Sheri so badly, but, in the end, Gloria was still family. If anything, Sheri felt utterly disappointed in Gloria. Sheri thought her cousin was above all of that. She looked up to Gloria. Those hard drugs didn't seem to go with Gloria's regal style. What had gone wrong?

She thought about how Skeeter had tried her best to explain what Gloria and Jimmy Budd were dealing with. Sheri just couldn't wrap her head around it at the time. She could still hear Skeeter's pleas that Gloria was battling a disease. Truthfully, a part of Sheri felt like she would never fully understand, but she loved her cousin, and she knew her cousin was good people through and through. She could never discard her.

Professor Howe walked down the aisle of the lecture hall, waving his arm in his usual dramatic fashion. "Materials away, scholars! Let's see what you know!"

Sheri loved how much her professor loved his work. Seeing someone genuinely love what they do inspired her. It let her know that better was out there.

In the year and a half that she had been in the city, Sheri had already seen a turnaround, but she felt the best was yet to come.

After she finished her exam, Sheri turned her booklet in to Professor Howe with a smile and a wave and walked back out into the brisk February darkness. She knew she had done well, and she scolded herself for leaving any room for doubt. Who's going to believe in you if you don't believe in you? Instead of making the trek back home on the MTA, she decided to let her two fingers pull a ride. This time a taxi stopped for her first, and she was finally on her way home.

Sheri stepped into the house to see Skeeter quietly sitting on the sofa with Peach lying in her lap.

"Fed 'em and gave 'em all baths. The boys are upstairs asleep, but Peach Mama wanted to stay down here and wait for you."

"Skeeter, I love you so much. Today was two days packed into one. Did Champ say anything else about his stomach? What about Popsee?"

"They really don't like these lights in here, Peanut." Skeeter's face clouded in worry. "They were carrying on and on about the lights just like a pair of cranky old men. I don't remember them doing all of this before back at Gloria's. Is everything okay?"

Sheri sighed and shook her head no.

Skeeter looked over at her cousin in an effort to read her face. "You eat? I made some beef stew and I have some dinner rolls in the oven."

Sheri leaned over to give her cousin the biggest hug she could muster, then reached down to pick up her baby girl to cover her in kisses. She quietly sat down on the other end of the sofa with Peach in tow. "Popsee is having school problems. I think Champ may be having them, too. I'm still trying to put the pieces together to figure this thing out."

Skeeter reached across the sofa to rub her cousin's knee.

"We had an appointment with a doctor at some type of treatment center, the Institute for Urban Children and Families. They screen children who are having behavior problems in school. Popsee told the doctor that he misses Titi and the family back in

Spruce Junction. I thought they were adjusting fine, but it looks like we still have some ways to go."

"Oh, Peanut, I'm so sorry."

"Girl, I'm doing the best that I can, but I know everyone is different. I have to remind myself that I didn't make this move alone. These babies have to process everything in their own way. This is still a lot for them."

"One day at a time. That's all we're required to do. You're doing a wonderful job. They love you."

Sheri felt the tears forming, but she was too tired to cry.

"It's late and it's cold. Stay here." Sheri figured Skeeter wasn't going to take her up on the offer, but she didn't like the idea of her cousin out there walking the streets by herself to get back to Gloria's.

"Girl, I got my own bed and my own space. You already know how I do." Skeeter flashed her usual dimpled grin. "But what I will do is use your phone real quick to call my patna, Lem. He's not far. He'll give me a ride back to the house."

Skeeter made her phone call and gathered the rest of her things to wait by the door. Sheri saw her answering machine light blinking and remembered that she needed to call Harold. She hoisted Peach over her shoulder and moved to the end of the sofa where Skeeter had been. She gently placed Peach's head in her lap and stretched the rest of her daughter's steadily growing body out along the couch.

The phone rang twice, then Sheri heard a sleep-tinged voice say hello. "I didn't mean to wake you, just wanted to say thanks so much for the flowers. They're beautiful."

Harold's baritone laughter sent chills down Sheri's body. "Just wanted to let you know that I was thinking of you. I'm always thinking of you."

Sheri peeked over to see if Skeeter was paying any attention, but her focus was on the door. "I had an exam today; I think it went well. Today was a long day, but it's a done day, so that's good," Sheri softly giggled into the phone. "How were things for you?"

Harold grunted. "One of my men got the flu, so we had to split up his route. Comes with the territory."

The two made small talk, but Sheri could feel the day pulling her down for the count. At first, she thought about inviting him to Gloria's game party that Saturday, then she reconsidered. She was just getting back on good terms with Gloria, and she didn't want to rope Harold into anything that wasn't fully resolved.

"Harold, I want you to know that I appreciate you and I enjoy your company. I don't want you to question how I feel."

There was a pause on the line. "You've got a pull on me, Sheri, and I just can't shake it. I don't think I want to, either."

"Ride's here!" Skeeter jumped up and blew Sheri air kisses as she made her exit.

"Call me when you get to Gloria's!" Sheri yelled at her cousin's back.

"Yes, Mom," Skeeter laughed.

Sheri slid from under Peach's sleeping head. She started to clean up the kitchen, which proved unnecessary since Skeeter had everything clean as a whistle. The Bethel Jeter way. Sheri was too sleepy to eat, so she packed up the food to take with her for lunch the next day. Then she saw the blinking light from the answering machine in her peripheral vision. She considered checking her messages in the morning, but she already knew that mornings in the Calloway house were far too hectic for such things.

Sheri pressed the play button. The first voice she heard was Dr. Rooney's.

"Yes, hi. Hi, Ms. Calloway, this is Dr. Rooney from IUCF. Please give me a call as soon as possible. This is in regard to Keyon's test from Saturday. I also tried calling your job and I left a message there as well. It's urgent, Ms. Calloway. Please contact me as soon as you receive this. Thank you."

Sheri slowly sat down at her dining table. Dr. Rooney's voice sounded jittery and nervous, and Sheri didn't like that at all. All three of her children had received clean bills of health from Sloane-Douglas regarding their blood tests, yet there Sheri was, fighting off a growing sense of dread that was trying to envelop her body.

No. No. Absolutely not. The headaches. *No. The lights. No.* The issues at school. *Please, God, not tonight. I will not do this tonight. I will call tomorrow and get to the bottom of this, but I will not give myself over to this tonight. I cannot.*

CHAPTER 15

Winter still had the city in a vice grip, and since the groundhog had seen its shadow, everyone had abandoned hope of getting an early reprieve from the cold. Yolanda Johnson stuffed her hands into the pockets of her knee-length leather coat and pulled her wool houndstooth cap further down over her long, burgundy braids.

She saw the woman again, deep in thought, as usual, although she didn't have her babies with her today. Even though other businesses had offices in the Beechfield building, Yolanda had a strong hunch that the woman was there for the Community Empowerment Center.

On one occasion, the two women did the "Hey, I see you" nod to each other because they were both raised right. Beyond that, Yolanda hadn't been able to get the sista alone to confirm her hunch that she was there to visit the CEC. She leaned her six-one frame against her '89 Nissan Sentra and breathed in the brisk winter air. There was a fresh stack of flyers in her backseat for parents who were enrolled in CEC's New Horizons program. Yolanda's heart was full of fury and vengeance as she dug her heels into her flat, knee-high boots and looked off into the distance.

Yolanda Ford Johnson was a warrior. She hadn't sought out a life on the front lines, but trying circumstances had forced the woman to find her power and voice early on. The fourth of Bradford and Glennis Ford's six children, Yolanda and her family had called 725 George Street, Apartment 507, home. She'd never felt any particular way growing up in the Murphy Homes. Once she became an adult, people turned their nose up at the mention, but Yolanda remembered her neighbors as good, hardworking people trying to carve out a life. The drugs and the violence definitely were a factor, but that wasn't until later. By then, much of Baltimore had already been taken under siege.

One July afternoon, Bradford hit Glennis. Then Glennis punched Bradford. So forth and so on, until the couple was rumbling like two junkyard dogs right there in the hallway of the fifth floor. Neighbors ran out of their apartments to break up the fight and calm things down. Later that night, Bradford randomly chose three of his six children, including Yolanda, and left for good. The fragmented family moved over to Walbrook Junction to live with one of Bradford's sisters. Every so often, Yolanda would sneak and call home to see if her mother had any plans to come get her, but each time the message was clear: Yolanda was to stay where she was.

Despite her rocky home life, Yolanda thrived in school. She was a decent student, and she was extremely popular. Yolanda started playing basketball and running track when she was in junior high school. She made the varsity basketball team at Walbrook Senior High, where she played forward. Yolanda also volunteered during mayoral and city council campaign seasons by going door to door, passing out flyers and standing on street corners with signs.

As active as she was, college still felt like an unattainable dream for the West Baltimore teenager. A small team of teachers and school staff formed a sort of "encouragement squad" for Yolanda as she navigated through the decisions that would shape the rest of her life. Then, on an unseasonably warm March day, Yolanda found out that she had received a basketball scholarship to play for Morgan State. Yolanda must have sat and read that acceptance letter a million times. She was going to college for real. She had made it.

Morgan was a whole new world for Yolanda. She felt like the proverbial little fish in a big pond. Everyone was smart. Everyone was motivated. Everyone had goals. How, exactly, was she supposed to stand out? Yolanda managed to make it through her freshman year, but finished the spring semester on academic probation, which meant she couldn't play until she brought her GPA back up. During summer session, she crossed paths with Leonard Johnson, a fast talker from Queens, New York. The ambitious young man always seemed to have some type of hustle or scheme up his sleeve.

Yolanda was torn. A part of her wanted to see how far she could go, while another part of her was completely done with school and was ready to move on. Her second mind won out, and she left Morgan before the start of her sophomore year. Leonard, now Yolanda's boyfriend, stayed on for another semester before he decided to call it quits as well. The pair found a cozy apartment over on Pennsylvania and Mosher and got married soon after. The twins, Man and Kelli, arrived first. Tater followed two years later. Ten months after Tater, Iesha joined the family.

Leonard got a job with the phone company installing telephone lines while Yolanda worked as a school secretary. The young family tried their best to hold things together until everything exploded on a warm June night in 1989. Leonard was good about being aware of his surroundings at all times. He had just finished cashing his check at the liquor store when the three masked gunmen stormed through the door. Leonard quickly jammed the money down the front of his pants, put his hands up and kept his head down.

"Where the fuck you put it?" was the last thing Leonard Johnson heard before a bullet tore through his back.

When Yolanda got word that she been approved for a house through the CEC's New Horizons program, she thought her fortune was turning. Then the headaches came, then the stomachaches, then the irritability and the fights at school. Although the CEC's staff had assured her that her babies would be fine in their house, as usual, a hunch kicked in. Yolanda had her children's lead levels tested by another medical provider. Through the roof.

Between Leonard's death and her children being poisoned, Yolanda underwent a metamorphosis by fire. She felt as if she were a lone, vigilante cowboy just like in those old Westerns she used to watch with her mother on Saturdays. Yolanda Ford Johnson was going to bring Baltimore City to its knees.

So far she had connected with six parents who were facing the same problem. Yolanda started a phone tree, and the crew of parents tried to meet every other week to discuss new strategies to inform the public about what was happening to their children. The most important goal was to try and reach other parents whose children may be victims as well.

Yolanda looked up and down the relatively quiet street. She hoped this was the day she would finally connect with the young sista who had the three children. The one who always looked deep in thought whenever Yolanda saw her. She wanted the young mother to know that she understood and that justice was going to be served.

◆ ◆ ◆

Arms folded and legs crossed, Sheri sat in the lobby of the CEC full of quiet, concentrated rage. After meeting with Dr. Rooney to get Popsee's test results, she took Champ and Peach to get retested at St. Christopher's. Their lead levels were just as bad. The feeling was beyond surreal. It was as if Sheri was in a living, breathing nightmare.

"Sheri Calloway?" the receptionist called from behind her desk.

Sheri grabbed her purse and waited for the buzzer to sound to be let into the back office area. Ms. Gibbs was waiting with her usual plastic smile. Sheri realized that if she were going to win, it would be imperative that she keep her emotions in check. The last thing she needed was to have a meltdown and them try to take her children away from her. As far as she was concerned, she was now living in hostile territory, and she had no other option than to move smart.

"When you called, you said that you had concerns about the house. Is everything okay? Should I set up a maintenance appointment with Mr. Cole?" the woman asked with seemingly genuine concern.

Sheri calmly took out three sheets of paper and placed them on the desk in front of her. She pushed them as far under Ms. Gibbs's nose as she could reach. "These are the blood test results"—Sheri took a deep breath—"for my three children Kareem, Keyon and Maya."

"Well, Ms. Calloway, I can assure you—"

"These are dangerously high levels of lead, Ms. Gibbs." Sheri spoke just above a whisper, never once taking her eyes off the woman.

"Ms. Calloway, when you signed your housing contract, you knew that you were moving into an older home. With that comes certain pre-existing hazards, and—"

"You promised that the house was safe. You told us that we would be okay. That the blood checks were just precautionary measures. What are you doing to my children? The CEC needs to fix this."

Ms. Gibbs continued her scripted delivery, "Well, as you know, we are working in partnership with Sloane-Douglas, and we would be more than glad to provide your children with full, comprehensive—"

"I. Need. You. To. Tell. Me. The. Truth." Sheri shot lasers directly into the woman's grey eyes. "I don't want your care. I don't want your charity. I don't want your house from hell. I want answers."

"Ms. Calloway…" The woman took a measured pause. "When you signed—"

Sheri got up and walked out of the office. The CEC, Sloane-Douglas and whoever else was in on this had made an enemy out of her for as long as she breathed air. Her mind raced with thoughts on what her next steps should be. She already knew she had to move out of the house. The money Sheri had managed to save for a car would instead have to be used to find another rental. Of course, there was always Gloria's, but Sheri had to approach that situation with some caution. Skeeter said Gloria and Jimmy Budd were in Narcotics Anonymous, but would it be wise to return?

Sheri stormed out of the building and ran right into the tall lady with the long braids. She had noticed the woman staring at her whenever she came down to the CEC. They had spoken once, but Sheri tried to avoid her. She made Sheri nervous. Sheri doubted the woman even knew her from anywhere, considering she had just arrived in the damn city.

When Yolanda saw the woman rush out of the building, she knew that was her chance. "Hi. Hello. Look, I'm really not trying to be weird, but I've seen you… well, we've seen each other," Yolanda said quickly. She could tell the woman wasn't in the mood. "My name is Yolanda Johnson, and I was wondering if you came down here to go to the CEC?" Yolanda stopped to catch her breath, praying that the woman gave her a chance.

"Why?" Sheri turned and gave Yolanda a long, hard look.

"Just… a hunch?" Yolanda pleaded with her brown eyes.

"Look, I don't want any trouble," Sheri said, shaking her head, "but am I supposed to know you? Have we met?"

"My children and I were a part of the New Horizons Housing Program. We were doing the testing at Sloane-Douglas, the whole nine and all that. I was told there were no issues, but I knew something was wrong with my children." Yolanda's eyes bore into the young mother, and she could see the woman fighting back tears. "I don't want to freak you out or scare you, but… I don't know… like I said, it was just a hunch that we may be in the same boat."

Sheri stared at the woman while trying her hardest not to have a breakdown right there on the sidewalk. She took a deep breath and the tears came. They flowed down her face and down her chest and under her bra. Tears for her babies. Tears for herself. Tears for all of the other families caught in this evil. Tears for being foolish enough to think she was going to make it. Tears for missing home. Tears for running through life like a jackrabbit and still not being able to catch up. Sheri was furious. She was tired. She was scared.

Yolanda lightly touched Sheri's shoulder and gave her a gentle smile. "I give hugs. Is it okay if I hug you?"

Sheri weakly nodded as the tears continued to fall. The two women hugged. It was a hug that contained all of the anger, the disappointment and the feelings of uncertainty about what was going to come their way next. Although she definitely seemed pleasant, Sheri could see the no-nonsense wasn't too far below the surface with Yolanda. She definitely seemed like a 'kick ass and take names' type of person.

"I'm Sheri." Sheri wiped her tears on her sweater sleeve. "Sheri Calloway."

Yolanda smiled at the young woman and nodded. "Sheri, can I give you a ride? I'm parked right here."

The two women slowly walked to Yolanda's red Nissan Sentra and got in. Yolanda started the engine and turned on the heat so they wouldn't be driving around in a moving icebox. She proudly tapped her steering wheel and looked over at Sheri. "This is my lil' putt-putt Millie, named for the queen, Ms. Millie Jackson."

Sheri leaned against the passenger side window and laughed. "I used to sneak and listen to her records whenever I was over my aunt's house."

Yolanda and Sheri, both lost in their own thoughts and memories for a brief moment, giggled to themselves as they waited for the car to warm up.

"Those bastards really have us paying rent for those poison houses," Sheri muttered, looking down at the floor of the car.

"Ain't that always the way? Out here paying them to get your babies sick. Like something from a damn science-fiction thriller movie." Yolanda shook her head and put the car in gear.

The two women swapped stories about their children's various symptoms since moving into their New Horizon rentals. Sheri told Yolanda about what happened at Champ's spelling bee and how that had been her first inkling that something wasn't right. She talked about the sensitivity to lights and how they were walking around in a dark house. Yolanda talked about how her normally easygoing eldest daughter got into a fight at school. The teacher told Yolanda that it looked like a scene out of *The Incredible Hulk*. Kelli just detonated, and no one knew why.

Yolanda admitted that she'd had misgivings from the onset because of the CEC's partnership with Sloane-Douglas. Black Baltimore had always been wary of dealing with anything Sloane-Douglas had involvement with. Whispers and rumors surrounded the hospital and, as the saying goes, where there's smoke, there's fire. Sheri told Yolanda about Jimmy Budd's warning to her about Sloane-Douglas.

"And since you're not from the city, they probably thought you were real easy pickings," Yolanda sighed.

This observation made Sheri slump down further in her seat, feeling even more defeated.

Yolanda gave Sheri a quick glance, and her eyes softened. "Predators are going to be who they are, Sis. You did nothing wrong. Remember that and keep it in the front of your mind through all of this. You wanted a home to raise your family, and they took advantage of that."

Sheri looked over at Yolanda. She saw some of Gloria in her. This woman was clearly on a mission, and Sheri, only knowing her for about thirty minutes, was ready to join her in battle. She felt a charge of electricity pulsating through her body, and she realized that she would never go back to her old life again. Something big was happening.

"This is some bullshit, but we're going to make it. I'm sure of that." Yolanda's eyes were locked onto the road in front of her. "They found the right ones this time, believe that."

Yolanda told Sheri about the crew of parents and their strategy meetings. The next meeting was coming up the following Thursday at Gethsemane Memorial off of McCullough and Gold. Yolanda assured Sheri that she and the children would have a way there and back home. The most important thing was to be there and connect with other parents going through the same thing. She pointed towards the backseat to show Sheri the flyers she'd made to pass out to families who were possibly impacted by the CEC's contaminated houses.

"So that's why you're always parked out in front of the building." Sheri leaned her head back on the headrest.

"Yup," Yolanda said, "at first, I was splitting my time between Sloane-Douglas and the Beechfield building, but I dropped Sloane-Douglas altogether. I figured I would have better odds reaching families as they were coming and going from the CEC."

Although there were multiple offices in the Beechfield building, over time, Yolanda had been able to figure out who was there for which agency through the process of elimination. Nine times out of ten, parents coming to the building with children were coming to the CEC.

"Have you had much luck?" Sheri asked.

"Well, you and I finally connected, so I take that as a win." Yolanda looked over and smiled.

The winter sky resembled orange sorbet as the sun began to set. Completely exhausted, Sheri gazed out the window as Yolanda rounded the corner onto Chase Street. Skeeter was again her lifesaver, watching the children while she dealt with the madness that was becoming the CEC. Sheri's mind had already drifted to the apartment-search stage. On that train from North Carolina, who would have even thought this would be her reality?

"It's tough, and it's going to be a battle, but the good news is that now you know that you're not out here by yourself." Yolanda looked over at Sheri as they sat in the parked car. "I really hope you can join us next Thursday. We'll get through this because we're the ones in the right. Every devil pays their due, eventually."

The two women exchanged telephone numbers and hugged again before Sheri got out of the car.

"I'll call you; I'll stay in touch." Sheri gave Yolanda a relieved smile. "Thank you."

Yolanda leaned over the passenger seat and called out to Sheri as she walked up the steps, "There's power in numbers, Sis. Remember that. We will win."

Streetlights illuminated the way as Yolanda drove off into the night. Sheri watched the car until it disappeared from view. She felt as if she had just come into contact with a force of nature. She was left in awe, and she felt her scattered rage and hurt gradually coalescing into something else—righteous fury.

CHAPTER 16

Sheri smoothed down her hair and tucked some of the reddish-brown strands behind her left ear. She'd decided that the pinned-up, French roll hairdo was a little too dramatic for her, and instead wore her shoulder-length hair brushed back with a headband. From the children's school, Sheri caught a hack to Gethsemane Memorial for the Thursday parent strategy meeting. Sheri figured it was going to be a long day, so she'd packed a separate bag filled with snacks and juice boxes.

"Church!" Peach yelled when she stepped out of the car.

Nervousness tugged at the young mother, but she realized that it was now or never. Her children's futures were at stake, and she could no longer afford to stay in a shell. She owed it to her children to fight for them. The family walked through the brown door and entered a long hallway.

A woman with silver barrel curls looked up at them from her desk. "Here for the meeting?"

"Yes, ma'am." Sheri nodded.

"It's in fellowship hall B." The woman pointed down the hall.

Sheri thanked the woman and headed for the meeting room. She looked around at all the stately portraits of former pastors and ministers that hung on the walls. Pictures of church events from years long past. The photos turned from color to sepia to black-and-white. So much history.

It made Sheri think about her own religious upbringing, or really her lack of one. For all of the yelling Bet used to do about the Bible, Sheri's mother, aunts and uncles were not big churchgoing people. Uncle Joe had stayed in the church as much as he had because of his pretty voice, not necessarily because of any relationship with Christ. It would be Sheri's cousins that would make up the first actively religious generation in the family.

They reached the doorway of a small, dimly lit chapel where a few parents were already sitting in the pews closest to the altar. At first, Sheri was taken aback by the room's darkness, considering they were there for a meeting. It hit her that the lights were low to accommodate the children's light sensitivity. Sheri could feel the tears forming in the back of her eyes. They were all dealing with the same bullshit.

A stout man with a round belly looked over and waved at Sheri and the children. "Come on up! We don't bite! We're still settling in over here."

Peach and Popsee gripped Sheri's jacket as they shuffled alongside their mother towards the front. Champ remained solemn-faced while carrying both his bookbag and the bag of snacks. The three children slid into the second pew from the front, and Sheri moved in behind them as she smiled and introduced herself to everyone.

"Yo found you, huh?" The round man folded his arms and gave a nod of approval.

"Yes, we met at the CEC." Sheri smiled as she got the children situated in the second pew.

"We call the CEC the House of Horrors over here," another man said, and let out a bitter laugh. He was a lean man with long arms and legs, and he looked much younger than the first man. His long locs were gathered in a ponytail that came to the middle of his back, and he was sitting alongside a beautiful, dark-brown woman wearing the most breathtaking multicolored headscarf and large, silver dangling earrings.

"That's for sure." The round man rolled his eyes at the lean man with the locs. "Let me introduce you to everyone." He started with the lean man. "This here is Alex and his lovely wife, Nishelle." The couple flashed dazzling, white-teethed smiles at Sheri and waved to her.

"This here is Paris." The round man pointed over to a young, light-brown woman with green eyes and a suspicious expression on her face. She looked as if she could have been the youngest in the group. Paris gave a mumbled greeting to Sheri.

"This one over here is Justin," the round man continued, "he's our detective. Him and Yolanda both are good at getting to the bottom of things. They put all the clues together."

Although his chiseled brown face had a stoic expression, Justin flashed Sheri the prettiest, dimpled smile, which completely caught her off guard. His smile reminded her a lot of Skeeter's.

"I'm Clarence." The round man had decidedly saved the best for last. "Baltimore born and raised and proud. Cherry Hill certified. My two knuckleheads are over there." He gestured toward the group of children who were either quietly keeping themselves busy or laying down on the pews, resting their eyes.

Right as Clarence finished the introductions, Yolanda burst into the room with the air of returning conqueror. Behind her was a young woman who looked no more than twenty years old with three children in tow, all of whom looked to be under the age of five.

"Hey, y'all! I was running a little bit late. Family, this is Tasha. Say hey, Tasha, this is everyone!" Yolanda had two large rolls of paper and a tote bag that she placed in the corner of the front pew.

Tasha smiled and waved as she quickly found a space on the second pew near Sheri and the children.

"My girl Sheri made it! Hey girl! Hey, Sheri's babies!" Yolanda gave a big wave to Sheri and the children.

Sheri waved back while Champ and Popsee looked at each other before giving a quick wave to the tall woman with the big voice. Peach had already fallen asleep next to Sheri.

Yolanda clapped her hands, and the cheerfulness of her voice gave way to a more serious tone. "Tonight is going to be a heavy night, I suspect, but we have to plow through all of the mess and trash to make it to the other side. I plotted out our New Horizons homes, and I have some maps with me. I think this may help with our recruitment."

Yolanda asked Justin to give her a hand with the two large rolls she had propped up in the corner of the front pew. The two of them rolled out two large street maps and placed them on the pulpit. "Clarence, help me find something that will weigh the corners down," Yolanda instructed while getting the maps in position. The man jumped up to find anything that could serve as a paperweight.

"See," Yolanda said, narrowing her eyes and pointing at the maps, "after I connected with Sheri and Tasha, I started to notice a little pattern." Yolanda waved everyone to come closer so they could get a better look. "At the very least, we know that there are two clusters of dirty houses. One cluster is on the west side and one on the east. Me, the Reeds, Clarence and Justin are on the west side. Sheri, Tasha and Paris are on the east side. It wouldn't surprise me to find out that the CEC, Sloane-Douglas and whomever else sectioned off a few blocks on both sides of town and began pulling families to fill the units."

Yolanda, eyes still on the maps, nodded her head and placed her hands on her hips. "We've been recruiting at the CEC, but it may be a better use of time to go door to door and see if any of your neighbors were accepted into New Horizons."

"That's a good plan; it makes sense." Justin's melodic baritone voice made Sheri do yet another double take. "The question we still need to find out is, what was the reason behind all of this?"

"Well, it's definitely clear that Sloane-Douglas was lying about the severity of our children's blood test results." Yolanda sat down on the pulpit step.

"What was the hypothesis, I wonder?" Nichelle spoke in a soothing accent that Sheri couldn't yet place.

Sheri thought back to when she'd confronted Ms. Gibbs, and how the woman continued to repeat her line about signing the contract. Was all of this some strange science project?

"Besides the recruiting, it's time to move on to phase two—protesting." Yolanda leaned in and made eye contact with all the parents. "I wanted to wait and try to get a few more folks in, but I don't want to waste everyone's time, either. For the west side, our council person is Charlene Rogers. For the east siders, y'all got the man himself—Mr. William 'Bill' Billups."

A collective groan went up in the sanctuary. Sheri and Tasha gave each other quizzical looks. Sheri thought back to how Jimmy Budd and Gloria said Billups only cared about the cameras. She guessed she would be seeing more of him in the future.

"We need to do a blitz attack." Clarence suddenly began rocking in his seat. "Calls to the office, protest signs outside City Hall and protests at any community event they attend."

"Spring is coming. As the weather gets warmer, we should go out to where the people are. Plot out a few busy intersections, pull out a bullhorn and let the city know what happened." Alex sat up in his seat. "The real goal is to get the attention of the news. Once this thing hits the press..." He swung his long arms to the right and made a whoosh noise to further accentuate his point.

"Hey!" Yolanda pointed over at Alex. "I do have a bullhorn."

"There's supposed to be some dedication coming up over at Sloane-Douglas in about three weeks. Saw it in the paper." Paris finally broke her silence. "Maybe that could be our test run."

"Where at, exactly?" Yolanda asked over her shoulder.

"Over on Harford Road. I think it's going to be another research wing."

"Sounds like a plan to me. Next meeting we can cover some logistics. Good stuff, Paris. Thank you." Yolanda winked at the young woman, who gave a self-conscious smile. "Also! I may have someone here next meeting who can help us with possibly getting a lawyer. Because y'all know that's the next step, right? We're suing these bleep bleeps, and I'm ONLY bleeping because we're in the house of the Lord, and little children are around, but y'all KNOW what I want to say. Bunch of mother bleepin' bleeps."

With that out of the way, Yolanda stood and stretched out her arms. Sheri looked around as the rest of the parents moved in to form a circle. Yolanda looked over at Sheri and made a quick neck motion to wave her over. Popsee had fallen asleep next to Peach, but Champ had remained awake through the meeting, so Sheri brought him with her to join the prayer circle.

Alex led the group in a closing prayer, thanking God for traveling mercies and continued blessings and protection over all of the families. He thanked God that the battle had already been won and that other children will not fall victim to the enemy's snares. Alex closed the prayer with a grateful "amen."

Everyone hugged and began gathering their belongings and children, most of whom had fallen asleep on the side pews.

A little boy with one of the happiest, sweetest faces Sheri had ever seen skipped over to Nishelle to hug her neck. He had a mane of gorgeous, dark-brown locs that framed his face, which his mother nuzzled with her nose. Sheri felt as if she were spying on this sincere act of affection between mother and child. It was so pure and honest.

Nishelle looked over at Sheri. "This is my little guy, Marlon. He's four." The little boy gave a shy smiled and waved.

"Hello, Marlon." Sheri smiled at the child with her whole face. Sheri looked over at Champ, who had gathered his bookbag and the snack bag that had gone fairly untouched. "This is my oldest son, Kareem."

Champ waved to the woman, and then did a wave/head nod combination thing with Marlon. To Sheri's surprise, Marlon responded with a head-nod back. This made Nishelle crack up laughing. "It's always something new with them, eh?" Nishelle smiled.

Sheri could only shake her head.

"Rides! Who needs 'em? Who's going where?" Yolanda was still in full general mode. "The Reeds, I know y'all are okay. Paris, you good?" She stretched her neck to check with Paris, who had since walked over to the side pews to get her son.

"My aunt should be outside already," Paris responded as she zipped up the jacket of a square-faced little boy with sweet eyes, fat cheeks and curly, sandy hair.

"Tasha and Sheri, I got y'all," Yolanda called out. "Clarence and Justin, I know y'all are good. How's the car runnin', Clarence?"

"It's holding, so I can't complain. I know it's going to be time for something else real soon, but that's the least of my troubles right now." Clarence shrugged while shaking awake a little brown girl with three perfectly round afro puffs.

Yolanda scanned the room and nodded her head. Sheri continued to be amazed by her. She noticed Yolanda hadn't brought her children with her to this meeting. Hopefully, she would be able to meet them sometime soon.

The temperature had dropped a bit as everyone cleared out of the building. Sheri was carrying a sleeping Peach while Popsee struggled to keep up his brother's pace.

"You'll sleep at home, Keyon!" Champ snapped at his brother. Sheri froze in shock. *What the hell was that?* This was completely uncharacteristic for her child.

"You do not talk to him that way. I know it's been a long day. We're almost home. We'll get something good to eat, a hot bath and you can sleep all night. In your own beds." Sheri leaned over, making sure Champ heard her clearly. Sheri didn't believe in whippings and poppings. She had seen enough of that in Spruce Junction. She communicated clearly to her children, and that was what she expected in return.

The three adults and the six children piled into Yolanda's four-door sedan. Tasha sat up front holding her youngest child, Ky. Sheri sat in the back, holding Peach and Tasha's middle baby, Jordan. Champ sat in the middle with Popsee on his lap, while Tasha's oldest daughter, Destiny, was pressed against the passenger side door. Yolanda dropped off Tasha first. Just as Yolanda had pointed out during the meeting, the young mother lived nearby off Biddle Street. Sheri wondered if her children attended Lexington Square also.

The Calloways were able to stretch out a bit once Tasha and her brood left. It was a fairly quiet ride back to the house. Sheri looked over at Yolanda and could see that the woman was in deep thought. She could tell that Yolanda lived and breathed everything she talked about. She wondered what the woman did to unwind.

Finally, Yolanda spoke. "I'm glad you joined us, Sis. We needed you there. If you need flyers about our meetings, just let me know. Don't go door to door if you're feeling uneasy. Just keep your eyes open. Our working theory is that the CEC targeted families with children ages six and under."

Yolanda pulled up in front of Sheri's house, where a single porch light tried its hardest to brighten up a relatively dark half of the block.

"I don't want to be nosey" — Yolanda looked over at Sheri and then glanced back at Champ, who was staring out the window —

"but the snapping? That's just irritability. A side effect of the lead exposure, by the way."

Sheri took a deep breath and shook her head. "I feel like I'm going to learn something new every day dealing with this shit."

"Those bastards took us on a ride, believe that—but we're going to make it. What's it say?" Yolanda narrowed her eyes and snapped her fingers as if trying to jog her memory. "Yeah, that's it. 'The race isn't even to the swift, nor to the strong but he that endureth to the end.' I'm not a Bible chick in the least, but I do believe that one."

Sheri leaned over to give Yolanda a hug. A smile teased the corners of her mouth. "How are you always so optimistic about things?"

Yolanda rolled her eyes and leaned back in her seat. "Girl. Every day is a damn fight. I'm out here fighting like Sugar Ray, chile. It's a battle to even get out of bed. They're hassling me on my job. Talking about I'm distracted. Well hello! These assholes poisoned my kids. That's enough of a distraction right there." She took a deep breath and looked at Sheri. "I get tired, but I know that I'm the only advocate my babies have. We're all they've got, Sher. It's tough, but we live to fight another day."

"It's never a dull moment. Ever." Sheri grunted and shook her head.

The two mothers said goodnight as Sheri herded her three, weighed down by the long day, up the steps and into the house.

CHAPTER 17

The telephone rang as Sheri bounced her left knee up and down out of both nervousness and frustration. Like clockwork, the syrupy sweet greeting came over the line once more: "Hello and good day, you have reached Millennium Management Partners—"

Sheri rolled her eyes and hung up the phone. She had already left three messages, and she languished on three waiting lists in hopes of landing a new apartment. She had already dashed her own dreams for a new car. The money had been reallocated to go toward her security deposit. Every day, Sheri toyed with the idea of not paying rent for that lead box they tried to pass off as a house.

The thought of returning to Gloria's place was always in the back of Sheri's mind, but something held her back. She deeply loved her cousin and wished her well; however, she didn't know if she wanted to go back down that road again. Skeeter talked about Gloria going to meetings to try and kick the habit. It would be an uphill battle for her cousin to get her life together and Sheri prayed for her victory.

One of the many things Sheri would always remain grateful to Gloria for was her current job. She had her own workspace. She didn't have a service-based job, and she wasn't doing manual labor. With all that was happening, Sheri doubted that she would have had the mental capacity to deal with the public or assemble furniture. She had her supervisor and her circle of coworkers to deal with, and that was it. That was completely enough.

Sheri thumbed through her growing stack of apartment-for-rent newspaper clippings. Although she wanted to rent another house, she doubted she would find one that would fit her budget. That was one of the main draws of the New Horizons program—

the cheap rent. Now Sheri realized why it had been so affordable. Everything comes at a cost. Living with Gloria came at the cost of seeing her cousin all drugged out. A decent home in the city going for a discounted rate came at the cost of her children being poisoned. God only knew what the long-term impact was going to be. Sheri had already noticed changes in such a short span of time.

Titi had called her earlier that week. Sheri hadn't gotten around to telling anyone about the whole Sloane-Douglas mess, so she kept the conversation relatively surface. Titi told her Kenneth was calling around and asking for her. This didn't make sense to Sheri, considering she had told him she and the children were moving to Baltimore and given him Gloria's number. Titi said Jackie was sick but wouldn't tell the family how serious it was.

"Syl thinks it's cancer," Titi lamented.

Skeeter instantly popped into Sheri's head when Titi mentioned Aunt Jackie. It would absolutely destroy her if her Ma Jackie were sick. Sheri debated whether or not to say anything to Skeeter, then decided she would just call over and make a general suggestion for Skeeter to call home. Just a 'Hey, have you checked in with the Spruce Junction folks?' should suffice.

"You need to call your Uncle Mike," Titi instructed her daughter matter-of-factly.

"Is he okay?" Sheri's stomach started to flutter. Something happening to Uncle Mike was the last thing she needed. Sheri was already kicking herself for not calling him more often.

"He just wants to hear from you."

"Well, did you give him my number, Ma? He can—"

"Just call him, Sheri." Sheri could feel her mother's eye-roll over the phone. "We're getting old. It's okay to be the one who reaches out."

Sheri agreed to call her uncle. All her life, he had always kept her in mind. A phone call to say hello wouldn't be a chore.

Titi asked how the children were, and Sheri gave some canned answer about how they missed Spruce Junction, but were doing well and making friends. Titi didn't try to mask her condescending tone when she asked whether or not she would see her grandchildren for the holidays this year. Now it was Sheri's turn to roll her eyes. She would come down when she was good and damn ready.

Sheri drummed her fingers on her desk and stared at her work phone, mentally willing the management companies to call her about an available apartment. Like so many other workdays since she'd received her children's test results, Sheri spent this one on autopilot. She made phone calls. She filed documents. She made copies. She faxed invoices. She greeted coworkers. She entered patient information into the database. Every so often, she would sneak off to gaze out the large picture window to get a glimpse of the breathtaking city views that she loved so much.

The clock next to Sheri's computer flashed five p.m., and Sheri grabbed her tote, her umbrella and her black-and-white striped trench coat. She flashed a beaming smile as she waved goodbye to her coworkers, who were shuffling to make their own dashes out the door. She lucked out and was able to catch an elevator as soon as she pushed the down button. Usually, waiting for an elevator in that building was just like waiting on a bus.

Sheri stepped out of the metal box, hastily walked across the granite floor and practically hurled herself through the sliding doors to escape into the soothing April warmth.

Sheri boarded the bus and rested on a seat to begin the trek back over to the east side. She watched the people as the bus jolted from stop to stop. Everyone seemed consumed in their own thoughts. A young man had his headphones on, but his loud music could still be heard throughout the bus. She watched as young children boarded the bus by themselves. They dutifully flashed a pass or slid a bus ticket into the meter. Sheri knew one day her children would be old enough to travel without her. She wasn't ready to face the reality that one day her babies would be adults. They already had their own minds, but what would she do the day she could no longer bring them close to her? The day she would have to schedule time to see them? To see if they were free to chat a bit with Mom?

She had taken them on a trip that previous Saturday to the Enoch Pratt Free Library . Sheri wanted to know more about lead poisoning and what her children may be facing. She had already mentally braced herself for the gut-wrenching discoveries that she would possibly uncover during her research. While Champ poured through the comic books and Popsee and Peach devoured all the picture and pop-up books they could get their hands on, Sheri meticulously read through every medical journal, science magazine article and encyclopedia entry the staff person brought to her. If she didn't understand a word, she looked it up in the dictionary. She was determined to find out what was happening to her children.

Sheri made photocopies of articles she planned to bring to the next Parent Crew meeting. She figured the other parents likely knew what they were up against already, but more information never hurt. Being around Yolanda had changed Sheri. She had never seen herself as being a leader. For most of her life, she had blended in. She had always been likable and relatively popular, but nothing more besides that. While Sheri had always credited her children for giving her purpose in life, Yolanda made Sheri ask herself, 'Who are you when your back is against the wall?'

Sheri got off the bus and walked the three blocks to Peach's daycare, then on to Lexington Square Elementary. This school year had been one for the books, and, thankfully, it was almost over. She thought back to a conversation she had with Harold's sister, Madilyn, about looking into schools over in the northwest part of the city. Madilyn raved about how clean they were and how much nicer the teachers were. Sheri didn't really have anything to compare Lexington Square to. The teachers at Horace L. Wagner, Champ and Popsee's school back in North Carolina, had been decent enough. The whole school comparison thing was new territory for Sheri.

Champ and Popsee did a little shake dance when they saw their mother and sister standing in the doorway of the cafeteria. Sheri always laughed to herself whenever her children cheered for her. It made her feel like a superstar. Champ asked if he could sign everyone out at the security desk. He wanted to practice his handwriting. Sheri nodded and let him have the honor.

Since it was a pleasant day, Sheri decided to walk the five or so blocks back to their house. She had started cutting unnecessary expenses from her budget, and hack rides were the first to go. Hacks were now used only in cases of an emergency or extremely bad weather.

"Champ, spell 'flower,'" Sheri called out to her oldest son, who was already walking ahead of the pack.

Champ turned to face his mother as if he had just been insulted. "Flower. F-L-O-W-E-R. Flower."

"Good job. Now spell 'themselves,'" Sheri continued.

Champ slowed down a few steps. He stared off into the distance. "Themselves. Them. T-H-E-M. Themselves." Champ started to hesitate.

"Don't overthink it. You know it," Sheri gently encouraged her son.

"Themselves. Them. Selves. T-H-E-M-S-E-L-V-E-S."

Sheri broke out into applause, which prompted Popsee and Peach to start clapping too.

"I WANNA DO ONE!" Popsee yelled out, never one for being left out.

"Okay, Mr. Keyon, spell 'hat,'" Sheri instructed.

"Ma..." Now it was Popsee's turn to be insulted. "H-A-T, and 'cat' is C-A-T!"

The waning April sunshine warmed Sheri as she laughed at her babies. Her scholars. She was fully prepared to fight for them until her last breath. Sheri swooped down to pick up Peach to carry her the last block.

"Miss Peach Cheeks, how was school today?" Peach loved when Sheri called her daycare school. Sheri didn't know when it happened, but she'd noticed her youngest would pitch a fit whenever Sheri asked her about daycare. School was where the boys went, and school was where she went, too.

"School was fun! We did the days by ourselves!"

"What! No way!" Sheri's eyes widened in excitement.

"Yes! Sunday, Monday, Tuesday, Wednesday, Thursday, Friday, Saturday! The days!" Peach recited triumphantly.

"Y'all about to be too smart for me. I don't know if I can keep up anymore." Sheri feigned nervousness as she looked into her children's faces. They strutted into the house feeling accomplished and proud.

Everyone knew the drill. Take off the school clothes and put on the running around clothes. This included Sheri as well. Popsee and Champ left their bookbags on the dining room table because Sheri checked over their homework every school night. Sheri would lay out Peach's running around outfit on her bed in the morning so she wouldn't have to rummage through her clean clothes. TV only came on once Sheri checked homework and made sure that the answers were correct.

While the children were still getting themselves together, Sheri decided to give Uncle Mike a call. The phone rang three times, and then a gruff voice answered.

"Yes?"

"Umm, hey. This is Sheri. How you been doing? I was trying to reach Uncle Mike."

"Oh... hey. Hold on." The voice never warmed once Sheri said who she was. She figured it was Maurice on the other end of the line. Between him and his sister Renita, Sheri didn't know which one was the funkiest. Only Uncle Mike and Mike Jr. greeted her with any decency. *Always breaking ugly on me. I didn't do anything to those people.*

"SHERI BERRY!" a warm tenor voice called out over the phone. Sheri immediately broke out into a giggle, and suddenly she was nine again.

Sheri could never see how her father and Uncle Mike were raised in the same house. They were night and day in every possible way. Although she had more memories with Uncle Mike than with Major, that one incident all those years ago was enough for Sheri to know that Major Calloway had been the devil himself.

"Uncle Mike. I've been meaning to call you. So much has been going on. It's a lot—"

"First, I wanna talk to my babies," Uncle Mike interrupted.

Sheri called up the stairs to Champ, Popsee and Peach. The trio came shuffling in a single-file line down the stairs, wearing their knock around clothes. Choruses of 'Hey, Uncle Mike!' filled the air, with everyone dutifully assuring him that they were behaving and not giving their mother any trouble.

Uncle Mike seemed to talk with Champ a little longer than the others. The boy nodded his head as if he were taking detailed mental notes, the usual serious expression never leaving his face. He turned toward his mother as he reported, "Uncle Mike says that we MUST visit them in Jersey." Champ's eyes widened to make sure his mother fully understood the instruction that was just given.

"Yes, sir!" Sheri yelled in the background, hoping her uncle heard her.

Popsee went over to speak with Uncle Mike again, then turned and thrust the telephone in Sheri's face. "He wants to talk to you again, Ma."

Sheri thanked her son and kissed him on the forehead.

"Girl, you got yourself a full house," Uncle Mike whistled.

Sheri cracked up laughing. "They keep me young."

"Talked with Tommy a little while back. How you liking Baltimore? I got happy when she said you had moved up north a little ways. A bit more closer to me."

Sheri smiled and talked to her uncle about the journey up north and the adjustments to the new city. She talked about living with Gloria and Skeeter, eating snowballs for the first time, starting college, visiting the Inner Harbor and the children adjusting to their new school. The two exchanged good news and pleasantries, but a sadness rose up in Sheri that seemed to hit her right in the throat. Suddenly, the tears started to fall.

"You don't got no man down there fighting you, do you? Cuz I still got my—" In an instant, Uncle Mike had turned back into his Vietnam self.

Sheri assured her uncle that she and the children were safe. Without going into detail, Sheri talked about having to find a new apartment as soon as possible. How she'd thought she was on the right track, but things beyond her control had sidelined her. Her budget was stretched, and she was just trying to make ends meet.

"Whatchu need? Money? That's all?" Uncle Mike's voice had softened to a whisper. "Listen, give me till Saturday, I'll wire you something. That's easy. Listen... I know you know that I love you, but I need for you to know that I've got you, too. Sheri, you're close to my heart. Always have been. I remember the first time I saw you when I came down to North Carolina. Had the sweetest little face and all that wild red hair on your head. The prettiest baby I ever saw." Uncle Mike laughed at the memory. "As long as I'm up and kicking, I'll be there. For you. For the babies. For your mama. Always."

"Uncle Mike, I just called to check in. Please, I didn't—"

"You really expected for me to hear you crying on the line and me not do nothing? Never. We blood, Sheri. You're a young woman out here raising your children, doing the best you can... let me help out some."

"Thank you, Uncle Mike. I love you." Sheri looked out at the setting sun as she wiped her tears. "I appreciate you."

"I love you, baby. You're not alone. Ever."

CHAPTER 18

Sheri had asked Yolanda for a ride to that week's parent strategy meeting. Yolanda told her it would be no trouble and that she would pick them up outside the elementary school. Sheri and the children were waiting on one of the benches next to the main entrance when a minivan pulled up with Anita Baker on full blast.

"Sheri! Jump on in. This is my sister's van." Yolanda waved from the driver's seat. A little girl with two pigtails had been in the passenger seat, but she quickly disappeared to the back.

"What is this?" Popsee's face was twisted in confusion. Sheri quickly hissed at her son and shushed him.

"Man! Can you help with the sliding door, please, baby? You know you've got the magic touch with that one," Yolanda instructed someone sitting in the back of the van.

Suddenly, with a loud creaking noise, the sliding door of the van flew open, and Sheri and her children came face-to-face with four different versions of Yolanda. Two boys and two girls.

Yolanda laughed loudly as Sheri helped the children into the van. "This here is my tribe. You got the twins, Man and Kelli. Then there's Tater, and right over here is Miss Fancy herself, Iesha."

All four of the children gave pleasant smiles and waved to Sheri and her three. Sheri could tell that Yolanda's babies were definitely going to surpass her in height. Man looked to be almost his mother's height already.

"Y'all, this is Ms. Sheri and her babies." Yolanda nodded toward the back.

"It's so good to meet you all. This Champ, Popsee and Peach." Sheri smiled at the squad of seven.

"Peaches!" Tater called out to the little girl.

"It's Peach," Popsee quickly corrected the little boy, who looked to be twice his size. "Short for Miss Peach Cheeks."

The entire van got quiet. No one knew exactly what to say after that.

"Well, alright now, Mr. Popsee." Yolanda let out a belly laugh. "Thanks for clearing that up for us. Make 'em come correct or not at all, that's what I say."

Sheri wanted to melt into the floor of the van. Her middle baby was just much too much sometimes.

"You like Anita Baker? Mom likes her, too." Champ nodded while looking around the van.

"Ms. Anita Baker, aka the living legend, aka the Songstress?!" Yolanda's face lit up. "Ask my babies, they'll tell you. We live in an Anita house!"

"She's my favorite, too!" Iesha piped in from the back of the van.

"So, how's it been going? Thanks for picking us up." Sheri straightened in her seat and put her seatbelt on.

"Sis, it's been going. Work stuff. Same ol' bull bleep." Yolanda sighed.

"Mom said 'bleep'! Bleeps means she's cussin'!" Tater yelled from the back with a laugh.

"I'm excited, though," Yolanda continued. "Our speaker is supposed to come through this evening. You ever heard of Alma Locklear?"

Sheri shook her head no.

"She's a member of the house of delegates, she's also a member of Gethsemane Memorial, and she sits on the board of A Better Way, a community organization that works with young parents. I volunteer with them about once a week. I do workshops with some of the moms. They have so many questions, and I talk about some of the mistakes and pitfalls that I faced coming along. Each one teach one, I guess."

Sheri ran a finger along her chin and looked over at Yolanda. "Do you think we're in a good position to pursue legal action? Like, fairly soon?"

"Labor Day, that's the goal." Yolanda nodded, looking straight ahead. "Yup, that's my own little internal timeline. Lawyer by Labor Day so we can kick this thing off for real in the fall. The whole lawsuit process is just so damn—ugh! I mean bleeping—"

"Bleepin' bleep!" A giggle came from the back.

Yolanda waved her hand as if she were swatting a fly. "This thing may be drawn out, and I'm trying to hit the ground running. So, how you been?" Yolanda gave Sheri a quick glance.

"Maintaining. I'm trying to get us an apartment. I feel like I've been driving into brick walls." Sheri rolled her eyes and watched North Avenue go by in a blur outside her window. "I don't want to spend another summer in that house. I'm trying to get something moving before the school year is out. Are you still in your New Horizons house?"

"Aww, nawl, no way." Yolanda squinched her nose as if a bad odor had just passed through. "No! Now, we were in there longer than I wanted us to be, but I eventually got out and moved in with my sister for a bit. Then we moved into our apartment right before Christmas last year."

"Did the CEC give y'all any trouble?" Sheri wanted to get a glimpse of how her story may likely play out.

"Girl, the CEC can go to h-e-l-l. You intentionally exposed MY children to toxins and poisons, and then you want to turn around and give ME grief? Over some raggedy rent? Honestly, I ended up throwing a lot of our stuff out. I kept clothes, art that the kids made, family photos—but I was just so paranoid about the lead dust. It was just a mess." Yolanda shook her head at the memory.

Sheri took a deep breath and closed her eyes. She tried to visualize herself and her children in their new space: clean, safe, affordable. A peaceful home in the midst of the growing chaos. She quietly prayed and meditated, choosing to visualize what she wanted instead of dwelling on what she didn't have at that particular time.

Yolanda pulled into a parking space on Gold Street across from the church. Someone let out a loud sigh, and Yolanda turned her head to give a warning glance. Champ held Peach's hand while Popsee and Sheri grabbed each other's hands. Sheri placed her free hand on Champ's shoulder as the pack crossed the narrow, tree-lined street.

Paris pulled up with her son and a folder full of papers under her arm. She nodded and gave a quick, tight smile to the group.

"This is information about the Sloane-Douglas dedication ceremony." Paris lightly tapped the green folder, then turned to open the main door to let everyone in.

"Good, because we're going to be talking about that tonight. Our first protest. It's time, Parent Crew. It. Is. Time." Yolanda reached over to give a quick hug and peck on the cheek to Ms. Leslie, the woman at the front desk with the thick grey hair worn in barrel curls.

"Hey, Corey!" Iesha waved to a little boy with sandy brown hair and unblinking grey eyes who looked to be right around three years old.

Corey gave a shy wave to all of the children, but made sure to stay glued to his mother's side.

Clarence, the Reeds, Justin and Tasha were already waiting in the sanctuary with their children. Cheers went up in the side pews when the children saw Yolanda's brood walk in. Sheri leaned over to see if her trio wanted to sit over on the side pews this meeting, but they all shook their heads no. Sheri shrugged and sat on the same pew from last time.

Once greetings were over, Yolanda took a seat on the top step of the pulpit and began the meeting. The first item of business was to discuss the crew's pilot protest, which was to take place at the Sloane-Douglas research wing dedication ceremony. Paris passed out the event flyers to everyone.

Yolanda rubbed her chin and narrowed her eyes. "This thing runs two hours. We should be able to stand that long, and it shouldn't be too hot that day."

Alex stretched his long legs and then shifted in his seat on the pew. "What's the messaging going to be, Yo? Like, should all of the protest signs say the same thing?"

"The wording doesn't need to be the same, but the overall message should be that these people, Sloane-Douglas, with the help of the Community Empowerment Center, intentionally exposed our children to harmful levels of lead and lied about it. I think if you're going to make a sign, and you don't necessarily have to, but if you choose to, make sure that the words 'lead' and 'poison' are on there somewhere."

Justin suggested that everyone meet at one assigned spot, maybe about a block away from the actual event location, so that the entire group could march in as a collective.

Clarence spoke up. "The twins' mother live over that way. There's a liquor store on the corner a block down for the Sloane-Douglas entrance on Saint Lo. Just park around there. The store can be our meeting spot, and we wouldn't have far to walk."

"You know the street name?" Justin asked from the side of the sanctuary.

"Abbotston. Shouldn't be too much of a hassle finding parking. I'm thinking we all should just carpool, though. Even the drivers. We don't need a caravan out there. We should sort that out today."

After some additional discussion, it was determined that Yolanda, Justin and the Reeds would be the designated drivers for the protest at Sloane-Douglas.

"Let the babies help you make the signs," Nishelle suggested. "They are as much a part of this as we are. In the end, this is about them and their future. Get them active. Yo, should the children come with us for the protest?"

"I don't see why not," Yolanda agreed. "I figure we should set up at the facility entrance right there on Hartford and Saint Lo. We'll still be visible from the street, but we won't be right on the street. See what I mean? Got a bit of protection just in case someone wants to drive wild."

"The event starts at eleven a.m.," Sheri spoke up from the second pew. "I say we get there around ten, ten-fifteen. They would have to pass by us as they entered the grounds."

Yolanda nodded her head as if she were listening to the greatest song ever played. "That's it. Now that's what I'm talking about! Make those moth—Make those BLEEPS see us. Let them know we're here and we won't go away quietly."

Sheri tried hard not to blush. She scooted back in her seat and picked some imaginary lint out of Champ's hair.

The air was charged with high energy, like a platoon ready to face their enemy. Sheri could feel the electricity, and it made her both excited and nervous.

A woman who resembled an understated Lena Horne quietly walked into the sanctuary. She had her salt-and-pepper hair brushed and pinned back with a beautiful turquoise barrette. Her attire was fairly nondescript, and she carried a stack of papers.

"Ms. Alma! Welcome!" Yolanda clapped her hands and bounced a bit. "Family, this is Delegate Alma Locklear, and she's been gracious enough to come and talk with us today about pursuing legal action."

Ms. Alma put a beige-colored finger in the air to speak before she got settled in. "I'm not here as a delegate; I'm here as a parent and as a friend of the community. Just wanted to be clear on that. I'm talking as a mother who understands."

Yolanda nodded her head and accepted the correction.

The older woman made herself comfortable on the front pew next to Nishelle, who slid down a little to give her more space.

"Oh, you're fine, baby." Ms. Alma took a quick breath and waved to all the parents, then turned and blew kisses at the children in the side pews who were off in their own worlds.

Yolanda sat on the pulpit steps, wide-eyed as if it were storytime. The parents went around and introduced themselves to Ms. Alma as the woman smiled approvingly at everyone. Something about her reminded Sheri of an older Skeeter.

"Well, Yolanda is a friend of mine, and she told me what has been happening. Let me first say that I am genuinely sorry. You were let down by the institutions that were supposed to help you and your family. I also want to be upfront and honest: this may prove to be a long battle. Both the CEC and Sloane-Douglas have formidable funding streams. While taking them to court will be essential, you may also have to plead your case in the court of public opinion."

The woman took another quick breath and looked around. She had everyone's full attention. Even the children had grown silent, seeming to hang onto her every word. "If anyone here writes well, then send a letter to the paper. All of them. Every local periodical in the city needs to get a letter from you all detailing what has been done. Go to public city council meetings. Work to get the attention of the local broadcast news stations."

Ms. Alma leaned back in the pew and scratched the tip of her nose. "Now that I'm thinking of it, you might want to expand your coverage to DC as well. Mail off a letter to papers down there, too. Don't get discouraged. Don't be hard on yourselves. This will be a fight, but you seem to be committed, and, truly, that is half the battle.

"Keep detailed notes of your children's behavior. Keep any documents that they may have received from school administrators and medical providers. Definitely make sure to keep copies of your children's blood test results. This includes the results provided by Sloane-Douglas, as well as the results provided by anyone else who may have tested them. Yolanda showed me the contract that everyone signed. I suspect the burden of proof will fall on all of you to show that you were not aware of the extent of the lead exposure."

"That damn Ms. Gibbs!" Clarence muttered in disgust, completely disregarding the 'no cussing in the church' rule in place.

"Who's Gibbs?" Ms. Alma turned to get a better look at Clarence, who sat next to Justin and Paris on the side of the sanctuary.

"That witch from the CEC forced us to sign them papers. Said we couldn't get our keys if we didn't sign."

"This thing goes far beyond some paper-filer behind a desk, honey. They were experimenting on your babies. We still have to uncover the 'why,' but for sure, that is what was happening. The New Horizons Housing Program was just a lure. Someone was in need of specific data. This is what we're dealing with."

The electricity in the air had fizzled out, and there was a stunned silence in the room. The gravity of the situation seemed to hit everyone at the same time. *Be careful. Be careful, Sheri. Always keep your eyes on them. Always.* Jimmy Budd's words played over and over in Sheri's mind as she fought to maintain her composure. She felt as if she were being chased through a maze, and there was no exit. No light. No release. Sheri counted backward from ten down to one as she took deep, measured breaths. Please don't let me have some kind of breakdown in front of all these damn people. In front of the kids. Just hold on. She needed water but didn't want to get up. *Sheri. Just. Breathe.*

Ms. Alma talked a little more, but Sheri could no longer hear her. All she could hear was a low buzzing noise that seemed to fill her ears. Sheri saw Yolanda get up to clap and walk over to hug Ms. Alma. She saw Nishelle lean over and whisper something to Alex. Paris snapped her fingers in the direction of her son, Corey, who Sheri assumed must have gotten into something he wasn't supposed to. Sheri saw Peach standing in front of her, jumping up and down. Then she turned and saw Popsee staring at her like she had three heads. Someone was tapping her on her shoulder, but Sheri didn't pay them any attention. All Sheri could hear was the buzzing.

"Ma!" Champ, Popsee and Peach's yells brought everyone's attention toward the second pew. Sheri struggled to inhale as she nodded her head and rubbed her temples.

"Peach gotta pee, Ma," Popsee whispered into his mother's neck.

"I can take her. No problem. Shelly has to go, too." Nishelle's voice seemed to bring Sheri back to herself. She watched Nishelle gather the two girls and walk out the side door of the sanctuary to the restrooms.

The strategy meeting wrapped up with everyone confirming their plans for the Sloane-Douglas protest in three weeks. Yolanda reminded the parents that both 'lead' and 'poison' should be somewhere on the sign, ideally. With arms outstretched, the meeting's closing prayer was led by Paris. Afterwards, Yolanda did her customary check of who all needed rides. Tasha let Yolanda know that her friend was picking her and the children up, so she was okay.

Sheri stayed seated to gather herself a little more. Champ, Popsee and Peach walked over to the side pews and began making what looked to be small talk as the children packed up their things alongside their parents. Sheri looked over at the little faces of the children as they laughed and joked with each other. Tiny humans with their own minds and personalities. So resilient without even realizing it.

Sheri knew she was going to be sitting with Ms. Alma's words for a good while. The part about the New Horizons program being a lure shook her to her core. What type of evil had she been dealing with? Sheri was very much still a country girl, and she was well aware of the razor-thin line that separated the saintly from the sinister.

Although Titi barely ever talked about it, Sheri knew her Aunt Myrtle had been a spiritual woman. A woman whose gifts reached beyond the physical realm. To Sheri's knowledge, no one in the family had really picked up where Aunt Myrtle had left off all those years ago. With everything crashing down all at once, Sheri believed it was time to seek out an extra layer of protection for her and her children.

CHAPTER 19

The last three weeks had found Sheri with a peace that she hadn't known since she first moved to the city. Uncle Mike wired her $4000 with the promise that more was available if she needed it. He made Sheri promise him that she would call him at the first sign of any trouble. Sheri had also accomplished the impossible. She talked her mother into making Aunt Myrtle's protection oil. It arrived in the mail two days before the protest.

"Why in the hell do you need this?" Titi demanded, suspicious when her daughter called her asking around about protection and coverings.

"Ma. Please? I don't ask for much, and I for dang sure never ask you about Aunt Myrtle's work. Trust me, I am fully aware that you don't like talking about it. I just need this right now. Stuff is going on," Sheri implored her wary mother.

"You not involved in some underhanded business, are you?" Titi pushed a little further.

Sheri again reassured her mother that she and the children were fine. She just needed something extra. Titi went on to talk about how Big Charlie and his guys swore by Aunt Myrtle's oils. Big Charlie's guys never got touched, even though black gangs were being taken out left and right by either the police, crews from across the bridge or guys from Atlantic City. In fact, a few of Charlie's men had pieced together that the oil their boss had given them was almost like some type of invisible cloak, and they used the cover to leave the city with their families.

It warmed Sheri's heart listening to her mother reminisce. Titi rarely talked about her Newark years. Although Titi loved Aunt Myrtle with all her heart, the young wife and mother had left it all behind when she packed up her infant daughter and made the journey back to Spruce Junction just a few months before the city exploded.

With an extra $4000 to her name and some extra protection for her and the children, Sheri was feeling pretty good the day of the protest. The Reeds had volunteered to pick Sheri up, and at 9:45 a.m. on the dot, a brown-and-cream Mercury Grand Marquis station wagon pulled up in front of the house.

Popsee was on lookout duty by the front window. Sheri did one last-minute check to see if she had everything. She had packed a small cooler filled with drinks and snacks as well as an activity bag with coloring books and Champ's newest favorite: word find puzzles. The family had worked as a team to make two protest signs: Lead Poison Hurts Futures and CEC/Sloane-Douglas Paints with Poison. Painted handprints lined the borders of the signs. Sheri nodded in approval once they had finished. The Calloways were officially activists.

Champ and Popsee each carried a sign as Sheri brought up the rear, carrying the cooler, the bag and leading Peach with her hip. Sheri steadied herself as she looped her left arm around the handle of Peach's stroller to balance it with her forearm.

"Aye now! We got the Bionic Mama here!" Alex, with his locs and long limbs, jumped out of the station wagon to give Sheri an extra pair of hands. He took the stroller from her and put it in the back of the station wagon, where there was already another stroller as well as protest signs. From the backseat, Marlon and Shelly happily waved to their new friends. Nishelle stepped out to give Sheri a quick peck on the cheek and one of those good, rocking hugs. The type of hug that let you know you were around genuine people who cared.

"I'm nervous, but I'm ready," Nishelle said to Sheri as they positioned the children in the backseat. Popsee and Marlon were granted permission by Alex to sit all the way in the back amongst the strollers and the protest signs. Shelly pouted her lips and turned around to stare at the boys, her big eyes full of longing to go back there and join them.

"I should have brought out my war music," Alex lamented as he checked under his seat where Sheri assumed he kept his cassette tapes. "For a day like today, we need some Peter Tosh. Gonna burn this city down."

"Maybe it's just as well." Nishelle continued to stare out the window. "Don't bring the rah-rah energy too soon."

"How long have you two been married?" Sheri surprised herself by asking a question so forthright, but she had been curious since she had met the couple. They seemed to be so in sync with one another, just like a seasoned married couple, but neither one looked older than twenty-five. Sheri figured they were high school sweethearts.

The question made the couple burst out laughing, which helped calm the sense of nervous tension that seemed to be growing the closer they got to the Sloane-Douglas compound.

Sheri learned that the couple met their freshmen year at the University of Maryland Eastern Shore. They both were education majors, Alex aiming to become a high school math teacher while Nishelle's focus was early childhood education. They would see each other around campus and at dorm parties, and the two struck up a friendship. One of the things they learned about each other was that they both had Jamaican heritage.

"Him only half, mi one 'undred percent yaadie ova ere." Nishelle turned to Sheri and playfully winked.

Nishelle said that she and her family moved from Clarendon to Brooklyn when she was seven, only to turn around and move to Edmondson Village right after her fourteenth birthday. Sheri figured that's why she loved Nishelle's accent so much—it was a mash-up of all of the places she had lived. Nishelle explained that it had been difficult settling in and making friends because she always felt like the new girl. UMES turned that around, and she had been able to connect with other young people with similar aspirations.

"Alex was this guy... always so full of life and energy and ideas." Nishelle smiled as she thought back to their early days. "I was drawn to him like a moth to a flame."

"I was the lucky one," Alex admitted, "brilliant and beautiful, the total full package. She says I was full of energy. That's an understatement. I was a wild bleepin' horse."

The couple laughed at Alex's imitation of Yolanda and her bleeps.

"I may power the ship, but Nish most definitely navigates it," Alex nodded matter-of-factly.

"We did all this talking and didn't even answer the question," Nishelle tutted at herself.

Alex explained that everything had fallen apart for them at the same time. His father died of a heart attack, and Nishelle's father had a major stroke while on the job. It was the beginning of their junior year at UMES, and the world was coming to an end. Nishelle's mother took her father back to Jamaica to recuperate, while Alex had to move back to Baltimore to help his mother pick up the pieces.

"We knew we needed each other." Alex stared straight ahead, bright and happy, as sunlit streets passed the windows of the station wagon.

Nishelle moved in with Alex and, determined to finished school, transferred her credits over to Goucher. Alex took a job tutoring high schoolers in math while also coaching basketball part-time and working a food delivery side gig on the weekends. It was a proud day when Nishelle walked across the stage. Alex realized he would be the biggest idiot of all time if he let her get away. He had saved up for a modest but thoughtful engagement ring and proposed to Nishelle at her graduation dinner.

"He was my rock when my father eventually passed away." Nishelle rubbed her bangled arm as she gazed out into the distance.

"I think we're here. The side street Clarence was talking about." Alex snapped his fingers to jog his memory. "What's it?"

"Abbotston," Nishelle said, shifting in her seat as she reached down for something on the floor of the station wagon.

"Yup, this is us." Alex turned down the street and saw a silver Honda parked on the opposite side, a safe distance from the fire hydrant. "Justin and Clarence are here. So I guess that means Yo got Paris and the new mom."

"Tasha." Nishelle scratched her chin and began stretching her neck to scan the area. "You think you can fit into this spot?"

"Ma'am! You know I'm the parking master. I can do this!" Alex shook his head at his wife's little faith as he backed into the space one car behind Justin.

"We're here!" Marlon shouted from all the way in the back. The car ride had been fairly quiet, as though everyone had been listening to Alex and Nishelle's story of how they met.

"It's Civil Rights time, guys." Alex exhaled loudly as he turned off the ignition.

Everyone began to quietly file out. Popsee and Champ appeared to be in deep thought as if they somehow already knew that something major was getting ready to occur. Peach had nodded off during the car ride and was trying to shake the sleep off of her. Nishelle picked some particles that only she could see out of Marlon's locs as Alex set up both strollers. Peach climbed into her stroller without being prompted and leaned back, ready to be pushed.

Justin and Clarence, along with two girls who both looked like pretty versions of Clarence, walked toward the station wagon. The little girls were holding large signs with black-and-blue lettering. Sheri tried to get a better look at what the signs said.

"Clarence and I were talking on the way up here," Justin started as he gave a quick dap to Alex and hugged Nishelle and Sheri. "Might not be too many people at this thing. Today is Preakness day."

"You all really think Preakness is going to factor in that much?" Alex asked, genuinely curious.

"You know those celebs and money men like to have their parties and private booths and all that." Clarence nodded. "I'd think this dedication might pull from the same pot of folks."

"I guess we'll see when we get up there. Definitely going to be a lot of research and science bigwigs there, that's for sure." Alex shut the back door of the station wagon and gave Marlon, who already had a full tank of energy, a high five.

Yolanda rounded the corner onto Abbotston in her sister's van, and the sounds of Miki Howard singing "Love Under New Management" suddenly flooded the block. There didn't appear to be any extra space on the side where Justin and Alex parked, so

Yolanda parked a little further down on the opposite side. She gave a big wave as she drove by the waiting group.

Sheri's watch read 10:10. She took a deep breath and turned her eyes upward, then looked to her boys, who were sitting on the steps alongside the liquor store.

"Are we ready?" Sheri smiled at them, giving her version of a pep talk.

Both boys shrugged as they rested their heads on their balled little fists. Peach remained stretched out in the stroller, staring at the bright, open May sky.

"Sheri, I didn't introduce ya to my kids!" Clarence suddenly remembered just as Yolanda, Tasha and Paris were making their way to the corner from further down the street with their children in tow.

"My girls! My two dynamos, Tyshawn and Tiffani. Y'all, this is Ms. Sheri! Say 'hi!'" Clarence beamed with pride while the girls didn't change their facial expression, most likely used to constant praise and adoration from their father. The two girls waved at Sheri and gave tight smiles.

"Family! It's go time." Yolanda walked up to the waiting parents and stopped to catch her breath. A black-and-grey bullhorn was slung over her shoulder by a black strap. Tasha and her children stood wide-eyed, as if the gravity of the day were slowly dawning on them. Paris, on the other hand, appeared rather nonplussed. She shifted from one leg to the other, and Sheri noticed she wore slouched socks of various colors stacked one on top of the other.

The crew of parents said a quick prayer and Yolanda did a head count. With everyone present and accounted for, the Parent Crew started out on their route: turn the corner onto Herford Road, then head up toward the entrance of Sloane-Douglas on Saint Lo Drive.

"THE CHILDREN ARE OUR FUTURE! SLOANE-DOUGLAS DEALS IN POISON!" Yolanda shouted into the bullhorn.

When Yolanda began chanting, Popsee and Champ, both holding protest signs almost as big as they were, exchanged frightened glances with each other before giving concerned looks up at their mother.

"SLOANE-DOUGLAS MADE US SICK! THEY BETTER FIX IT QUICK!" Tyshawn and Tiffani roared their own chant from the middle of the pack.

Yolanda quickly turned around and flashed an impressed smile at the little girls.

"Told ya they were some dynamos!" Clarence grinned as the caravan got closer to the intersection.

Yolanda nodded her approval and resumed chanting on the bullhorn: "SLOANE-DOUGLAS MADE US SICK! THEY BETTER FIX IT QUICK!"

Everyone joined in at the top of their lungs as the caravan crossed the intersection in the direction of the Sloane-Douglas research center's main entrance. The time was 10:21, and cars carrying guests were beginning to drive through the main gates. It was a pleasant day, and the sky appeared to be an extra-vivid shade of blue. The caravan stopped right outside the main gates in front of a low sloping hill just off the sidewalk. Nishelle covered part of the grass with a large, heavy blanket that had been stashed in the undercarriage of Shelly's stroller.

"For the little ones, just in case they want to rest," Nishelle said.

Sheri, Nichelle and Paris parked their strollers at the base of the hill as the group started to spread out a little, still chanting and carrying their signs. Some people honked their horns or pumped their fists in support as they drove past the intersection. Champ and Popsee furiously shook their signs and stomped their feet. Initially unnerved by Yolanda and the bullhorn, the two brothers had a change of heart. They seemed to have come alive right there at the gates of the Sloane-Douglas entrance.

Sheri looked into the cars as they continued to drive through the Sloane-Douglas gates. Some simply drove by and looked at the protesting parents with blank expressions, while derision covered the faces of others. Cold eyes. Just like the men who had visited Robinson Brothers. That chapter seemed like ages ago. One could never fully prepare for the twists and turns of life.

A couple out exercising stood off to the side, watching in fascination as the parents and children chanted and held up their signs. Alex's eyes lit up as he jogged toward the couple and began talking with them about why everyone was out. The couple's eyes grew wider and wider the longer Alex talked with them. The woman covered her mouth in disgusted shock.

Yolanda was clearly in her element. She chanted a bit, then she would pass the bullhorn to the children and let them get a few chants in. Then, for good measure, she would press the siren button as the children danced on either side of her.

"THE WORLD IS WATCHING YOU, SLOANE-DOUGLAS!" Yolanda screamed into the bullhorn. The children shook their signs on either side of her.

Just then, a security guard with a face like an angry eagle came marching down the hill. Sheri braced herself and looked over at the boys, then checked to see where Yolanda was. She wanted to be ready just in case things took a turn. It looked like the other parents had the same idea as they turned their backs to the street and began directing their chants toward the Sloane-Douglas gate and the incoming man.

"Who's in charge and where's your permit?" the man growled. His name tag read 'Lewis.'

Justin and Clarence both stepped up and walked toward the guard. "We're all in charge. We're concerned parents, and we're exercising our right to assemble and our right of free speech."

The guard's face turned beet red. "You all need to provide a permit or else I'm calling the police." The guard jutted his non-existent chin out and looked down his nose at the protestors.

"Sir, we are fully aware of the law." Yolanda gave the guard a dismissive sneer. "We are on Baltimore City property. Like my comrade said, we have a right to assemble. We are not on Sloane-Douglas grounds."

Sheri checked her watch. 12:38. Just twenty-two minutes to go. For a pilot run, it had been a good showing. Sheri held her breath when she saw Yolanda ball her free hand into a fist, but quickly exhaled when she released it. *We can go now, Yo. We did good.*

149

A brief stare-off ensued between the clearly frustrated guard and the families, which ended with the guard nodding his head, mumbling something into his walkie-talkie and marching off.

"We made our statement today. Great job, family, we did it!" Yolanda tried to bring the energy back up.

Alex began to loudly clap his hands as if his favorite performer had just gotten off the stage. The parents hugged and happily slapped each other's backs. Not to be left out, the children started clapping and giving each other high fives.

"We're gonna fight, we're gonna win," Nishelle laughed to herself and clapped in time with the beat. Yolanda stepped over to hand her the bullhorn as a sign to lead the closing chant.

"WE'RE GONNA FIGHT! WE'RE GONNA WIN!"

The sound of the claps seemed to slice straight through the balmy spring air as the protestors crossed the intersection.

"WE'RE GONNA FIGHT! *clap**clap* WE'RE GONNA WIN! *clap**clap* WE'RE GONNA FIGHT! *clap**clap* WE'RE GONNA WIN! *clap**clap*" echoed throughout the east Baltimore streets as people settled into their Saturday. The chant rang over the music coming out of the houses, carry-outs and cars. People stuck their heads out of windows and doorways to see what the commotion was. Campaign volunteers, perhaps? Was it another Stop the Violence rally?

Who were these people?

CHAPTER 20

The two women sat in silence around a small brown table near the window in Dr. Rooney's office. Popsee was on the other side of the office, seemingly in his own world as he played with Legos, racing cars and other small toys. He had earned his 'Rockstar' certificate, which came with a grab bag of gifts and goodies.

"This is a lot." Dr. Rooney took a deep breath and rubbed her temples.

Sheri could only shake her head as she sat with her arms folded. She told Dr. Rooney the slightly abridged version of what she was currently dealing with.

"The IUCF blood test really got this whole thing rolling. Without it, I would have been none the wiser. The whole thing still doesn't feel real to me."

Dr. Rooney ran her fingers through her hair, which appeared to be growing out of the chic cut she'd had when Popsee first started his appointments. Her skin flushed red, and she looked as if she was barely controlling her rage. After many deep breaths, she spoke: "I say this not just as a doctor but as a human being with a conscience. If you need anything for your case, I will be more than happy to assist. We took an oath to protect the community."

Dr. Rooney drummed her fingers on her desk, lost in her own thoughts, then continued, "To call this an ethics violation would be a gross understatement. This violates the cardinal rule of medicine—'First, do no harm.'" She leaned over to make direct eye contact with Sheri. "Ms. Calloway, I sincerely apologize. To you and to Keyon and to your other children. I know my apologies likely hold no weight in the grand scheme of things, but please know that I am so sorry."

Sheri thanked the woman for her offer to provide assistance. The information that the IUCF had collected on Popsee could quite possibly prove to be a big help as the parents continued to gather documentation to build their case. Dr. Rooney gave Sheri some literature about lead poisoning and its impact on a child's development. Sheri made sure to get a few of Dr. Rooney's business cards as they made their way out the door.

Sheri and her son held hands as they walked to the corner to catch the bus home. Skeeter was back at the house watching Champ and Peach. On top of ending things with the IUCF, Sheri was officially closing the door to the lead box. The management company had called a week ago to let her know her unit was available. A two-bedroom apartment in a building that was about five years old. Sheri breathed a sigh of genuine relief when she received the news.

Harold had asked Sheri out on another date. It would be their first solo date since the incident. The two had started to develop a little bit of a rhythm. They talked about once a week. Their time together had been converted into family dates, which was perfectly fine with Sheri. Their most recent family date had been a trip to the drive-in theater out by Westview to see some cartoon movie that had already slipped from Sheri's mind. The children had loved it, and Sheri couldn't recall a time when she had laughed so much. Harold had her in stitches the entire night.

Harold had told her he wanted her, and not in that creepy, only sexual type of way. He'd said it without a single trace of hesitation in his voice. He was aware that Sheri had her priorities, and he respected that, but he said he needed more of her. Sheri knew that she would need to start making adjustments in her personal life. She didn't want to leave Harold floating around the margins. There was so much to process. Sheri drowned in her thoughts daily, a trait she got honest from Titi. Sometimes she wondered if a part of the reason she was so hesitant with Harold was because she felt as if she wasn't worthy of the type of love he wanted to give her.

On the bus ride home, Sheri's thoughts drifted to the Parent Crew. So many lives impacted by the CEC and Sloane-Douglas.

Sheri knew that things would never be the same. Ms. Alma's words continued to ring in Sheri's head. *They lured us. Yolanda called them predators, and that's exactly who they are. She was right. These people truly are predators. Just like on those nature television shows. Damn.*

Sheri shook herself out of her reverie and looked over at Popsee, who was usually good for an astute observation or two. "Whatcha thinkin' 'bout?"

Popsee shook his head and continued to stare out the window. "I'm so glad it's over," the little boy sighed. "I really, really did not like Ms. Dennis. I hope I like my teacher when I get to the second grade. I like school, Ma. I don't know what I did."

A pang hit Sheri in her stomach, but she quickly swallowed it down. She looked at her son and lifted his chin with her thumb and forefinger. "Keyon Calloway, you are and will forever be a scholar. We all are entitled to have a bad day. Never ever think that you are a bad person. If your heart is good and you try your best, then you have won. This year nearly took all of us down for the count, but we're still here. We are winners. Never forget that."

Popsee gave a shy smile. "Ma... we're on the bus. With people."

"I don't care! You're my baby." Sheri looked around the bus. She turned back to her son and smiled lovingly at the work of art she had created. "I love you, Pop. You mean the world to me."

"Love ya, Ma."

◆ ◆ ◆

Sheri wanted to do a praise shout once the last of the boxes were brought into the second-floor apartment. She had decided to throw out the little furniture she had been able to amass in the time that they'd lived in the house. Sheri was so paranoid about the dust particles now, she thought it best to just start fresh. A new place and new furniture. For the time being, she had bunk beds for the boys and a full-size bed that she would share with Peach. She was grateful for new beginnings.

Yolanda and the children stopped by and gave a housewarming gift of new dishware. Sheri gave her friend the biggest, tightest hug. By far, one of the highlights of a rather hellish year had been connecting with Yolanda Johnson. Sheri knew the woman was only human, but that did nothing to diminish her sincere admiration.

The children bounced around the new apartment, and Sheri had to remind them that they were living over people now and they needed to be considerate of their neighbors. Yet another adjustment amongst so many they'd had to make in the last two years living in the city. They always took it in stride, but for Sheri, it stung seeing her babies not able to rip and run and be as free as they wanted to be.

"Next week, it's camp!" Champ yelled.

"Camp, lamp, stamp!" Popsee added his sentiments.

"Camp!" Peach added her piece.

Sheri had registered all three children in a summer camp program offered through the Baltimore Department of Parks and Recreation. It was an eight-week all-day summer camp that would take the children through the bulk of their summer break. Between the money that she had already saved and the money Uncle Mike had wired, Sheri was in a good place. She'd even paid two month's rent in advance. Despite a level of financial comfort she wasn't used to, Sheri continued to live on a strict budget and made cuts as needed.

◆ ◆ ◆

Although they had been back on speaking terms for some time now, it had been a while since Sheri had spoken with Gloria. Despite working for the same company and in the same building, it felt like Sheri hadn't seen her cousin in a month of Sundays. When Gloria called to say she had a gift for the new place, Sheri was a little surprised but happy that her cousin had taken time to think about her.

Sheri was sitting on the concrete-and-brick front stoop, watching the children play as the July humidity nipped at her from all angles. She had put a cool, wet washcloth in her bra to fight off the sweat, and she was readjusting it as Gloria's blue Buick pulled up in front of the building. Gloria was always known for a sleek, pinned-up hairstyle, but this time around her thick black hair was pulled into a ponytail. She wore a breezy linen skirt and a matching sleeveless top that was cinched around the bustline. Black sandals and a pair of Chanel sunglasses finished her look.

"Hey, Cousin Glo!" Popsee yelled from up the block.

"Mr. Popsee Poo!" Gloria blew the little boy a kiss and flashed him a dazzling smile.

Sheri had to admit Gloria was looking really good, practically magazine cover ready. Thanks to her statuesque figure, Gloria had always worn clothes well, but something was different that day. She was radiant. She seemed to be in a good place. On her hip was a fairly large box covered in purple-and-gold wrapping paper.

"I come bearing gifts. Or really a gift. It's a real nice one." Gloria carefully placed the box on the step just under Sheri's feet.

"This is real sweet, Glo. Thank you. We appreciate you," Sheri said softly.

Gloria took a seat on the steps next to her cousin. She chided her about sitting on the ground wearing white, to which Gloria corrected her and said she was actually wearing alabaster. This resulted in an eye-roll and a slight push from Sheri as she playfully sucked her teeth.

It was quiet on the stoop for a good minute. A few neighbors came and went, saying hi as they passed the two cousins. After a while, Sheri stood up to yell out for her three to play closer to where she could see them. The siblings groaned as they marched towards their front entrance.

Finally, Gloria took a long, deep breath, leaned back on her elbows and put her fancy glasses to the test as she stared up into the sky. "I was gone for four weeks. Rehab. Detoxing my body."

Sheri stayed quiet as her cousin continued.

"Linda liked to have raised all kinds of hell, but I made sure my paperwork was straight. Really gotta be Teflon when you're dealing with certain people. Always looking for a damn 'gotcha.'"

Gloria shifted from leaning back on the steps to leaning forward, placing her arms around her knees.

"All of my demons came out to play while I was trying to set my body free. Everything and everyone. It was like the Ghost of

155

Christmas Past in real life. Saw Juniper. Saw my dad. Saw Bet. Even saw Ms. Hazel and that mean, hateful sister of hers that used to despise me so bad. She would always stare at me like I was a living, breathing, walking pile of trash."

Sheri rubbed her shoulders and stared down at her yellow flip-flops. A single row of ants snaked along the concrete step.

"My mama and Ms. Hazel were dying at the same exact time." Gloria leaned her head back and looked off into the distance. "I begged and begged and begged Daddy to let me go home. Let me get back down to Spruce Junction to see my mama. Let me be there when she took her last breath. Told me no. Straight up. Flat out. No. That man yelled at me and stared me down like I was some stranger. Like I wasn't his own flesh and blood. Told me, 'We raised you! Hazel raised you like you were her own! You're so ungrateful! We gave your ass a life!'"

A little boy rode past on a green-and-grey Huffy bike, a younger girl holding tight to him.

"All of this Ms. Hazel talk, but Daddy always managed to find his way back into Juniper's bed whenever we came down to Spruce Junction. Told me that what he and Juniper had going on was none of my damn business. I love Gregory Shaw with all of my heart, but he was straitjacket certified." Gloria lightly scratched the tip of her button nose. Her profile was an exact duplicate of Bethel's.

"I was posted by Ms. Hazel's side like it was my paid job. Did her nails. Brushed her hair. Read to her out of the *Reader's Digest* magazines that she liked so much. Even swallowed my pride when her family would come over to the house to see her. My dad cried like a newborn baby when she finally died. I had never seen my father cry the way he cried. This man was the same man who created a child with a whole 'nother woman while married. Sheri, I tell you, he just wept and wailed. By the time everything was said and done with Ms. Hazel, it was too late. I had missed Mama."

Sheri remembered when Aunt Juniper passed. The air around Jeter Hill was heavy with sadness. Although hers had been a lengthy battle, no one was really fully prepared when Juniper eventually succumbed. Everyone had taken turns calling up to Baltimore in hopes of reaching Gloria, but to no avail. Bet had cackled in warped delight at the family's attempts to reach her teenaged granddaughter. "I TOLD Y'ALL SHE WAS A DAMN SHAW!" the lady yelled at anyone within earshot.

Juniper had been in the ground for about three days by the time Gloria was finally able to make it down to Spruce Junction. She arrived wearing a sensible black dress, sheer black stockings and black flats. Her thick hair was styled in a chic, yet age-appropriate, shoulder-length feathered cut. Sheri had been one of the few family members who greeted and embraced the grieving young woman. Many decided to keep their distance, figuring that Bet had been right about Gloria the whole time.

"Drugs have been my friend. They've been my priest. They've been my counselor. They've been a comfort for me for a real, real long time, girl." Gloria shook her head, then turned to look at Sheri, who had drifted down her own memory lane. "I'm not excusing my behavior. I was wrong. Jimmy was wrong. We messed up, Sheri. We fucked up. Bad. I am sorry."

"I think you're a good person. You just fell. It was a lapse. Just got to do right by yourself, Gloria. You have to love yourself enough to keep fighting for yourself." Sheri spoke slow and low, eyeing the golden-brown hair along her forearms. "Honestly, I'm talking to myself right now just as much as I'm talking to you."

Gloria turned and gave Sheri a look of concern. "Sheri… you okay?"

"I'm tired, Glo. I'm just tired." Sheri let out a deep sigh and looped her arm through Gloria's arm. Still family. "But I'm here."

Later that evening, Sheri had finished the last of the baths. Everyone sat clean and fresh in their t-shirts and pajama pants. Champ and Popsee begged for their mother to open the box. Peach said the paper was too pretty and that they should all just leave the box alone. Sheri actually agreed with her daughter on this one, although she eventually relented. She made a careful effort to open the package, lifting the tape with her fingernail.

"What is that?" Popsee asked with a slight tinge of disappoint-ment in his voice.

"A MICROWAVE! That's cool! Wow!" Champ seemed to have enough excitement for everyone.

Sheri shook her head. This was too much. Gloria didn't have to do all of this. These children didn't need a microwave. Still, the small, white appliance fit perfectly on her kitchen counter.

"We can make our dinner in the microwave now!" Champ was still on Cloud Nine.

"Alright!" Sheri clapped her hands. "Enough festivities for one day. It's time for bed."

It had been Peach's suggestion that the family start saying nightly prayers. Sheri tried to be mindful not to forget the nightly ritual, since it wasn't a practice she had grown up with. The family bowed their heads and said a quick prayer of thanks for the day.

Sheri walked back into the kitchen to clear off the wrapping paper from the dining table. As she did, a white card slipped out. On the card were two little birds on a tree branch surrounded by autumn scenery, and inside was a simple message: You remembered me. You loved me. You mourned with me, and I will always thank you for that. I love you always. Gloria.

There were ten one-hundred-dollar bills tucked neatly in the card.

CHAPTER 21

On a hill overlooking the harbor, Harold sat deep in thought, occasionally taking sips from his jumbo, fresh-squeezed lemonade. Sheri sat alongside him, eating hand-cut French fries doused in salt, pepper and malt vinegar. Between bites, she told Harold about the entire ordeal of the last five months.

"I knew something was going on, but I didn't want to overstep," Harold admitted with a thoughtful expression on his face. "I don't know anything about the CEC, but I do know those Sloane-Douglas folks have always been on the shady side. Growing up, we always went to Sinai." Harold ate a few more fries and took another sip of lemonade.

"They were making us go up there for blood tests as a precautionary measure." Sheri sucked her teeth before drinking from her jumbo cup.

"This city has a history when it comes to lead in the home." Harold turned and leaned closer to Sheri. In the distance, children laughed and played while the adults lay out and enjoyed the July sun minus the usual humidity. "I looked your place over, and it looked good. Honestly, it looked like a fresh paint job. No chipping at all, and I didn't notice too much dust."

Harold stroked his chin as if the wheels in his brain were working overtime. "They had you bring the babies in as a precaution… I just…" Harold shook his head as if trying to force the thought out. "I told you my brother does rehabs, right? He's told me in the past about how a few independent landlords and management companies had contacted him to see if he offered lead abatement treatments. They all seem to want something cut-rate. The thing is, some treatments work better than others. My brother doesn't really fool with that type of work much at all."

Sheri sat on the edge of the bench, hanging on to every word.

"I wonder…" Harold took a deep breath. "I wonder if they used different treatments in the houses. Like, one block may have gotten one type of treatment, and a different block could have gotten another type of treatment. Your 'check-ins' could have been to see which treatment had been more effective."

"You think Sloane-Douglas or the CEC had something going on with some of these landlords?" By now, Sheri's fries were cold and her mind was going a hundred miles per second.

Sheri suddenly got dizzy and wanted to throw up. She went from cold to hot back to cold only to turn hot again. She placed her head between her knees and took shallow breaths. Harold pulled Sheri close and could feel her shaking as he held her.

"When we pick up the kids, we need to talk to Yo. We need to sit with Yo and tell her about this. We suspected—" Sheri took a deep breath to steady herself. "We knew there was something deep behind all of this. We just couldn't connect all the dots."

Sheri buried her face in Harold's neck as he continued to rock her. She was stressed and sick of playing cute. At this point, she didn't give a damn.

"Let's go." Sheri jumped up and clapped her hands twice. "We have time."

"Go where?" Harold asked, still sitting down. Confusion covered his face as Sheri spun in a strange, misplaced frenzy.

"My place. Come on, we have time. It's okay." Sheri did a sort of sweeping hand gesture. Harold slowly stood up and grabbed hold of her small shoulders.

"Listen, now, you and I both know that I've wanted you far longer than you probably wanted me, but I don't want you like this. I'm a man, and I guess that means I'm supposed to be ready at any given moment, but there's a lot going on right now and things aren't clear."

"You don't know what I've been dealing with." Sheri sniffed and threw Harold a petulant glare. She felt embarrassed and wanted to have a breakdown. She also knew he was right.

"Sheri, I love you, and I care about you too much to take advantage of where you are right now. Hell yeah, it would feel good, but I wouldn't feel right. I've been trying my best to show you that my feelings go deeper than the physical. I don't want to throw that away."

Sheri sat back down and leaned on the armrest. "This has been some shit. The whole thing. All of it. I'm all cried out. I don't know if I'm coming or going anymore. My children are going through it, and I feel like my hands are tied. I just want to set everything on fire. This rage that I'm carrying scares the hell out of me. I've been fighting hard not to be eaten up by it." Staring down at the ground, Sheri was talking more to herself than to Harold.

"Let's take a drive before we have to get the little folks. We can drive through the park a little. Just to clear our heads. It's a pretty day and, as you already pointed out, we have time." Harold didn't like seeing Sheri so despondent and tried to lighten the mood.

Sheri nodded, and Harold tenderly helped her to her feet. The sounds of laughing summer revelers filled the air as the couple headed to the car.

◆ ◆ ◆

"I DON'T CARE WHAT SONG IT IS, TURN IT OFF! TURN IT OFF! We got baby children in this house, and we don't want to hear that filth. TURN IT OFF! And if I hear even as much as one chord, I'm gonna full well kick the stereo down the street!" Yolanda's face was twisted in annoyance as she argued with a thin, pleading voice coming from the basement. "Who even bought that tape for you? Did Yvonne buy that mess? IT'S FILTH!"

Just because Yolanda had to move back in with her sister didn't mean her rules went out the window.

Yolanda opened the door to Sheri and her cute man friend, Harold. "Hey, y'all!" Yolanda's face immediately dropped when she saw the couple's somber expressions.

"Yo, we gotta talk," was all Sheri could say.

Harold sat down and proceeded to explain his Sloane-Douglas testing and landlord lead abatement theory as Yolanda sat on the brown chenille sofa. Legs crossed, she shook her right foot viciously and chewed on her left thumb. Once Harold finished, Yolanda massaged her temples and let out a loud sigh.

"We figured as much. We knew some experimenting was going on, just couldn't figure out for what. Used our babies as human guinea pigs."

"Just like Tuskegee." Harold's voice trembled slightly.

"How can we prove all of this? I mean... we know what it is, but what could we provide that would hold up in court?" Sheri leaned forward in the high-backed brown-and-gold plaid chair, her elbows resting on her knees.

"It's all connected." Yolanda twirled one of her long braids between her fingers and stared out into the distance. "We just need to find the connections. Find out who sits on boards. Who donates money to campaigns. The answers lie in the connections."

"Would this information even be available to the public?" Harold gave a skeptical look.

"Media. TV, radio, all of it. We need to whip up some attention and fast." Sheri felt her heart racing.

Yolanda popped up with a jolt and stared at Harold. "You deliver, right?"

"Yeah."

"I made flyers. Actually, I made two sets of flyers. One is just a general information flyer detailing what those henchmen did to us, but the other one is for our next protest rally. We're going down to the CEC and we're bringing the reckoning." Yolanda nodded to herself proudly.

Another protest. Sheri was far more comfortable after the first protest, but this time, she would try to find someone to watch the children. Hopefully, Skeeter would be available. Sheri knew the boys had enjoyed themselves, but it still was a lot, and she didn't know how comfortable she truly was about them becoming warriors so soon.

Yolanda looked at Harold. "If you could, I would really appreciate it if you could take a good handful from both stacks and just leave them in high-traffic areas where they'll be seen. Be discreet! I don't want your money messed up on account of us, but it would definitely be a huge help."

Harold looked over at Sheri. He smiled and gently rubbed her knee.

"Okay, y'all. I can step away."

"Oh, Yo. No." Sheri shook her head.

"Don't 'Yo, no' me. I know when to get gone. Don't have to tell me twice."

At this point, Harold had turned deep red and all Sheri could do was cover her face.

"Just remember, when you start looking at bridesmaids' dresses, shades of purple really highlight my undertones." Yolanda gave a casual shrug.

Harold and Sheri stared down at the floor like two bashful teenagers at a church dance.

"Alright, dancin' machines! Mom is here!" Yolanda called up to the second floor.

For a split second, Sheri felt a little weepy as she heard the heavy footsteps coming down the stairs. Her babies were getting bigger every day. Their personalities were becoming more and more defined, and sometimes it was just too much for Sheri to take.

"Sheri, listen!" Yolanda's voice boomed through the room, full of amazement. "Your babies can cut a rug, did you know that? They just about burned the grass up back over there in the yard. Girl, I put on 'Square Biz,' and they were moving like in the discos. Who's dancing around them like that? Even Mr. 'Just the facts, ma'am' himself was over here groovin' to beat the band!" Yolanda gave Champ's cheek a little pinch. "Champ, you never told me you were a fan of Lady T!"

This made Sheri erupt in laughter. Mr. 'Just the facts, ma'am' was the perfect way to describe her oldest child. About business since the day he was born. Sheri was happy that he had been able to loosen up and have a little fun.

"I saved y'all some crabs, too. Can take 'em back with you, but you're also more than welcome to eat here. It's Saturday. No rushing going on in this house."

Harold and Sheri looked at each other and gave a shrug.

"I figured as much." Yolanda smiled and went to find some newspaper to cover the dining table.

"Ma, can we go back upstairs and finish watching the movie? It got right at the good part." Champ served as the spokesman while Popsee and Peach stood behind him with eyes wide like saucers.

Sheri shooed them back upstairs and walked over to the table with Harold.

"They're the real-life Musketeers." Harold laughed as he pulled out Sheri's chair.

"Who are you tellin'? That's exactly who they are." Sheri shook her head.

Yolanda, Sheri and Harold sat around the table talking more about the Parent Crew and the upcoming plans to raise awareness about what had happened to their children. They brainstormed until every last piece of Old Bay-covered crab meat was gone. Although tired and mentally drained, a sensation still vibrated deep inside Sheri. She always felt charged after conversations with Yolanda. Even Harold had a look of determination in his eyes as Yolanda handed him a stack of flyers she had printed the previous day.

"I'm going to take these and make some more copies, if you don't mind. The whole city is going to be covered once I'm done," Harold assured the two women.

"Don't do anything that'll get you in any hot water. Just a few here and there as you see fit," Yolanda reminded him.

"Nah, I got this." Harold glanced over the flyers, then looked back up at Sheri and Yolanda. "That old saying about what's done in the dark?"

Fire was in Sheri's eyes as she stared at the stack of flyers under Harold's arm. "Light those bastards up."

CHAPTER 22

S keeter had started picking up more shifts at the factory with the goal of purchasing her first car, so Sheri had been super appreciative when her cousin said she would be available to watch the children that Saturday so she could have that day free. Sheri slipped Skeeter a little money on the way out the door. Sheri truthfully could never put a price tag on Skeeter's support, and she was fully aware that her cousin definitely deserved way more than the few twenties that slid across her palm from time to time.

Sometimes Sheri wondered if babysitting was a type of catharsis for her cousin. Perhaps it soothed feelings that still went unacknowledged. Skeeter never talked about Patrick, and outside of the Polaroids that she'd brought when she first moved to the city, Sheri never brought the young boy up. Sheri's musings would have to remain flyaway thoughts trapped in her maze-like mind.

Sheri wore a crimson-and-grey jogging suit and matching grey tennis shoes. Her hair was brushed up into a loose bun, and she had channeled Gloria by wearing a pair of sunglasses. She had also brought a tote bag stuffed with flyers in various bright colors. At last count, Sheri, Yolanda, Clarence and Alex were going to be in attendance, with Paris and Justin penciled in as maybes. There was a knot in Sheri's stomach, and she didn't know if it was her gut giving a warning signal or just her adrenaline spinning out of control.

She thought back to the park and how Harold had to set her straight. Sheri hated feeling as if she were unraveling. She had three children to raise, and she couldn't afford to not be in her right mind. Although her mother never spoke on it directly, Sheri had heard the whispers concerning Titi's breakdown. The one that had rattled Bet so badly and led to Titi being sent up to Newark. Sometimes Sheri felt that it was only a matter of time before her own number was called. Having a healthy mental state wasn't discussed much in the family. Some folks prayed while others drank and smoked. Whatever it took to cope and survive the day.

Sheri got off the bus and walked the three blocks up to the Beechfield building. A cursed place in Sheri's eyes, right along with the numerous Sloane-Douglas buildings scattered around the city. As she got closer, she saw a group of about fifteen people in front of the building, including a group of women wearing white t-shirts and jeans. A head stood out over the crowd. *Chile, what is Yo over there up to now? Are these a whole new group of parents? Lord... what is going on?* Sheri slowed her pace to get a better look at the happenings taking place directly in front of the main entrance.

Yolanda wore a bright-yellow t-shirt and a pair of black shorts. Her hair was out in a full burgundy-and-dark-brown mane contained by a black headband. The women in white shirts looked to be in their early twenties or possibly even late teens, and they were all holding signs that read "Will My Child Be Next?" Sheri counted about eight of them. When Yolanda spotted Sheri walking up the street, she gave her signature beaming smile and waved to her.

"Sher! We're just getting started!" Yolanda adjusted the strap of her bullhorn, looking like a woman who had come fully prepared to set the entire block off. The CEC opened in thirty minutes, and Yolanda was steadily getting people into position. She instructed the young women with the signs to flank both sides of the main entrance—four on the left side and four on the right. The remaining bystanders had flyers in their hands similar to the flyers Sheri had in her bag. Like a true field general, Yolanda pointed out different places along the block for the people to stand.

Sheri scanned the block and noticed a police car parked about two blocks further up the street with two officers inside. She walked over to Yolanda and gave her a heads-up that eyes were already on them. Yolanda shot a quick glance in their direction and turned her attention back to getting everyone in order. She had brought the twins with her today, and Man sat on a blue-and-white cooler while Kelli sorted out flyers, placing them in neat, rubber band-bound bundles.

Alex and Clarence rounded the corner, each carrying a sign. Yolanda waved them over and positioned them at the east and west corners of the block where the Beechfield building stood.

Sheri stood there feeling like she should help in some way. Yolanda hadn't given her a specific assignment, so she found a spot and waited. She assumed the plan was to pass out flyers to pedestrians. It was the last weekend in July, and the humidity was starting to nip at the back of Sheri's neck. She had a bottled water stashed in her tote, which would have to get her through the day until she got home. Sheri was thankful her monthly visitor had moved on. That would have been the last thing she needed.

A few more people showed up to the building. Iesha handed everyone their own stack of flyers, and Yolanda had the new arrivals stand across the street at different positions. Once that was done, she scanned the block as if she were looking for someone. Iesha pointed in Sheri's direction and Yolanda waved her arms again.

"Sher! I need you down here. Near me."

Sheri walked back to where she originally had been standing, near the front door of the building.

"You and I have special roles today. Do you feel comfortable speaking in public? The plan is for us to chant a little bit, then I'm going to speak and then you're going to speak. If we have time, I'll bring Alex and Clarence over to speak."

Yolanda made a gesture with her hand in Man's direction, and the young, exceptionally tall boy slowly got up from the comfort of the cooler lid and carried a blue milk crate over to his mother. Kelli took that time to quickly claim the cooler lid for a seat. Yolanda stood on the milk crate and turned on the bullhorn while the seat-less Man sulked over to a shady spot and stood against the wall.

Yolanda got a chant going of "THE CEC AIN'T BEEN GOOD TO ME," with everyone on both sides of the street chanting in unison. After she felt comfortable the chant could ride without her, Yolanda spoke into the bullhorn: "The Community Empowerment Center has been actively luring families—families seeking better lives for themselves—posing as an affordable housing program when it's all just a deceitful medical experiment. 'It's affordable rent!' they told us, but in reality, they made us pay on houses that were contaminated by lead. Our children have been living with the effects of lead poisoning, and neither the CEC nor Sloane-Douglas have made any attempts to reach out to us to rectify this!"

Chills ran through Sheri's body as Yolanda laid bare the entire situation. Never in her wildest nightmares could Sheri ever imagine that she and her children would have gotten caught up in a tumultuous event such as this one.

"They used our babies as human test subjects! Their lives and futures were disregarded and treated as nothing more than an afterthought! You can BEST believe that this wouldn't have happened to their children, but ours are seen as disposable."

The protestors still had the chant circulating as they passed out flyers to passersby. Yolanda continued to speak as the crowd in front of the Beechfield building grew larger.

"You're going to hear our stories today! We want you to see how the Community Empowerment Center and Sloane-Douglas violated the trust of the people!"

Yolanda glanced quickly behind her to see where Sheri was. Sheri took a deep breath and exchanged places with Yolanda on the milk crate in the middle of the sidewalk.

"My name is Sheri Calloway, and I'm a mother of three from Spruce Junction, North Carolina. I doubt anyone here knows anything about Spruce Junction. We're a little two-stoplight town in Wilson County. I lost my job at the furniture factory, and I saw that loss as an opportunity to dream a little bit bigger and go farther than I had ever been. I moved up to Baltimore to stay with my family, who lived here already. Life was real good. I started school. Got a job. I was happy. I wanted more space for me and my babies, and I just happened to hear about the CEC's New Horizons Housing Program. I thought this would put me closer to my dream of having my own home for my family."

While she was speaking, Sheri noticed a large orange-and-white news van pull up. Butterflies started waking up in her stomach, but she couldn't stop. She had to finish her story. She felt it was her responsibility to let the people know what was truly happening out here under the guise of "trying to help the community."

"My family had our home and we were happy. We were stable. Then the headaches started. My babies could no longer tolerate too much light. It bothered them so bad they would hide their faces in their shirts for a little bit of peace."

Tears rolled down Sheri's face and her voice began to crack, but she continued, "So I ended up having to keep my house dang near fully dark just so my babies could move freely in their own home. There were issues at school. My boys had a hard time focusing and concentrating on their work. They never used to struggle before, but suddenly everything seemed to be a challenge. Behavior troubles. Being a distraction in class. Here we were at a new school, living in a new city, and everything felt upside down."

Sheri took a deep breath. The people who had been in the news truck had set up their equipment. A tall guy in a polo shirt and faded jeans with shaggy blonde hair held a camera in Sheri's direction. A young woman with a shoulder-length bob wearing an expensive-looking mauve blouse and black slacks stood off to the side holding a microphone. The young women in the white t-shirts lowered their signs as they all focused their attention on Sheri, seeming to hang onto her every word. Sheri stood on that milk crate feeling as if the entire city of Baltimore were watching her, but she knew she needed this. She needed to finally speak aloud what had been tormenting her for months.

"Then, the test results came back. We were getting tested by Sloane-Douglas, and I was told that everything was fine. This was a blatant lie. I went someplace else for testing, and I learned that each of my children had significant levels of lead in their bloodstream." Sheri pointed to the Beechfield building's front door as she continued talking into the bullhorn. "They knew the whole entire time. The CEC. Sloane-Douglas. They were prepared for this scheme to run for as long as it could run. Until they had gotten their full use out of us. Baltimore needs to know what is happening in the dark. Underhanded isn't a big enough word for this. We deserve answers! We deserve justice! Thank you."

Sheri jumped off the milk crate and handed the bullhorn back to Yolanda. Loud applause broke out amongst the crowd, and Yolanda softly rubbed Sheri's back.

"You did good, Sis. You did it." Yolanda's voice shook as she fought to hold back tears. Before Sheri could get her bearings, the young reporter with the fancy blouse thrust her microphone between Sheri and Yolanda. The tall, shaggy-haired cameraman stood directly behind her while Man and Kelli stood directly behind him, eyeing the man warily.

Alex had managed to swoop in and claim the bullhorn from Yolanda to start a chant and keep the crowd going. The reporter began asking questions but, by that point, Sheri was all talked out, and was content to 'that's right' and 'amen' all of Yolanda's points as she watched the reporter slowly come to the realization that her interview had been completely taken over by the tall woman with the big hair.

"...And what about you, ma'am? Your speech left everyone so emotional. What should be the takeaway from today's rally?" A microphone was pushed right under Sheri's nose.

"We want answers and we want justice," Sheri responded, then quickly turned to walk away, desperately in need of a place to sit down.

"Sheri!" A voice came from further down the block.

Sheri nearly collapsed in happiness and tears when she saw Harold walking up the street to meet her.

"I wanted to come through, see how you were doing. Y'all got a crowd out here today, boy. It looks good." Harold slipped his hand around Sheri's waist as Sheri leaned up to give him a kiss.

"I need to sit down," she whispered in his neck.

Harold steadied Sheri as they walked back in the direction of the Beechfield building. Sheri saw Clarence off to the side getting interviewed. Paris stood on the edge of the curb leading chants along with Alex and a few other protestors. Some of the young women in the white tees had left; Sheri saw only four of them this time. Harold gripped Sheri tighter and nodded his head forward. About a block up the street, six police officers were walking toward the Beechfield building. Sheri noticed that Man and Kelli were in their direct path.

"Yo! Yolanda!" Sheri tried to get Yolanda's attention as she grabbed Harold's arm and began walking quickly up the street to reach Man and Kelli first.

"Come!" Sheri made it to the twins in time. Man and Kelli stared at their mother's friend as if she had three heads, but Sheri didn't want to risk them getting hurt if the police chose to react.

"This is an unauthorized gathering! Who's responsible?" An officer who resembled a tall Uncle Fester stood legs apart with his hands resting on his belt. "Everyone needs to vacate the premises immediately. This is an unauthorized gathering! Disobeying a command will result in an arrest!"

An officer with a mousy brown crew cut reached to grab something off his belt. He furiously shook the silver-and-red tube as he looked to his fellow officers as if waiting on further instructions.

"This is an unauthorized gathering, and you are impeding foot traffic!" The tall Uncle Fester officer continued yelling at the crowd, who had since quieted down and were now all looking in the direction of the six officers.

"Yall ain't nothing but some ol' Carroll County hillbillies!" Clarence screamed from further down the block.

Everyone turned their a.ention to the officers who had now walked directly in front of the Beechfield building. Yolanda managed to make it over to where Sheri, Harold and the children stood waiting, but she felt she had an obligation to go back to the building to calm the situation down.

Sheri grabbed Yolanda's arm when she noticed the woman walking back towards the front of the building. "You are NOT going to go face down those cops!" Sheri growled through gritted teeth.

"I put this rally together, and I have to resolve this. Make 'em go away. I'm responsible," Yolanda reasoned.

"Yo, they're all adults. They know enough to walk away. The rally was ending anyway. You can't be everybody's mama." Sheri stared at her friend in disbelief. *What in the hell is she going to do up against six police?*

Although the crowd had stopped chanting and had grown silent, no one moved. The protestors and bystanders had managed to form a loose semicircle around the officers, with the Beechfield building at the officers' backs.

"WE ARE ASKING YOU TO LEAVE THE PREMISES IMMEDIATELY!" another officer barked to the crowd.

"JUSTICE FOR THE PEOPLE!" Alex screamed back at the officers.

A chorus of "justice for the people" rippled through the crowd as the officers appeared angry and agitated. One radioed something in while two others started patting their belts. The mousy-haired officer still had his silver-and-red wand ready to go. The officer with the drill sergeant bark had a stare-off with Alex, while the sixth officer decided to unsnap his gun holster.

"JUSTICE FOR THE PEOPLE! JUSTICE FOR THE PEOPLE!"

Three officers began pepper-spraying the crowd, which made everyone scatter. A camerawoman wearing a blue baseball cap stood off to the side, recording footage.

"C'mon! Get in my car!" Harold yelled as the suffocating mist started wafting in their direction. Kelli started choking as they all ran behind Harold. His car was parked on a side street in front of a stately home that doubled as a church: Full Life and Grace Tabernacle of Prayer. Harold unlocked the car doors and Sheri, Yolanda, Kelli and Man piled in.

"Shit! Shit! Shit! Shit!" Yolanda fought back tears and completely forgot about her no-cussing rule. "I gotta call Alex and Clarence and Paris to make sure that they're okay. Gotta call my girls from A Better Way to make sure that they got home safe." Yolanda shifted in the tight corner seat, chewing on her thumb as she stared out the window in a daze.

Harold and Sheri exchanged concerned glances while Yolanda shook and Kelli rubbed her back. "It's okay, Mommy. Everything's going to be alright."

"Mom's car is parked on Dolphin Street," Man said flatly, staring out the driver's side backseat window.

"Umm… thanks." Harold gave Sheri a quick what-is-up-with-this-child glance.

Sheri reached back to rub Yolanda's knee. "Yo, we're not going anywhere. We will sit here and wait. We can drive you home if you want." Sheri quickly looked at Harold, who nodded his head. "It's Saturday. It's been a long, heavy day. We have time."

Yolanda raised her head and rolled her neck back to lay on the backseat headrest. She let out a sigh and rubbed her temples. "I think I left some stuff in front of the building. Can we drive back there?" she whispered.

Harold gladly obliged and started the car. He did a U-turn in the street and turned the corner to pull up directly in front of the Beechfield building. There were a few colorful flyers stacked in the corner of the doorway. Yolanda instructed Man to get the flyers. The boy huffed out of the car, ran over to the doorway and quickly grabbed the papers up. He returned and slunk back in his seat.

"I'm parked about two blocks up. Thanks, y'all." Yolanda's usually bombastic voice had turned into a gravelly whisper.

Harold pulled up in front of Ms. Millie, Yolanda's faithful car. Sheri and Yolanda tried to do a quick cheek peck, but it turned out clumsy and they were both too drained to care. Sheri told Yolanda she would call her as soon as she got back home. Yolanda blew an air kiss as she, Kelli and Man unfolded themselves to get out of Harold's car. Harold waited until Yolanda drove off before he started the car up.

"You want to go eat?" Harold looked over at Sheri, as she had been through it all and then some.

"I just want my babies. I was hungry at first, but now I'm just tired. I feel like I've been through a war." Sheri sighed, then reached over to place her hand on top of Harold's gearshift hand. "Thank you for coming by." A little bit of color returned to Sheri's face as a smile broke through. "Things might have gone different if you weren't here."

"I always deliver." Harold gave Sheri a guilty grin, already aware of the corniness of his line.

"Oh, boy, stop!" Sheri playfully rolled her eyes.

On the way home, Sheri changed her mind and decided to go to McDonald's for a Filet-o-Fish meal to go; Harold went with a McChicken meal. The harmonies of Debarge filled the air as the couple sat in the car, parked in front of Sheri's building. They held hands as Sheri stared out the window and Harold stared at Sheri.

Sheri was leaned back in the seat, deep in thought. "It's going to be a fight." She looked up at the sky but could see no stars. She was a long way from Spruce Junction. "We're battling people with deep pockets and no care at all for our lives. We're just bodies to them. Something to tinker with. They don't give a damn about our fears. They don't give a damn about our hopes, our dreams. We're nothing of value to those folks. It's going to be a real dogfight."

Harold squeezed Sheri's hand as she turned to look at him. "And you're going to win."

CHAPTER 23

Champ slid out of bed and went to the bathroom. Afterward, the conscientious eight-year-old navigated his way around the dimly lit kitchen and pulled a bowl from the cabinet and a spoon from the dish drainer. His mother didn't believe in sugary cereals, and the sweetest she would allow was Cap'n Crunch. Champ poured some cereal into his bowl, then carefully sealed the inner plastic bag and closed the cardboard flap. He went to the refrigerator, got the half-gallon jug of whole milk and poured it over the cereal. He punched at the wet cereal a few times with his spoon for good measure, then put the milk back in the fridge and the cereal on the counter before he sat down to eat his breakfast.

Champ was enjoying the sugary sweetness of Cap'n Crunch when the telephone rang. It rang and rang until the answering machine finally clicked on: "SHERI, CALL ME! PLEASE TELL ME WHAT IS GOING ON! ARE YOU OKAY? I KNEW SOMETHING WAS WRONG! PLEASE CALL ME! YOU ARE NOT IN THIS CITY BY YOURSELF!"

Champ stared in the direction of the answering machine. He knew it was Cousin Gloria's voice, but what was she yelling about? What happened? Everyone was safe in the apartment, so they were all okay. Champ shrugged and continued to eat.

Popsee dragged his feet as he wiped the sleep from his eyes. Before he could even get himself situated, Champ ordered his younger brother to go back to the bathroom to use it and wash his hands. Popsee made a noise that sounded like a hiss and furiously stomped back down the narrow apartment hallway toward the bathroom.

Champ got up, took two more bowls out of the cabinet and pulled two spoons from the dish drainer. He went through the same routine as he filled his brother's bowl with cereal.

Champ left the third bowl and spoon on the counter just in case Peach got up before their mother.

"Thank you," Popsee grumbled as he scooted in his chair and started in on his bowl.

The morning silence was disturbed by more telephone rings. This time a softer, calmer voice spoke back: "Peanut, you don't have to tell me everything, but I need to know what's going on. Are you safe? Are the children okay? You didn't say anything last night. Did anyone go to jail? What's happening? You're probably gonna get a call from Gloria, too. I love you. Bye."

Both brothers' eyes grew wide at the mention of jail. What exactly happened? Their mother had been very tired when she got in the night before, but, other than that, she looked okay to them.

Champ rubbed his head when the answering machine clicked for the third time. It was Gloria again: "BECAUSE YOU KNOW WHAT? WE KEEP TOO MANY DAMN SECRETS IN THIS FAMILY AND THAT'S OUR PROBLEM! WE NEED TO STOP THAT! BETHEL DID THIS TO US! CALL ME!"

"Did Mom go to jail?" Popsee appeared genuinely confused as he continued to devour his Cap'n Crunch.

"I don't know. I don't think she did." Champ stared into his bowl and then lifted it to his mouth to drink the sweet cereal milk.

Champ and Popsee put their spoons and bowls in the sink. Champ went to the cabinet closest to the fridge and pulled out two paper cups. He placed the cups on the table, then got the gallon of Sunny Delight out of the refrigerator. Champ remembered how he, Popsee and Peach had joined together to beg their mom to buy the orange drink they had seen in all the commercials. It was imperative that they got a chance to try the drink just to see if they liked it or not.

Champ handed Popsee one of the half-filled cups, then put the drink back into the fridge. He wiped his hands on one of the blue dishrags before enjoying his morning cup of Sunny Delight.

Sheri was a mirror image of Popsee as she dragged herself down the hall, rubbing her face. She pinched herself for forgetting to put a scarf on the night before. It was one of those nights when her mind had been everywhere, completely scattered in a million pieces.

"Ma, did you go to jail?" Popsee's eyes were wide with concern. Champ peeked behind him with the same concerned look on his face. The two boys had made themselves comfortable on the couch watching a cartoon.

"What? What're y'all talking about?" Sheri gave her sons a cautious, inquiring look.

"Cousin Skeeter and Cousin Gloria called, and they both sounded scared. Talkin' about jail and secrets." Champ tried his best to summarize the messages from earlier.

"Shit," Sheri whispered under her breath. She quickly fixed her face, because the last thing she wanted was for the children to be worried. She clapped her hands and forced a smile. "Well! I'll have you know that I did not go to jail, but I did go to a really fun rally. We talked about justice and rights and doing right by the people."

Sheri watched as Popsee and Champ looked at each other as if trying to decide whether they believed her or not.

Sheri walked over to the end table and picked up the phone. A part of Sheri didn't want to bring either one of her cousins in on what was going on. She had enough on her plate, and neither one was really in a position to help. Sheri did feel a slight feeling of guilt for not letting Skeeter in on some of the madness. She felt torn.

The phone rang twice. "Hello? Peanut?" Skeeter's steady voice was music to Sheri's ears at that moment.

Sheri put the small talk and pleasantries aside and just began talking. "Hey. I got the message. I'm okay. No jail. Things just got wild toward the end. Thanks for checking in on me. I should have said something last night. I'm sorry."

There was a long silence on the line, then Skeeter finally spoke. "I'm glad you're okay. Thanks for calling us. I just got back in myself, and Gloria's walking around here snipping, but I can tell her everything is fine. You looked good on the news, too. They showed you up there speaking. Everything is going to work out. We really miss you around here, Peanut."

Sheri took a deep breath and gently tapped her fingers along the edge of the oval-shaped end table. "I love you, cousin. Always."

♦ ♦ ♦

It had been unseasonably cool for most of the week, and the heavy rain made the dreariness more pronounced. Sheri chalked the weather up to it still being hurricane season. She didn't know if Baltimore got hurricanes much. Spruce Junction got its fair share of flooding rains but not much else.

Sheri got to work and took a few minutes to get herself mentally situated. Although her office job didn't have the family feel of the furniture factory, she still liked her coworkers, and for the most part, enjoyed coming to work. Sheri knew she had some files to locate in preparation for a big meeting that was taking place the following week. She'd also gotten asked to assist with an interdepartmental project, so she was a little excited about that. Sheri didn't know if she wanted to be at Polaris Health long-term, but now she was content.

She had just returned from the canteen for lunch when she saw a note on her chair. She was to go to Linda's office immediately. Sheri slowly placed the pack of M&M's down on her desk near her computer and walked back out the glass doors. She looked around and didn't see any of her co-workers. Sheri counted backward from ten to one as she pressed the up button on the elevator. Usually, when she stepped onto the 12th floor, she made a left to check in on Gloria. This time she turned right to go to the HR offices.

Sheri walked through the glass double doors and was greeted by a man with slick hair and curious blue eyes. He tilted his head slightly to the side when he asked Sheri who she was there to see. Sheri mentioned that someone had left a note on her seat to come up to see Linda. He nodded his head and adjusted his tie, then stood up to walk down a narrow hallway. The man returned and told Sheri to follow him.

The man escorted Sheri to a corner office with a tall but narrow picture window that looked out over downtown Baltimore. It was the view Sheri loved so much, but she preferred the view from the conference room on her floor.

"Thank you, Nelson." Linda smiled as the man quickly hurried out of the office. Then she skipped the handshake and jumped right into it. "Ms. Calloway, according to your personnel file, you've been with us for a little over two years."

Sheri nodded yes as she resumed counting backward in her head.

"Well, you should be aware that even when you're not in the office, you represent Polaris Health. It is essential that our employees conduct themselves in a manner that is up to standard."

She's about to fire me. Okay, Sheri, just breathe. Breathe and count. Count and breathe. I wonder if Polaris has any dealing with the CEC or Sloane-Douglas? Definitely Sloane-Douglas, I would imagine. This is the type of shit I was telling Harold about. I wonder how deep it all goes. Who's connected to who? This is too damn much, chile. I'm done. I'm just... done.

Linda was still droning on and on, but Sheri had reached her limit. She was tired and, at the moment, she was feeling downright insulted.

"Ms. Calloway? Ms. Calloway?" Linda paused and gave Sheri a strange look.

"If you're talking about what happened at the Beechfield building, then yes, I was there. I protested. I spoke. Linda, I don't know if you were aware, but my children were poisoned. My children were poisoned and no one seems to want to take responsibility for what happened to my babies. Like we're just some trash."

"Well,"—Linda took a quick, measured breath—"we have decided as a company that we are relieving you of your dut—"

Sheri laughed and looked down at her lap. This made Linda squinch her nose and flash Sheri a cold stare.

"You're firing me because you know you can't fire Gloria, and this is the closest that you're ever going to get. Gloria's smarter than you; she can do your job better than you and you know you can't touch her."

"I beg your pardon?" Linda asked loudly.

"You heard me." Sheri dismissed the pinched-faced woman with a wave of her hand. "I'll get my stuff. This place can go straight to hell. Right along with Sloane-Douglas and right along with the CE fucking C."

"Ms. Calloway! Excuse me!" Linda yelled at Sheri's back.

Sheri decided to take the steps back down to her floor. She picked up her umbrella, work tote and red cardigan that she kept on the back of her chair. She made sure to put her pack of M&M's in her bag and stepped back out without a word. She considered saying a few quick goodbyes to her co-workers, but Sheri realized that she was no longer in a headspace for social graces. She wanted to just get away.

As Sheri waved goodbye to the two security guards on the ground floor, she breathed a sigh of relief. She was scared, but she felt free as well. A part of her wanted to scream to the heavens, but the other part of her wanted to twirl and dance in the afternoon rain. Sheri opened up her pack of chocolate candies and popped a few into her mouth. She would miss the view of the city the most. Those views had calmed her down, they gave her peace, they made her smile—yet the people who had access to those views on a regular basis never gave it much thought. Such was life.

Sheri was grateful that she had thought enough to pay her rent a few months in advance. Between the money from Uncle Mike and Gloria, she was okay—for now. School was starting in a few weeks, and this year all three of her babies would be enrolled. Sheri knew she wouldn't have too much time to kick back and sleep in. The job search for something new was just around the corner.

A covered bus stop served as a shelter for Sheri to sit down and collect her thoughts. A man walked up and showed his cup to Sheri, and she reached into her wallet for her last few coins. She watched a row of children in matching bright-blue t-shirts walk by on what she assumed was a field trip. Sheri checked her watched to see how much time she had before it was time to get the babies from camp. Maybe she could swing past the apartment to take a shower before she headed over to the rec center.

Sheri remembered when she was a little girl, her Uncle Syl would talk about something called "provin' time." It was when a series of tests would come, and a person had to prove what they were made of. Sheri also thought back to the question Yolanda had posed: "Who are you when your back is against the wall?" Sheri hadn't intended to move to Baltimore to be tested like Job, but, at this point, she felt she had come too far to flinch.

CHAPTER 24

The mood was low in the fellowship hall of Gethsemane Memorial. Clarence was talking about something that no one seemed to be paying attention to. Sheri, Yolanda, the Reeds and Paris all seem to be lost in their own thoughts. Justin couldn't make the meeting due to a death in the family, and, despite Yolanda's persistent entreaties, Tasha had decided that the Parent Crew wasn't for her.

Yolanda leaned against a wooden railing and rubbed her shoulder. Usually, she was fine being the engine to rev things up, but she had been mentally drained since the showdown at the Beechfield building. When Sheri told Yolanda she had lost her job, Yolanda blamed herself. The usually high-energy Yolanda definitely wasn't out, but she was for sure down.

"It's time for lawyers, y'all." Yolanda looked up at the parents from her usual perch on the pulpit steps.

"Yo, how are we supposed to pay?" Nishelle asked in her soft, melodic voice. Usually light and airy, today, it was laden with weariness. The summer seemed to have taken a lot out of everyone.

"Might be one of those things where the lawyer wouldn't get paid unless we win a settlement or something like that," Yolanda reasoned.

"Like an ambulance chaser?" Clarence sniffed from the side pew.

"We should find someone who specializes in medical class-action type cases. Like when people sue for getting cancer or respiratory diseases from their jobs. Something up that street." Alex nodded, his sandy brown locs lounging over his shoulder, almost reaching his waist.

"It's an outside shot for now, but there may be a chance that we'll be able to get Teddy Atkinson." Yolanda's voice took a hopeful tone.

A few surprised grunts went up, but the name rang no bells for Sheri.

"That would be a pretty big get." Clarence folded his arms in disbelief.

"Ms. Alma's looking into it. She said that he saw us on the news at the CEC protest, and he was interested. Nothing's set in stone, but we at least have a connection. In the meantime, we need to keep gathering materials, documents, stuff like that. If you've been taking your children to the doctor, get copies of any medical notes. We want a real for real paper trail. This is Sloane-Douglas we're up against. We don't want to give them any reason to write us off."

Yolanda called the meeting to a close a little early. She asked the group to put their feelers out for a possible lawyer who may be willing to review documents gathered so far pro bono. The group did their closing prayer and said their goodbyes. Sheri got the children together, and they walked out with Yolanda to head to the car. Yolanda's son Tater was the only one of the brood with her that evening. The stocky young boy had a playful, easygoing demeanor. He seemed especially fascinated by Champ. On the days when Champ would bring his computer, Sheri would find the two boys spelling words from off the computer screen or figuring out math problems aloud.

It was a fairly quiet drive back to the apartment. Yolanda looked to be having an intense conversation in her head. Every so often, she would shake her head "no" or purse her lips as if begrudgingly agreeing with something that only she was aware of. The children talked quietly in the backseat, with Champ leading the conversation. The topic for the evening drive was a new video game that had just come out.

Sheri stared out the window, lost in her thoughts as the sights and sounds of Druid Hill Avenue flashed by in a blur. As the year dragged on, Sheri's initial disbelief and shock regarding her and the children's undeserved misfortunes had gradually turned into a calcified rage. It wasn't an inferno type of rage. It wasn't loud and unhinged. It was quiet and steady. It went to bed with her at night and sat with her at the dining table in the mornings. It stood with her on the bus stops as she took the children to camp and it walked alongside her when she was at the grocery store.

Yolanda pulled up in front of the apartment. Tater let out a lively shriek that made everyone in the car jump. Yolanda quickly looked behind her to check on her son. "We on the level today? We okay?" She gently placed her hand on his knee and gave him a nod. The young boy nodded back yes and put two fingers up against his lips.

Yolanda turned to Sheri. "I remember our chat. I think I got something that you might like. It's not the Monday through Friday downtown life, but it's rewarding."

Sheri tilted her head, waiting to hear more.

"You remember those girls with the white shirts from the CEC rally? They're my girls from A Better Way. It's an organization that works with young parents. Didn't we talk about this? I thought we did. Anyway, they have an opening for an office manager. It would be Mondays, Wednesdays and Fridays from nine to three. When I heard about it, I thought about you."

Sheri smiled and thanked her friend. Despite all the madness, it seemed like Sheri always had angels along the way: Gloria, Skeeter, Uncle Mike, Harold and now Yolanda. Life had been hard as hell for her, but Sheri was grateful for the grace that still managed to get through.

"I want you to come by and tour the place. I feel like you'll really like it, Sher. They'll definitely be thankful to have you, too. All of them are still talking about the speech you gave at the rally."

Sheri reached over and hugged Yolanda tight. She thanked her friend again and placed Yolanda's hand on her cheek. Sheri didn't know if she was about to laugh or cry. She felt as if she were navigating life while walking a tightrope, taking one step after the other while hoping that something would catch her if she were to fall.

◆ ◆ ◆

The sunny August morning found Sheri walking into a storefront community center off of North and Bentalou. For some reason, this visit to A Better Way made Sheri far more nervous than she had been the day she sat down with Mr. Heath at her Polaris Health interview, which seemed like a million years ago. Yolanda said the lady's name was Louette Charles, but everyone called her Ms. Lou. Ms. Lou was the Director, Fundraiser and Marketing Manager for the community-based organization that served around two hundred families annually.

Sheri walked through the front door and was greeted by a custodian who reminded her of James Earl Jones. The older man gave Sheri an inquisitive once-over and asked her who she was there to see, since she clearly wasn't one of the "regulars." Once Sheri said she was there to see Ms. Charles, the man nodded and walked her down a narrow hallway lined with children's artwork.

"Thank you, Mr. Crockett." A woman with a short, neatly shaped salt-and-pepper afro stood up from her desk covered in papers, pictures and other miscellaneous items. Jazz played softly from a radio on a bookshelf filled with books, pictures and little figurines of black children. Sheri nodded her head to thank the custodian and reached out to shake Ms. Charles's hand.

"Thank you for seeing me, Ms. Charles. I really appreciate this."

"First off, call me Ms. Lou, and you are more than welcome. If Yolanda vouches for you, then you're good in my book. Go on and have a seat."

Sheri sat down in the surprisingly comfortable blue office chair. Although Sheri had just met the woman, she already liked her style. Petite in stature, she wore colorful, afro-centric earrings that Sheri had loved so much from the first time she saw Nichelle wearing them at the parent's meeting. Like Gloria and Yolanda, Ms. Lou seemed to possess the same majestic presence that could easily fill a room. She wore tortoiseshell reading glasses as she signed some papers and put them in a yellow folder, which she then placed in her top drawer.

"This song is so pretty. I don't listen to jazz much, but I've always thought the music was beautiful." Sheri shifted in her seat, trying her best not to look awkward.

Ms. Lou nodded her head and looked over at the radio on her bookshelf. "Jazz is my comfort when the whole world is going to hell. Dizzy, Dinah, Lady Day. That's my favorite song playing right now, 'Naima'. A gift from the genius himself, John Coltrane. I call him my cousin. Our families are from the same town back in North Carolina. I don't know if we're actually blood kin or not, but when it comes to our people, we're all related at the end of the day."

Sheri's heart fluttered when Ms. Lou said she was from North Carolina. Sheri told her she was also a North Carolinian. There was a sparkle in Ms. Lou's eyes as she gave Sheri an approving wink. She told Sheri she was coming up on her fortieth year living in the city.

"I tell people that I'm a Baltimorean Carolinian." Ms. Lou laughed at her own joke. Sheri smiled as she let herself get comfortable. A Better Way would definitely be a welcome change of pace from Polaris Health.

"Let's have a tour, shall we?" Ms. Lou turned off her radio, and the two women walked out of the cozy comfort of her office.

Despite the center only having two windows, the layout still felt open and airy. There were mirrors placed in strategic locations, which made the space seem bigger than it was. Support groups, workshops, meetings and other gatherings were held in one of four color-themed rooms. The red, blue, gold and green rooms were immaculate and tastefully decorated with comfortable-looking furniture. African statues and drums were situated around the rooms; paintings and photographs from Black American artists hung prominently on the walls.

"We wanted our parents and their babies to feel affirmed when they walked into this place. We wanted them to see themselves and to recognize their own beauty. It's tough facing a world where your very being is despised at every turn. We come from people who beat the odds. It may not have been easy, but we survived, and it's important that we honor and draw strength from that."

Ms. Lou talked about how difficult it was to reach some of the parents despite their desire for a better life for themselves and their children. The pressure from toxic friends and family members.

The pull from the streets. Ms. Lou and her small yet formidable staff faced it all head-on.

"It's generational. So much of it is generational. We try to step in and work with our young people to help them break the cycle. It gets hard sometimes because the traumas are so entrenched to the point where you could just chalk it up as normal." Ms. Lou made a sweeping hand gesture as the two women walked past a group session that was taking place in one of the classrooms. "When your mother and grandmother and great-grandmother have always handled things a particular way, who are you to say 'let's try something different'? That's one of the reasons why I named this place A Better Way, because sometimes there is a better way out there. You just have to push through all of the muck and stuff to get to it."

Sheri thought about her own family. The cycles. All of the things left unacknowledged and unaddressed. She thought about Titi and how she never allowed herself to be vulnerable, how she always seemed to mentally close herself off to the world. All these years later and she had never fully opened up to her daughter. She never told stories about herself and her girlhood. They really didn't have too many mother-daughter bonding memories. Then Sheri thought about Bet and how she held the family together with an iron fist. Violence and isolation were tools that she didn't mind using to maintain order. Sheri wondered how far back the cycles went and what she could do to make sure that it stopped with her. So that her children would have a different reality.

"Well, Ms. Calloway," Ms. Lou's voice brought Sheri back to the moment, "we have a position for you if you're so inclined. It would be three days a week — Monday, Wednesday and Friday — from nine a.m. to three p.m. The pay would be eight-fifty per hour. You would start the Wednesday after Labor Day."

Sheri hadn't expected to get paid that much, so she was pleasantly surprised at the hourly rate. She could breathe a little bit easier again. One less thing to worry about as fall approached and the Parent Crew's legal battles loomed ahead.

CHAPTER 25

Theodore "Teddy" Atkinson sat in a silver chair on the floor directly in front of the altar. At five-ten and weighing over three hundred pounds with thinning, wavy black hair and coal-black eyes, Teddy Atkinson was a formidable man. His clipped, no-nonsense tone spoke of generations of Atkinsons who had called Baltimore home since before Emancipation, and Atkinson knew the city and its power players like the back of his hand.

The lawyer had agreed to take up the case against the CEC and Sloane-Douglas. Known to be a shark of a litigator, Atkinson had won large settlements for people exposed to asbestos. He also won a major class-action lawsuit against Simmons Power when it was discovered they had discriminated in their hiring and promotion practices.

"I'm going to be real and direct with you all. This is going to be a fight, but I'm confident that we'll pull through. The CEC is just a front; it's Sloane-Douglas that we're truly up against. As parents, the burden of proof is going to fall on you to prove what you did and did not know regarding the lead levels in those homes."

"Sloane-Douglas and the CEC put our children through all of this to track cheap lead abatement methods in houses. They're working with the landlords." Sheri spoke up from the second pew.

Atkinson looked up at the woman with the tired eyes and nodded his head sympathetically. "No disrespect, sista, but right now that's just kitchen table talk. We have nothing concrete to prove any of it. I hear you, believe me, I do. Our best bet is to bring information that will hold up when put before a judge."

Yolanda and Sheri exchanged glances with one another. Sheri shook her head. *This is some ol' bullshit. It's more than 'kitchen table talk.' It's the reason behind all of this mess. Harold called it.*

Just because you can't prove a thing outright doesn't mean it isn't true.

Atkinson talked a little more, but Sheri had mentally checked out. As he made his exit, he gave a business card to each parent. The legal titan told everyone to "hold on to hope" and to remember it was the children they all were fighting for. Atkinson slipped on his straw fedora and headed back out into the sticky, late August humidity.

"Since the babies are going back to school soon, this is going to be our last meeting for a little bit, but I want you all to mark your calendars for October ninth." Yolanda placed her knee in the first pew as she leaned forward as if she were guiding a ship.

"We're going to pay the Baltimore City Council a visit. I read some old articles and found out that Bill Billups's wife sits on some type of research advisory panel for Sloane-Douglas. I'm still looking for anything that may tie Charlene Rogers to them. Might not find anything, who knows? I plan to keep on digging, though. I refuse to believe that they didn't know what was going on."

◆ ◆ ◆

For what may have been the thirtieth time within three hours, "Tootsee Roll" blasted from the stereo as the family and friends of the Parent Crew enjoyed one last summer cookout. Labor Day weekend had brought an extra celebratory feeling into the humid city air as the parents were still riding on the high of finally securing a lawyer for their case.

"We stompin' asses now!" Clarence whooped loudly while tending to the burgers, hotdogs and chicken legs on the grill.

Harold sat in the backyard, keeping an eye on Champ, Popsee and Peach. He'd brought along Amir and another one of his nephews, a happy little round-faced boy with missing front teeth and cornrows past his shoulders named Dylan. They got a game of catch started that came right on time in an attempt to tire the group of young revelers.

It was obvious that Harold was the favorite uncle in his family, and all the children seemed to gravitate toward the jovial, easygoing man. Clarence and Alex had given Harold a little lighthearted ribbing, telling him that it was time to start looking at minivans and asking if the reception was going to be open bar or not.

Yolanda's daughters, Kelli and Iesha, were diligently working on a step routine in a small corner of the yard. Kelli had confided in her mother that she had her heart set on trying out for the New Edition Marching Band the next time tryouts came around. The young girl secretly held some concerns that her weight could prove a hindrance in her being picked for the squad, but she would never let her mother know this. Kelli already knew that Yolanda would tell her to go out for what she wanted, if she really wanted it. With this in the back of her mind, Kelli fought hard to beat back any feelings of insecurity that tried to rise up and make her doubt her abilities.

Justin started a game of Pin the Tail on the Donkey near the backyard fence, and Paris had set up a station close to the steps where she painted the children's faces. The backyard had been transformed into a carnival wonderland, and the children danced, skipped and hopped from point to point with sticky faces and goofy grins.

"Mr. Atkinson is filing on Tuesday." Yolanda sat inside the quiet, cool living room with Sheri and Nichelle, away from the noise and jubilation outside. The humidity had been too much for Nishelle, so she'd snuck away to cool down to clear her thoughts. Marlon and Shelly were busy wearing themselves out in the backyard with the rest of the children, so Nishelle was free and clear. Sheri and Yolanda ended up joining her, and the three women talked about all the madness that had taken place during the year.

Sheri nursed a can of generic lemon-lime soda as she massaged her temples. She had made sure to thank Yolanda again for connecting her to A Better Way. Her first day was that upcoming Wednesday, and she was grateful for being in a more understanding workplace. Nishelle sat on the sofa with a glazed-over expression. She looked radiant and beautiful as usual, wearing a loose-fitting ocean-blue jumpsuit with earrings made with white-and-silver Ankara fabric to complete her look. She closed her eyes as she took slow, deep breaths.

Sheri and Yolanda exchanged a quick, worried glance. Both knew that something was weighing heavy on their usually even-keeled friend.

"Even before I had children, I knew I wanted them to be raised in Jamaica. But everything seemed to happen so quickly. Then Marlon came. Just as soon as I could get myself together, I found out I was pregnant with Shelly. My parents were already in Jamaica because my dad was recuperating from his stroke. Then my mom got sick. My sister went back to take care of them both."

Nishelle took another deep breath and slowly opened her eyes. "Honestly, I wanted to just up and leave. Get Alex on board, take the babies and go, but I knew I wouldn't be able to do that. I tried to connect with some of my extended family to see if the children could possibly live with them, but things were just never able to come together. Then all this happened."

Yolanda reached over to rub Nishelle's knee. Nishelle took Yolanda's hand in hers and held it tight. "I remember what you said, Yo. I remember you said it's not our fault and that they're predators doing what predators do, but I..." Nichelle's soft voice started to crack. She stared long and hard at the floor as large teardrops rolled down her brown face, then finally took a deep breath. "I'm pregnant again. I haven't told Alex yet. I just... I don't know."

She looked at Sheri and Yolanda with eyes filled with pain and guilt. "I always wanted a large family, but this place... it's such a wicked place. With wicked, wicked people. I just wouldn't feel right bringing another..." Nishelle closed her eyes as the tears continued to fall.

Sheri and Yolanda both went over to hug Nishelle and hold her tight. The sounds of laughing children and party music filled the air, along with the aromas of grilled hotdogs, burgers and chicken. In the distance, an ice cream truck played a happy carnival tune.

Nishelle's tears fell onto both women's arms as they embraced her. "I will live with this forever," Nishelle whispered. "What happened to my children, I will never forgive myself. A part of me will always believe that I let my children down."

Tears covered Yolanda's face as she lifted Nishelle's chin to look the remorseful mother in the eyes. "Nishelle. You did nothing wrong. I need for you to keep saying that and saying that until it sticks. You wanted a place for your family. This is not your burden to bear. It will never be. I know how you're feeling, I understand. I also know that your babies are the luckiest children in the world right now because you are their mom, and you're fighting like hell for them."

Sheri softly rubbed Nishelle's hand as tears trickled down her own face. "Nishelle, you are dear to me. I consider you a friend, and whatever you need, I'll be there. I will do all that I can to help. Please know this. If you need a babysitter, I'm there. If you need an alibi, I'm there."

"Yes. Yes. Yes," Yolanda seconded. "If you need a ride to the place. If you need us to have a story ready, just in case. I really didn't mean to make that rhyme. Just know that whatever you need, we're here. We love you, girl."

Some of Nishelle's signature glow came back. She smiled as she began to wipe her face.

"Napkins! I can do that! Napkins!" Yolanda ran over to get napkins from the kitchen.

Sheri sat by Nishelle's knee as she continued to gently rub her hand. Sheri knew the decision would be a hard one, and she definitely understood everything Nishelle was feeling. After what had happened over that year, the thought of bringing another child into this chaos was too much for Sheri to fathom. Sheri never figured herself as being naïve, but she now fully realized how depraved the world could be. One could never afford to underestimate evil.

Yolanda came back with the napkins, and the three women dabbed their faces and tried to shake the sadness off. Harold came in through the back door looking for something in the kitchen and saw the three ladies huddled in the living room. He flashed a concerned look, and Sheri blew him an air kiss. He gave another quick look over his shoulder before he ran back outside to rejoin the party.

Loud, energetic chatter filled the entire drive back to the apartment. The children laughed themselves silly at knock-knock jokes that apparently only they could fully appreciate. All five children sported painted faces, and Sheri's three also had a serious, lingering case of sugar rush.

"You okay over there?" Harold asked Sheri just as the light turned green.

"Yeah." She smiled and took his hand in hers and kissed it. "It was a good day. Mr. Atkinson is filing on Tuesday. Yolanda mentioned something about depositions, but she doesn't know when those will be. It's September already. Next thing you know, the holidays will be here."

"New job is coming up, too. Right?" Harold slowly pulled up in front of Sheri's building.

"Yup, on Wednesday." Sheri smoothed down some hair by her ears.

"It's going to be different not seeing your face on the route. I'm serious. Got me through the day." A sneaky grin came across Harold's face.

"Well, you are free to stop on by A Better Way on Mondays, Wednesdays and Fridays because that's where I'll be," Sheri said, nodding with mock-seriousness.

"So, what are you doing on Tuesdays and Thursdays?"

"Whatever I feel." Sheri threw Harold a silly, come-hither stare, then shrugged. "I don't know. I'm thinking about setting up a volunteer schedule at the school. Be a parent helper or something like that, if they need one. I'm not taking classes this semester because I suspect the lawsuit stuff is going to keep me busy. I guess we'll see."

Harold and Sheri continued to talk as if they were the only people in the car. Talking about how fast the year was going. Harold giving updates about his move to independent contracting. He asked when the next rally was, and Sheri said it wasn't a rally, per se, but the crew was going to drop in at a city council meeting in a few weeks. Finally, Popsee and Peach both announced that they had to use the bathroom, so all car talk had to conclude.

Harold helped Sheri take the children inside while Amir and a sleeping Dylan stayed in the car. He gave Sheri a kiss in the doorway, and, in a flash, he was back out in the humid September night.

Everyone in the Calloway household already knew the drill of bath, prayers and bed. Sheri turned on the air conditioner to cool everything down and hopefully speed up the children falling asleep.

"Mom?" Champ called out to Sheri as she walked past his bedroom door.

"Yeah, babe? What you need?" Sheri sat on the edge of the junior-size twin bed.

"That Mr. Harold. He likes you a lot and you like him, I can tell," Champ surmised.

"Yeah?" Sheri leaned in closer.

"Well… we like him enough, too. He's okay." Champ nodded thoughtfully.

"I'm glad." Sheri broke out into a full, toothy grin as she caressed her son's face. "I'm happy you all like him like I do. Regardless of who I meet, you and Popsee and Peach will always come first. Know that."

Champ nodded and reached over to hug his mother. He gave her a quick peck on the cheek and lay back to get cozy under his blankets.

Sheri breathed a happy sigh of relief as she got herself ready for bed. Although Sheri had learned not to get ahead of herself, she did leave room for hope. Perhaps there would be calmer days ahead just yet.

CHAPTER 26

S heri walked into Mr. Matthews's second-grade class with a haul that included cupcakes, ice cream cups and two jugs of fruit punch in honor of Popsee's seventh birthday. Sheri knew that it had been a trying year for all of her children, but especially her middle child. Sheri and Popsee both were already big fans of his teacher that year, Cedric Matthews. A studious-looking young man with a neat goatee and a very slender build, Mr. Matthews looked to be only a year or two in his twenties. He also looked to be the best person to keep up with a class of rambunctious young learners.

"Ma!" Popsee screamed when he saw his mother coming through the door of the classroom.

Mr. Matthews set up a space in the back of the room for Sheri to set up the cupcakes, ice cream and punch. The class formed a single-file line as Sheri handed each of them a plate containing a cupcake, an ice cream cup and a spoon along with a half-filled cup of punch. After Mr. Matthews placed napkins at each desk, the children wasted no time diving into their sweet treat courtesy of their classmate's special day.

Mr. Matthews went to the filing cabinet behind his desk and began looking through the top drawer. He pulled out a small boombox and a few cassette tapes. The first tape Mr. Matthews chose was cartoon party songs, which prompted a steady stream of boos from the finicky crowd.

"That's for babies, Mr. Matthews!" one of the students yelled.

"Tough room." Mr. Matthews shook his head with a laugh. He looked over the tapes again and put in a second one that he knew would definitely get the party jumping. The sound of thumping bass filled the brightly decorated classroom as Heavy D's high energy flow got the entire class up on their feet. Popsee stepped away from his birthday cupcake to do a few spin moves and hip wiggles.

"Can't go wrong with Heavy D or DJ Jazzy Jeff and the Fresh Prince. They always come through in a clutch when I want to get the children loosened up and still be able to keep my job." Mr. Matthews laughed as he took a seat next to Sheri, who was fully enjoying watching the little folks show off their best moves.

Sheri thanked Mr. Matthews for letting her have that time to celebrate with her son and his classmates. That year marked Popsee's third school year in Baltimore and his second school in the city. So far, Sheri really liked Mitchell Elementary, and she had hopes that all three of her babies would succeed there. Sheri told Mr. Matthews how both she and her son had been anxious at the start of the year because of how things played out at his previous school. Sheri decided not to mention the ongoing lead poisoning fiasco; that was an area she didn't want to visit on such a joyful day.

Mr. Matthews revealed that Popsee was one of his most engaged and earnest students. It was apparent that the young boy loved to learn. He was an excellent communicator, and he always spoke with confidence. Popsee was always considerate toward his classmates, and the students seem to gravitate to him. Mr. Matthews observed that Popsee's opinion on things held a lot of sway amongst his peers, and it wasn't uncommon for his classmates to agree with his points during story discussions.

"Ms. Calloway, you may have a future trial lawyer on your hands. Keyon is very sure of himself without being mean or overbearing. To have that presence at seven is a testament to your excellent parenting."

Sheri knew all of her children were exceptional children, and she knew that she should feel more secure when receiving compliments, but there was still a mental barrier in place that made her feel uneasy. "Let people praise you!" Sheri could hear Yolanda's booming voice in her head. It was something she knew she would have to work on, day by day.

Mr. Matthews told Sheri that his fraternity offered young men's leadership workshops during the summer, but the boys had to be at least in the third grade. He went to his desk to get Sheri a flyer. If all of the men were like Mr. Matthews, Sheri figured this may very well be a perfect opportunity for her boys. Sheri knew these were important years for all three of her children. They were growing and developing at a rapid pace. There was going to come a time when they would prefer the company of their friends over being with her. Sheri realized that keeping her babies around people going places would be the ticket to them wanting better and doing better.

♦♦♦

It was decided that black and gold would be the Parent Crew's designated color scheme for that evening's city council meeting. Yolanda reasoned that the Parent Crew represented the true Baltimore City, so it was only right to wear the city's colors. In a change of pace, Sheri decided to wrap her hair in gold fabric. She wore black slacks with a black turtleneck and a black blazer with gold embroidery along the cuffs. A sensible pair of black shoes and some gold hoop earrings finished Sheri's look.

Sheri sat on a brick wall in War Memorial Plaza as she waited for the rest of the team to arrive. She crossed her legs at the ankle and kicked like a child waiting to be picked up from school. The fall air felt good on her skin as she continued to replay Mr. Matthews's words over and over in her head. She had been on pins and needles worrying about who her son would get this year, and it appeared he had been paired with a teacher who saw him for who he really was.

Sheri mentally prepared herself for that evening's meeting. "You're the meat and I'm the sides, Sher," Yolanda had said during their phone conversation earlier that week. "When the floor is opened for public comments, you're going to lead us off—hit 'em fast and early."

Sheri was more than ready. As far as she was concerned, she was far past the point of second-guessing herself.

Talk slow. Talk sure. Make them feel what you've been feeling these last eight months. Let them know the toll that this has taken on everyone. They work for you. Remember that. They're in office to serve the people. Never forget that. This is for your babies. Remember them. Always.

Justin, Paris and Clarence rounded the corner in their black and gold. Justin and Clarence had kept it simple, with both men donning black button-up shirts with black pants. Paris had decided to sport a new look for the season; her hair was platinum blond and cut in a feathered, pixie style. She wore a black leather jacket over a black-and-gold knee-length sweater dress, black fishnet tights and a pair of black Doc Martens with gold studs around the toe.

Sheri walked over to meet her crewmates at the bottom of the stairs of City Hall.

"We're dealing with the fat cats tonight, you ready?" Clarence smiled at Sheri as she rubbed her arms to beat back the pesky October chill.

"As ready as I can be. No time to tuck tail now." Sheri shrugged matter-of-factly, as only a person from Spruce Junction could.

Yolanda did a light jog through War Memorial Plaza to meet the rest of the group. For that evening, Yolanda had chosen to go with a black knee-length dress, sheer stockings and black pumps that accentuated her six-one frame. A luxurious-looking black-and-gold silk scarf and gold earrings capped everything off. The burgundy was gone from Yolanda's mane, and her dark brown hair was in waist-length braids.

The waiting four members of the Parent Crew broke out in applause as Yolanda reached the steps of the building.

"Fashion week!" the usually quiet Paris yelled out.

Yolanda's cinnamon-brown skin seemed to radiate as she did a silly curtsey to the group. Everyone quickly got serious again and circled up to have a quick prayer. Once that was done, the parents walked up the steps and entered City Hall.

In the meeting hall, Sheri looked around, taken aback by how large the room was and how high the ceilings were. The sense of history was extremely heavy. Sheri fought back the nervousness that wanted to try to break its way through. She didn't have time for the nonsense that evening. She studied the city council members as they droned through the agenda. Sheri was finally able to see the infamous—at least to Gloria and Jimmy—Bill Billups. He was a big man, big and tall with balding, light-brown hair. He wore glasses and kept taking them off and putting them back on his long, jowly face.

Sheri squinted as she looked for the other council member they were targeting, Charlene Rogers. When Sheri finally found the woman, she had to do a double take. Normally, Sheri was good at spotting her people, but this Charlene Rogers woman had her genuinely stumped. Her hair was honey blonde and shoulder length. She wore a conservative blue suit with pearl earrings and a pearl necklace. Sheri wondered how old she was.

Sheri's mind went to her children, who were being watched by their next-door neighbor, Mrs. Lee. Mrs. Lee was an older woman who usually watched the infant babies in the building during the day. Since it was one of Sheri's off days, she'd picked the children up from school, fed them an early dinner and packed a snack bag for their visit with their neighbor.

"The floor is open for public comment," a man who resembled an owl said into his microphone.

The Parent Crew stood up and made their way to the front. From the corner of Sheri's eye, she saw a woman in a red pantsuit trying to get to the podium first, but Sheri zoomed ahead to stake her claim. Sheri smoothed her jacket and did a quick check to see if her team was behind her. She faced the front and looked into the faces of the city council members. Some looked more engaged than others. Regardless, it was now her time to be heard.

"My name is Sheri Calloway, and I am here as part of a group of concerned parents who were selected to be a part of the New Horizons Housing Program sponsored by the Baltimore Community Empowerment Center. New Horizons houses are located in your district, Mr. Billups, as well as your district, Ms. Rogers. At the time we moved in, the homes were contaminated with high levels of lead. Our children have been dealing with the effects of lead poisoning, and we are looking to you for help."

"Please be mindful of time," the owl-faced man spoke up.

"We are looking to you for help because, as residents of this city, we should be assured that our children will not be used as human test subjects. Our children's lead levels were supposedly being monitored by staff at Sloane-Douglas hospital, yet no one thought to tell us about the danger we were in. Exposure to toxic levels of lead greatly impairs a child's cognitive development. Living in these houses will have life-long consequences for our children, and we are looking for justice. Mr. Billups and Ms. Rogers, we have a list of demands, and we would appreciate the opportunity to—"

"Time," Owl-face spoke dryly into the mic.

Sheri felt hands gently rubbing her back. That was it. That had been her moment. She looked over and made eye contact with Yolanda, who quickly nodded and walked up to the podium as if taking the baton in a relay race.

"Councilwoman Rogers, you're still fairly new in this city, and, to be quite honest, I don't know where you came from or what you're about. You were my councilwoman when I lived in my New Horizons house, and I distinctly remember trying to find some time on your schedule, but we never managed to connect. That's unfortunate. I would hope that you are here on behalf of your constituents, but I can't call that, at this moment." Yolanda turned her head slightly to the left. "But Councilman Billups, I come to you surprised and disappointed.

"Councilman Billups, it was a proud day when your father and your uncle were elected to represent our city, our community. There were a good number of people who left this city for dead after the riots, but the Billups brothers vowed to restore what had been lost. They vowed to take Baltimore City forward... but that's not what we got. We got photo shoots and lies, along with more photo shoots and corruption. The people—the lifeblood of this city—were left high and dry. Our babies were poisoned. Doesn't that bother you? Our babies' futures were brokered away, and for what? For whom?"

"Ma'am!" Mr. Owl yelled into his mic.

"Sir!" Yolanda leaned into the mic and looked over at Mr. Owl. "You all made a deal with the devil and went against the very people you were put into office to advocate for. Sloane-Douglas stood silent while our babies were intentionally poisoned. Everyone should be up in arms about this! Our children look just like yours, and yet you sold them down the river!"

"Time!" another person shouted into the mic.

Yolanda took a breath and gripped the podium. "There is going to come a day when all of you will have to answer for the evil you let slide in the name of kickbacks and a few extra dollars. Councilman Billups, you're just another name on the list of do-nothings who never really gave a damn—"

"Please yield the floor!"

"Never really gave a damn, just like your daddy, Calvin, and your uncle Jeffery. If there's any true justice in the world, you will end up in jail just like them, too. I yield the floor, thank you."

The Parent Crew, in their Baltimore black and gold, walked out of the meeting hall with their heads held high. It was done. They had made their voices heard and put the city council on notice that they were going to do all they could to fight for their children.

"That was... a lot." The usually impassive Paris was visibly shaken as everyone stood outside in the October chill.

"I could really use a drink right now, and I don't drink but I feel like I need something." Sheri rocked back and forth on the heels of her black flats.

Yolanda's braids swung from side to side as she paced along the foot of the City Hall steps. "Pieces of shit." Substituting bleeps in place of curse words was not an option that night. "They are some dogs, for real. All of the years I spent volunteering for campaigns when I was younger. I believed in change. I believed in all of this. I thought all this city needed was the right combination of people to really push it all forward. I was a real dumb-ass."

"You ever thought about running for office, Yo?" Clarence took off his cap and scratched his head.

"I'd definitely volunteer. Heck, I'll be your manager, if you want." Justin laughed, but it was clear his words were sincere.

Yolanda stopped her pacing and stared at the ground as she chewed her bottom lip. She looked as if she were about to say something, but quickly changed her mind. Her faced relaxed and she smiled at her people. "We showed up and we showed out. Sometimes this thing gets so overwhelming, but we can only take it one day at a time, last time I checked. I know I don't say it much, but I really appreciate you all. I would have had a breakdown a long time ago if it were just me dealing with this by myself."

Yolanda's voice cracked and she looked as if she were holding back tears. "Y'all, I've been on 'go' ever since Leonard was killed. Just go go go. I love you all. Between you guys and my children, you've really kept me together. Kept me sane. Thank you."

Yolanda's candid words caught everyone by surprise as Clarence took a few hesitant steps to reach in for a group hug. A collective sigh of relief rose in the air. City Council night with the Parent Crew was done.

Sheri playfully bumped hips with Yolanda as the two walked over to where Yolanda's car was parked. They talked about A Better Way and events that were coming up on the calendar. Yolanda gave Sheri a heads-up that the center got really busy during the holidays, and they would likely need her to cover more hours. Sheri told Yolanda about how much she enjoyed working with Ms. Lou.

Sheri appreciated how intelligent Ms. Lou was and how easily she could take even the most complex subjects and break them down into easily understood concepts. She explained how she and Ms. Lou talked a lot about generational trauma and how to sort through it all to ensure that the cycles of dysfunction could finally end.

Sheri got out of Yolanda's car and waved bye as she bounded up the concrete steps to get back to her babies. Between leaving the city council meeting and getting dropped off by Yolanda, Sheri had gotten a second wind. She had work the next day, though, so she knew staying up late wasn't an option. Sheri went up to the third floor to Mrs. Lee's place to pick up the children. Mrs. Lee said all three were wonderful, but she was concerned about Peach. The little girl had gotten extremely frustrated about a crayon that was broken in the pack. Mrs. Lee figured Peach was just sleepy and likely missed being in her own space; she just wanted Sheri to be aware.

Sheri thanked Mrs. Lee and took out some money to pay the older woman. Mrs. Lee waved the young mother off and said it was fine. Sheri hustled the sleepyheads down the stairs and into their dimly lit apartment. She didn't know if she should just do showers in the morning and let them go on to sleep. Although Sheri was still running off her second wind, she could clearly see that the day was done for everyone else. After doing a round of bathroom visits, Sheri tucked the children into bed and went back into the living room to collect her thoughts.

The light of the answering machine flickered in the darkness. Sheri wondered if Harold had called her. She doubted Yolanda had made it home to call her that fast. Maybe something happened down in Spruce? Sheri slid off her flats and walked over to the machine to press the play button.

"Sheri, please call as soon as you get this. Doesn't matter how late," Skeeter whispered over the line. "Some boys shot Jimmy. He's dead."

CHAPTER 27

According to the detectives, two twelve-year-old boys were responsible for Jimmy Budd's death. There had been a rash of shootings that summer involving the gang that claimed the park across from Gloria's house and a crew that hung around the Flag House Courts. The detectives said Jimmy was in the wrong place at the wrong time and got caught in the crossfire.

One of the detectives mentioned that Jimmy was found with a vial of crack and two vials of heroin on him. Gloria politely asked the officer what the fuck that had to do with anything as she leaned back on her steps and waited for someone to answer her. The two detectives exchanged uncomfortable glances with each other as one turned beet red.

Sheri had been rattled since she heard the news. Just shot down like a dog. Bled out right there in the park that she had gazed upon so many times from the bedroom window. Sheri wondered if Gloria would sell her house. To live directly across the street from where Jimmy was killed would be too much to take. Gloria wanted Sheri to spend a few nights at the house with her like old times, but Sheri had the children and work as well as all of the stuff with the Parent Crew. So much had changed since the last time she was on Preston Street.

On Sheri's off days from work, she came by the house and cleaned up for both Gloria and Skeeter. Skeeter had met a new lady friend, a woman named Joyce, and wasn't around the house as much anymore. After Gloria had taken her pills and finally drifted off to sleep, Skeeter would find Sheri and talk her ear completely off, going on and on about Joyce. Skeeter lit up like a Christmas tree every time she mentioned Joyce's name. Sheri had never seen her cousin so over the moon. If anyone deserved genuine love, Skeeter did. It made Sheri's heart happy.

The glorious colors of the season seemed muted the day of Jimmy's service. There were two repasts happening on the deceased's behalf, one at Gloria's place and the other at Jimmy's aunt's house. Jimmy's family had washed their hands of their prodigal relative a long time ago, so for one of them to offer to hold a repast completely blew Gloria's mind. As far as Gloria was concerned, she and Jimmy's close circle of friends were his only true family.

Someone managed to turn on the stereo, and "Stay In My Corner" played softly as Jimmy's chosen family filled their plates and quietly made conversation. Champ, Popsee and Peach sat silently in the corner of the living room eating their baked chicken, green beans and rice as they tried to make sense of the fact that Mister Jimmy was gone. Sheri considered having Mrs. Lee watch them again, but she figured Gloria would get offended if the babies weren't there.

Upstairs, Gloria sat on her bed, still in her funeral outfit. Sheri was up with her, leaning against Gloria's wood-and-glass wardrobe while trying her best to ignore the smell of men's cologne that hung heavy in the room. Had it been sprayed in remembrance of Jimmy, or did it drift up to the second floor of Gloria's home some other way?

"Babies with fresh milk still on their breath killed my damn man. What are the odds on that one?" Gloria leaned against her wood-and-leather headboard. "Just shooting at everything and everyone to prove that they're the new men on the block, is that what it is? Shit. The crazy part is, they're going to be back at it when they turn eighteen. This is just a bump on the road for those lil' raggedy bastards."

"Probably got pressured by the older boys." Sheri stared down at her black-and-silver low-heel slingbacks.

"Regardless. Their lives are over just as much as Jimmy's is. Just one big cycle. I need a cigarette." Gloria folded her arms and narrowed her eyes at Sheri. She decided to change the subject. "How you like Skeeter's friend, Joyce?"

"She seems nice. Skeeter's really in love, and I'm happy about that." Sheri crossed her ankles, trying to figure out what Gloria was getting at.

"They down there wearing those damn men's suits. Both of 'em. Can you believe that mess?" Gloria shook her head in frustration and looked out the bedroom window. "I begged Skeeter. I said, 'Skeeter, just for one day, can you please wear a dress? For Jimmy's sake?'"

"When's the last time you saw Skeeter in a dress? Skeeter doesn't wear dresses. Why would you want her to do that for a dead man? Jimmy wouldn't care about any of that, God rest his soul." Sheri tried to reason with her cousin.

Gloria huffed and turned her body around to bring her legs up on her grand, king-sized bed. Sheri shook her head at her cousin and figured she was just in some kind of grief-induced fog. She didn't want to think Gloria would be singling Skeeter out to give her any trouble. She knew better than that.

"They found drugs on Jimmy. I thought you said you got clean." Now it was Sheri's turn to narrow her eyes at Gloria.

"How dare you? I am clean! Jimmy had that shit still going on, I didn't. He stopped shooting up in this house a long time ago anyway. He would cop at the park and shoot with Rico and 'em."

Gloria shook her foot and closed her eyes. "He had a hard life. A real hard life. He didn't deserve it. None of it. I know people saw him as just some kind of raggedy drug addict. Like addicts don't have value or nothin'. Jimmy grew up over there 'round by Pig Town. He had a good life. Daddy had a good job as a longshoreman, making some real good money, especially as a black man. Then one day he just up and shot Jimmy's mama, then he turned the gun on himself."

Eyes still closed, Gloria wiped her face as tears began to fall. "Jimmy and his brother were a few doors down, at a friend's house, when the shots rang out. Everyone ran out into the streets. Jimmy and his brother ran back to their house, and that's when they saw them. Nobody knew why. Was making decent money, too. Living a good life as a black man, and then this happened. Jimmy told me that he and his brother used to take violin lessons. Can you even imagine? Jimmy Budd on a violin?"

Gloria laughed bitterly and swiped at her eyes. "Some neighborhood corner dude back from the war put Jimmy on to the stuff. He was never the same person. The drugs just masked his pain, but they didn't free him from it. Jimmy had a heart. Jimmy was good people, and the only thing people will say is that it's just another addict dead."

"It doesn't matter what the world thinks, Gloria. All that matters is what we know, and we know that Jimmy was a thoughtful, caring, kind man who still remained genuine even as he battled his addictions." Sheri sat on the edge of Gloria's bed and rubbed her feet.

"I just feel like everybody I love has left me. My mama. My daddy. Ms. Hazel. Jimmy." Heavy tears rolled down Gloria's rouge-tinted cheeks. "I just have you, the babies and Skeeter left. You've gone off to your place, and Skeeter... I don't know what's going to happen with all that. She might end up leaving too. I'm alone. All these years and I have nothing to show for them. Alone."

"You know you're never alone, Gloria. We're here. We may not be down the hall like we used to be, but we're still here." Sheri tried her best to soothe her clearly distraught cousin.

"Jimmy wanted babies. He begged me for babies. I kept telling him 'no.' Truth is, I can't have them. I've known about it for a while, and I even relished it when I was younger, but I look at it all differently now." Gloria shook her head and stared down at the dark-blue bedspread. "The same thing that got Ms. Hazel ended up getting me, too."

Gloria laid back all the way on the bed and rested her head on a faded gold pillow. She closed her eyes and breathed deeply as the tears continued to fall. Sheri rubbed Gloria's side and gave her cousin a kiss on her cheek. She tip-toed out of the bedroom and walked back downstairs.

The mourners were beginning to clear out and say their goodbyes while Skeeter and Joyce got down to business tidying the house back up. Both women had taken off their suit jackets and rolled up their sleeves.

Skeeter saw Sheri coming down the steps and gave Joyce a little nudge. The two women stood in the dining room like two nervous teenagers as they waited for Sheri to come a little closer. "Peanut, this is my friend, Joyce." Skeeter's face was flushed as she smiled nervously at her cousin.

"Hi!" Joyce gave Sheri a friendly wave. "Usually I hug, but we just met so I don't want to overwhelm you. It's a heavy time right now. I'm rambling, but I'm very glad to meet you. I got a chance to meet your children, too."

Sheri smiled at Joyce and leaned in for a hug. As the two hugged, Sheri gave her cousin a quick wink. She took to Joyce immediately, and she could see why Skeeter was so enamored by her. She was about Skeeter's height, with a beautiful mahogany complexion. Long lashes provided cover for her thoughtful brown eyes. The way her lips curled up at the corners let Sheri know she probably smiled a lot, just like Skeeter, and one deep dimple dotted the left side of her oval-shaped face. Her hair was cut in one of those short styles that Toni Braxton had made famous not too long ago. It was very cute on her and gave her a youthful appearance.

"I'm so happy to meet you, Joyce. I wish that it didn't have to be under these circumstances, but Skeeter's told me so much about you, and I needed to meet the person who made my cousin so happy." Sheri held both women's hands. "Skeeter means everything to me. My cousin loves with all her heart, and it's good to know that she's getting that love back."

Skeeter tried to hide her blushing just as Joyce leaned over to give Skeeter a quick peck along her jawline. Sheri cracked up laughing as she watched her cousin furtively try to keep her composure. By this point, Skeeter had turned two different shades of red and playfully shooed Sheri and Joyce away so she could get back to cleaning.

CHAPTER 28

Raindrops hit the plexiglass pane of Sheri's bedroom window as she lay in her bed, lightly tracing her finger down Harold's broad chest. He'd decided to use his off day to spend time with Sheri while she continued to do research about lead exposure and the possible short- and long-term impacts on her children. Sheri pored through journals and medical encyclopedias, trying to make everything make sense.

After spending much of the morning at the Pratt Library, the two had lunch at a cute café on Charles Street, then returned to Sheri's apartment, where they enjoyed each other. Sheri looked up and kissed along Harold's jawline as he slept. Harold had ended up being the thoughtful lover that Sheri hoped he'd be. The warm feeling that enveloped Sheri's body was a much-needed change from the morose energy that hung in the air after Jimmy's death.

Jimmy Budd's killing was still very raw for Sheri. For the first time since she had moved to the city, a part of her felt unsafe. Sheri knew Jimmy lived a risky lifestyle, but the ages of the boys who killed him rattled her immensely. Only a few years older than Champ.

Harold let out a groggy moan as he wiped his eyes. "What time is it? You want me to drive you to the school to pick up the folks?"

Sheri came down from her thought cloud and kissed Harold on his shoulder. "They have afterschool, and that wraps up at six. I think I'll pick them up a little earlier today, but we still have time."

Harold shot up in bed and flashed Sheri a mischievous grin, which made her laugh so hard her body shook. He pulled her close to him and decided to pick up where they had left off.

◆ ◆ ◆

Yolanda told no lies when she said that A Better Way got busy during the holidays. It had been all hands on deck at the center since the first week of November. Women in plain, yet expensive, clothing dropped off bags of toys, clothes and books by the carloads. Good toys. The type that children would circle in catalogs or tear out to show to their parents. Sheri did the inventory to make sure that there would be enough items so that the children could go home with a nice haul of goodies.

In between the holiday prep work, someone from the Baltimore Weekly called up to the center looking for Yolanda. It appeared that Sloane-Douglas and the CEC were out doing damage control amid allegations that they were "deliberately exposing low-income children to toxic levels of lead." Apparently, the reporter had been keeping track of the Parent Crew's attempts to raise awareness about the issue, and Yolanda had emerged as the person in the center of it all.

The fact that the reporter knew to contact A Better Way unnerved Sheri, considering Yolanda didn't actually work at the center; she just volunteered there. It made Sheri wonder how much of the crew's personal information was known. All types of nefarious scenarios ran through Sheri's mind. What if Sloane-Douglas sent someone to follow all of the parents or, worse yet, their children? What if someone tried to harm them?

Sheri told Yolanda about the call, and Yolanda said that she had already spoken to the reporter since he had also contacted her job. To Yolanda, the questions the reporter asked seemed like bait. Yolanda had already mentally prepared herself for the fact that the article would likely be a puff piece extolling the virtues of Baltimore's most beloved hospital and community partner, Sloane-Douglas. After the protest and the showdown at the city council meeting, there was a very real possibility that the Parent Crew now had targets on their backs.

Paranoia wasn't a state Sheri was too familiar with. She didn't like feeling anxious in her own damn skin. She had already lost her job at Polaris Health due to her speaking out about what had happened to her children. What was next? Despite the persistent feelings of unease, Sheri was determined to stay mentally strong and keep fighting. She owed it to her children to stand firm.

At the center, Ms. Lou was in full hostess mode as she gave tours to various philanthropic groups, business leaders and public officials. Sheri would watch in awe as Ms. Lou glided from room to room, speaking of the importance of engaging marginalized parents and their children.

"A Better Way is a part of a family's village. We aim to be a resource for parents, providing them with the tools necessary to raise their babies from a place of confidence."

Ms. Lou was in full command, and A Better Way was clearly her kingdom. Sheri didn't know how long she would be at the center, but she knew that she intended to soak up as much as she could from Louetta Charles.

After Ms. Lou concluded yet another center tour, she pulled up a seat next to Sheri's desk and let out an exaggerated sigh. "Sher, I tell you true, they are making an old girl work for her pay today!" Ms. Lou slapped her knee with a laugh.

"You just flow with it, Ms. Lou. You make everything look so easy, and I know it's not." Sheri looked over at her supervisor while she continued to file donation slips.

"This is the life of a public servant—a real one," Ms. Lou noted. "I've been trying to look for ways where we can be a little more self-sustaining. So we can keep a steady flow of money coming in. I was thinking about possibly making crochet dolls or something like that for us to sell. That's going to be high on my to-do list in the new year. How is everything going on your side?"

Sheri told Ms. Lou that the children's new school seem to really agree with them. She was grateful that all three had gotten teachers who seem to be invested in making sure the children do well. She mentioned that she was still struggling with Jimmy Budd's death, and she was taking it all one day at a time. Sheri suspected that Ms. Lou already knew the story of what had transpired with the CEC and Sloane-Douglas, so she didn't see the need in poking at that for the time being.

"Are you taking time out for you?" Ms. Lou asked Sheri, her brown eyes wide with concern.

Sheri nodded yes, but she knew it was a lie. Even on her off days away from the center, she could easily be found nose deep in a medical textbook at the library. Her occasional rendezvous with Harold were a welcomed distraction, but all of that was few and far between.

"Make sure you do that this holiday," Ms. Lou ordered. "I know you're a mama with a full plate, but don't wear yourself down to the nub."

Sheri assured Ms. Lou that she would find time that would be hers and hers alone. The matriarch of A Better Way smiled and gently squeezed Sheri's hand. Ms. Lou then stood up and began massaging her temples, then both of her wrists. She sat back down and let out one more sigh, then told Sheri that every year, she and a few parents from the center volunteered to help Ms. Bea serve Thanksgiving dinner to those in need. Ms. Lou and Ms. Bea were good friends, and both of them were Baltimorean Carolinians, so it was extra special.

"She's dynamite on two legs. Energy for days." Ms. Lou laughed to herself, thinking about her friend. "Yo volunteers with us every once and again. If you're able to make it, that would be wonderful, but you better not break yourself in half to do so. I mean it, mark off your 'Sheri time' first."

◆ ◆ ◆

Sheri awoke to "Great Is Thy Faithfulness" being sung softly. She sat up to get a better look. "Who taught you that?"

"Cousin Aunt Skeeter." Peach picked at her pajama sleeve.

"Woke up with a song in your heart, huh? You sound beautiful, Peach." Sheri smiled at her five-year-old roommate.

The little girl thanked her mother, then stared wistfully out the window, past the bars and out into the late-autumn morning sky.

"What's on your mind?"

"Mr. Jimmy Budd," Peach responded with no hesitation.

"What about him?" Sheri prepared herself.

"He's never coming back, and he's gone forever. We're never going to see his face again. I'm sad about it."

Sheri paused and reflected that Jimmy's was the first death that fully registered with her children.

"How much do you think about Mr. Jimmy being gone?"

"A lot. I think about Mom-Mom being gone forever, and I get very sad and mad. I miss Mom-Mom, and I don't want her gone." It looked as if a burden had been lifted off the kindergartener's small shoulders.

Sheri reached over to get Peach and hold her tight. She wanted to gather all three of her children and just love on them from the protective fort of her bed. It was Aunt Jackie who always said to never underestimate what a child knows. Young brains were like sponges, just retaining everything.

"Death is a part of life, Peach," Sheri spoke into her daughter's halo of coils. "It's okay to feel mad and sad. Feeling scared is okay, too. Mr. Jimmy's death surprised all of us, and everyone is very upset. I want you to always know that you can always come to me about anything. I love you, Peach. Saying how you're feeling—on good and bad days—is important. You're using your big girl words, too. I'm proud of you."

Sheri got up quickly and picked up the small radio from the dresser. She adjusted the dial to see if the radio had enough reception to catch one of the gospel stations. A clear sound came over the waves when Sheri turned the AM dial to 1400. Sheri didn't know the song, but she knew it was gospel, so hopefully, Peach would take to it. Skeeter had the ear for exposing her children to new music, and Sheri genuinely appreciated her cousin taking the time out to do that.

As she held her daughter, Sheri reflected on a year filled with twists and turns. From the principal meeting for Popsee to the IUCF meetings with Dr. Rooney. The New Horizons-CEC-Sloane Douglas nightmare. Connecting with Yolanda and the Parent Crew. The lawsuit. The protests. The police. Jimmy Budd dying. 1994 was on its last legs, and Sheri prayed that the year wouldn't attempt for a grand finale.

CHAPTER 29

1995

Exhausted beyond words, the February cold felt like daggers as Sheri hustled her way back home from the law office. The deposition had both drained and unsettled her. She dragged her body through the front door to find Popsee doing wild karate moves in the middle of the living room floor while a steady percussion beat pounded from the stereo.

"You like this?" Skeeter nodded over at the stereo as Popsee continued his kicks and leg sweeps. "Joyce put me on to him, Chuck Brown. You know Joyce is a DC girl, and they listen to all of that down there. Go-Go, they call it." Skeeter bobbed her head while wiping down the stove.

"Well, Pop definitely seems to be a fan." Sheri slid into a dining chair.

"Girl, she has me listening to everything. Chuck Brown, Rare Essence, EU—all of it. I really like it, though. You know Joyce is a musichead, just like me. That's why we get along so well." Skeeter was fully prepared to talk about Joyce all night if Sheri gave her the green light.

"Made you a plate. I can heat it up for you if you'd like." Skeeter gave Sheri's shoulder a slight squeeze before she turned to start clearing off the counter.

"You don't have to do that, cousin. Just sit with me, please." Sheri's voice had dwindled down to a thin croak. She had never talked so much in her entire life. Question after question. Cross examinations and clarifying statements. Having to walk through the last year of her and her children's lives over and over again in some twisted, cruel loop.

"Times like this, I wish I had a little alcohol in this place," Sheri admitted.

Sheri reached over to grab Skeeter's hands, which still maintained their softness despite her years of factory work. Popsee turned down the music a little, but he still had a few more kicks in his system. Sheri closed her eyes, took a deep breath and slowly exhaled.

"Cousin, my time here is winding down." Sheri opened her eyes and looked across the table at Skeeter.

"So where to next? Up to Jersey with your uncle and 'em?" Skeeter looked as if she were already on the verge of tears.

"North Carolina. I don't plan to return to Spruce Junction, though. That particular chapter is done. I talked with Eunice over the holidays, and she just moved to Greenville. Got a job at the college. She said we can stay with her and Unique while I get myself back together." Sheri leaned back in the chair and stretched her legs under the table.

"What about Harold?"

Sheri's stomach dropped. She hadn't even begun to think about the conversation she would have with Harold about her leaving.

"And what about your friends and those meetings? The lawsuit and all that?" Skeeter continued to gently interrogate.

"Skeeter, damn. It's not like I'm leaving tomorrow." Sheri folded her arms.

"I mean... it's just that you got so much done here. You met some really good people; why give all of this up?" Skeeter questioned.

Sheri rubbed her left wrist. She thought about the endless barrage of questions. The intrusive poking and prodding into her and her children's lives. She took a long look at Popsee, who had since fallen asleep on the sofa.

"You step out on faith. You search for something new. You go to a place where the air feels different, the smells and the sounds hit you differently, but you press on anyway. Change is good sometimes, right? What's the worst thing that could happen?"

Sheri gazed at the eggshell-white apartment walls. "Never in a million years would I have expected for all of this to happen. To me. To my children. I just feel that it's time to go back to the devil I know."

♦ ♦ ♦

Sleep provided no respite to Sheri as she violently tossed around on her side of the bed. She found herself back in front of the looming office building under slate-grey Baltimore skies. The dusky fragrance of Aunt Myrtle's covering oil wrapped around Sheri, gradually relaxing her. She sniffed her wrist, inhaling the amber resin as she glided into the law office.

A well-dressed woman walked Sheri to a back conference room. The brightly lit office boasted a captivating view of the Inner Harbor. Even the greyest of days could never take away the beauty that was the Harbor. Six lawyers, including Mr. Atkinson, were seated around the long, oval-shaped table. Notepads were strewn about and recording equipment covered the middle. At the head was an empty black office chair with an overly padded seat and swivel wheels.

Sheri felt as if she were on one of those carnival twirl-a-whirl rides. The barrage of questions started immediately. She steadied herself in the black swivel office chair and dug her nails into the fabric. Questions about her children's behavior. Questions about their performance in school. Questions about their home life. Questions about their father. Questions about what made the single mother leave North Carolina. Questions about where Sheri lived before she moved into the New Horizons house.

As the questions continued to land like prize fight punches, she felt herself drifting further and further away. First above her chair, then out the office window. Out beyond the city limits and down 95 South. Sheri hovered over Highway 102 until she finally landed on what appeared to be Clary Cove Road, the main drag through Spruce Junction. The road looked familiar, yet it didn't. She recognized the church and some of the houses, but something felt out of place.

Sheri stood at an intersection of Clary Cove and another road that ran east to west. The amber scent gently wafted past her nose as she tried to make sense of where exactly she had been transported. The sound of blood-curdling screams and loud whoops suddenly exploded in the air and shook Sheri to her core. In the trees, across from where she stood, heavy footfalls punctuated the air like steady drumbeats. Men, women and children emerged from the woods, looks of pure terror covering their faces. All running toward Spruce Junction.

Before she could make sense of what she had just witnessed out on Clary Cove Road, Sheri found herself in the corner of the dimly lit living room. A man, hat in hand, had just informed the family that their beloved father, grandfather and uncle had met their tragic fate in the massacre that took place two nights before. A little girl wearing a defiant look on her face leaned against the wall, arms folded, with her hands balled into small fists.

"Bethel!" A copper-toned woman with sharp yet weary eyes looked over in the girl's direction. The woman pointed to a spot directly to the left of her. Bethel walked over to where her mother pointed and reluctantly took a seat.

The grieving family quietly talked amongst themselves. Word was Mr. and Mrs. Whitaker's son had returned home sporting his military uniform, and some of the local yahoos felt offended at the sight of the colored man strutting like a proud peacock. A rumor quickly circulated in the white part of town that the disrespectful veteran had shot at a white man. That was enough motivation for a roving posse to form and torch their way through an innocent community.

Peach woke up to find her mother shaking her head and talking in her sleep. "Ma? Mom, wake up! Mom, you are mad at something. Mom. Get up!" The little girl had never seen her mother this way, and it scared her. Peach tried her best to shake her mother awake, but Sheri was far beyond her daughter's reach.

"Mama!"

A lanky teenaged boy with luminous dark-brown eyes and a head covered in chestnut-brown curls screamed from outside the bedroom. "Mama! She's okay! She's okay! She's okay!"

Sheri found herself back in the same house where she had been when the family received the devastating news about the massacre. Bethel now looked to be about twelve. Another girl who appeared to be in her teens stood with her arm wrapped around Bethel's shoulder. The grief-stricken young man continued to yell for his mother while everyone else stood silent as the doctor covered the deceased with a white sheet. Her once rich, copper tone was now muted and sallow.

Sheri felt a strange sensation, as if her body were vibrating. She looked over to find that the teenaged girl holding Bethel was staring directly at her. Sheri opened her mouth to speak just as she was transported back to the conference room. Mr. Atkinson was talking, but Sheri could only hear the loud blaring of car horns coming from the street below.

"What's happening to me?" Sheri called out to the void.

The grey Baltimore day transformed once again. The sun was shining high and bright over Jeter Hill. Sheri was standing in the living room of the house she knew like the back of her hand. A young man with horned-rimmed glasses, strawberry-blonde hair and a slight gap in his teeth stood in the middle of the room.

"No one is helping us," the frustrated man lamented to Bethel and her husband.

The police, the sheriff, no one had made themselves available to find out what happened to the two volunteers who were supposed to meet up with the rest of the members of the East Carolina Justice Council in Raleigh. Emmanuel Hayes and Patricia Ann Jeter hadn't been heard from for seven days.

Bet sat on the sofa with her arms folded, indifferent to the sadness that surrounded her. "I warned her. Told that girl to stop hanging around those troublemakers. Talkin' 'bout some 'it's my right,'" Bet scoffed to no one in particular. "Patty Ann just thought she was too fancy for an honest day's work."

Sheri watched as her mother and aunts loudly wailed and comforted each other in the kitchen. She wanted to run over to join the circle and grieve with the Jeter sisters, but she couldn't move. She could only stand as a helpless witness to their pain.

The cold, persistent questions from the lawyers could still be heard over the mournful cries that filled the Jeter home. Did you have any difficulty learning while in school? What's your highest level of education? Did you fully read the contract that you were instructed to sign by the Community Empowerment Center? Were you aware that you had received prior notice that lead would be present in the rental unit? Ms. Calloway, what is your history with abusive relationships?

Sheri's eyes came into focus on an older woman standing calmly in the middle of a country bridge. Beams of sunlight formed a circle around Sheri's leafy perch. The older woman looked as if she were waiting on the next scheduled bus arrival. The sounds of screeching tires and shattering glass caused Sheri to jump. A car came roaring over the bridge, landing top-down in the swamp water below. Nature stood silent as the older woman now appeared to be standing by the passenger side of the overturned vehicle.

"Mom..." Sheri's hand covered her mouth. She stood frozen. Although she had never met her in person, she knew from pictures that the older woman standing in the water was her late Aunt Myrtle.

Aunt Myrtle looked up and made eye contact just as Sheri was teleported once more back to the law office conference room. She was done with the interrogation. She stood up to address the men in the room:

"I'm a damn good mother. I try. I have always put my children first. I come from hard times. My family comes from hard times, but my babies are going to make it. And I'm gonna make sure of that. I took a gamble thinking that the CEC cared about my children as much as I did. I made the wrong choice, but they are the ones who will have to answer for what was done. You ask me these disrespectful questions. You think you have me and my children all figured out without even knowing us. We don't exist to be pieces in your games."

"Mom? Ma?!"

"Mom, you sick?!"

Small hands gently kneaded Sheri's shoulder, leg and foot. "Ma, Peach said you were in here yelling at something in your sleep. She came to get us."

219

Sheri opened her eyes and stared at her children, who stared back with concern covering their faces.

"You want a bowl of cinnamon and sugar oatmeal?"
Popsee nodded his head, sure that this was the perfect remedy.

"Come." Sheri clapped her hands and patted the bed. "We have space, come. I need my babies with me tonight. I need y'all."

Popsee furrowed his brow and gave his mother a questioning look.

"I'll eat some oatmeal in the morning, Pop. I promise." Sheri smiled at her little guardian.

Champ and Popsee joined Peach and Sheri on the queen-sized bed. Sheri reached over and kissed them all on their foreheads.

The last thing Sheri wanted was her children worrying over her. The deposition had her beside herself. It was imperative that Sheri hold herself together. The CEC, Sloane-Douglas, the lawsuits—Sheri couldn't let the situation take any more than it had already stolen.

CHAPTER 30

Teddy Atkinson paced the worn carpet of the split-level house like a coach trying to stir up a second wind amongst a defeated sports team. "We took one on the chin. We're wobbly, but we're still standing."

In the corner of the room, Sheri sat with her ankles crossed and her mind a thousand miles away. She wasn't surprised about the ruling, and she knew the Parent Crew was fully prepared to appeal and continue the fight. She also knew that the fondness and attachment she had toward her adopted city had frayed.

"Well, we're going to appeal. That's already a done deal." Yolanda leaned forward on one of the carpeted steps, resting her arms on her thighs. "We're up against major hitters, so I feel we all expected this. We just have to keep showing them that we're just as tough."

"Imma be honest." Justin scratched through his beard while he leaned against the railing. "I appreciate you and your team, Mr. Atkinson, but those other lawyers were some undercutting sharks. I didn't think it would be easy, but I definitely wasn't expecting what I got. We should have been prepped a little bit better. Some of their questions were just unnecessary and disrespectful. It just threw me off."

Paris ran her fingers through her son Corey's sandy curls while she, like so many of the others, looked to be in a daze. "Yolanda, I'm tired," the young mother sighed dejectedly. "I believe in us, but, at the same time, I feel like I'm running on empty."

Yolanda nodded sympathetically. "I know, Sis. On top of just daily survival, we all had to turn around and deal with all of this bullshit. This is an uphill battle, and some days you'll be in it, and then there will be other times when you just want to tap out. I understand. Paris and Justin, y'all are my originals, and so you know how much has come at us these last two years. I appreciate you both and what you bring." Yolanda placed her hand over her heart. "I appreciate all of y'all."

"So this is the cycle we're on?" Justin leaned against the wall, holding a can of grape soda. "We're just going to go round and round with these bastards? Like a damn—excuse the language, I know Corey is up here—like we're just on a hamster wheel right now, huh? This isn't directed toward you, Yo. Just like you appreciate us, I know we all appreciate you for having the vision, but all of this is just…" Justin's warm brown skin flushed a deep red. "They see our babies as collateral damage, and I'm just frustrated, man. How much are their futures worth?"

Teddy Atkinson sat stoically in the oversized chair, one of the rare times the lawyer and master orator was at a loss for words. Seeing this hardscrabble group of parents go up against one of the city's long-standing titans was a victory in itself. The lawyer knew saying that would likely bring little comfort at that particular moment, but what they had accomplished so far was a major feat.

"I'll file the paperwork for an appeal tomorrow morning," the lawyer said, nodding to the parents.

"We live to fight another day," Clarence said to no one in particular as he leaned back on the sofa, kneading his forehead. It seemed like each day left fewer and fewer strands of salt-and-pepper hair on the older man's crown, and, despite his quick wit and fairly high energy, time was still insistent on making its presence known.

An air of fatigue hung heavy over the faithful crew members who had been through so much over the last year. Protests, police and Sloane-Douglas propaganda pieces that masqueraded as news articles, it had been a whirlwind roller coaster ride that didn't appear to be letting up. Sheri had already made up her mind that this would be her last summer in Baltimore. She'd asked Eunice to put out some feelers for her as to who was hiring in town. Sheri knew no job would make her feel as fulfilled as A Better Way did, and she realized it would just have to be yet another thing she would learn to do without.

After the meeting concluded, Sheri and the children caught a ride with Clarence and his girls. The drive back to the apartment was a fairly quiet one for both the adults and the children. Champ worked on a connect the dots puzzle in his activity pad while Popsee and Peach stared out the window. Tyshawn sat in her twin sister's lap, lazily sucking her thumb while admiring Peach's neat, intricate plaits with the blue, silver and white beads on the ends. Patti Austin filled in the quiet spaces and seemed to invoke a hypnotic lull in the rickety, tan Oldsmobile.

"I don't know how much you've learned about Sloane-Douglas since you've been in the city, but these are some real-deal mofos, believe that." Clarence broke the silence.

"I've seen. Up close and personal." Sheri sighed and leaned back in her seat.

"Deep-pocket devils, basically. It just is what it is, I guess."

"Listen, at this point, something has to break." Sheri tried to look on the bright side for her beleaguered comrade.

"Yeah," Clarence grunted, "us."

◆ ◆ ◆

Thanks to the generosity of an anonymous donor, A Better Way had been gifted two new computers and one laser printer. The day the delivery came, Ms. Lou looked as if she had seen a ghost. She kept asking the delivery guy who she should thank, but the short, gruff man just shook his head and shrugged his shoulders.

Sheri sat in front of one of the computers and instantly saw why Champ was so mesmerized by them. It felt like some kind of space-age device, and she felt as if she were touching the future. One day, after her shift was over, Sheri sat down and clicked on the word processing system. She wasn't a computer whiz by any means, but Sheri had learned enough to type up a flyer.

Sheri decided that others needed to know what she'd had to learn about the hard way. All of her visits to the library spilled out onto a neat, eight-and-a-half-by-eleven page with LEAD POISONING: FACTS YOU NEED TO KNOW typed in all-caps in large, block font. Sheri tried her best to translate the complex, technical terms into everyday language to ensure the vital information could reach the people who needed this knowledge the most. On an off day, after dropping the children off at school, Sheri went to Mercury Printing near the University of Baltimore's campus and had the clerk run off copies of the flyer.

Sheri stood underneath the blue-and-white awning with two full tote bags resting on both shoulders, flyers printed and ready. She shifted her weight from one leg to the other as she thought of the best strategy to reach as large an audience as possible. She considered just selecting different corners around her neighborhood. She thought about asking churches to post the flyer on the bulletin boards used to broadcast community news.

Sheri firmly pressed two fingers on her right temple and took a deep breath. While she didn't feel overwhelmed, the gravity of the information she was literally carrying on her shoulders made her body pulsate.

Sheri returned to her apartment as she continued to think through some type of game plan. She pulled out a notepad and listed the places she would go to hand out flyers. Benefits offices. Clinics. Churches. Community centers. Sheri also listed the children's school as a possible flyer drop-off location.

The desire for a few quick pulls of a Newport tried to snake its way through Sheri's thoughts, but the focused woman tapped two fingers on her full lips and focused on the issue at hand. She counted off ten stacks of flyers and placed a slip of paper on top of each stack with the name of the location she would pass out or leave the flyers. After a quick shower, Sheri changed into a t-shirt and jeans and headed back out into the streets. In her tote was a stack for Mitchell Elementary, a stack for Full Truth Gospel and a stack for the benefits office on Eutaw Street.

Sheri spoke with Mrs. Pender in the front office and left her flyers on the community table. Mrs. Pender also said she would post a flyer on the News You Can Use bulletin board by the front door. Sheri prayed her string of good fortune continued for the remaining stacks of flyers. At Full Truth Gospel, she received a full lecture about the history of paint in Baltimore from one of the elders.

"The effort is appreciated, young sister, but don't expect for these to do that much. The people already know about what lead can do," the small-statured older man with the thick, salt-and-pepper mustache advised Sheri. The elder went on to talk about redlining and how certain parts of the city were only available to certain people. "The housing conditions revealed who the houses were for."

Sheri thanked the man for the history lesson and thanked the front receptionist again for allowing her to leave a stack of flyers. For all Sheri knew, everyone in the city of Baltimore were already well aware of the effects of lead, but she was still determined to reach the one person in the city who didn't know. Just thinking about the early trips to the library made Sheri stop in her tracks. She had never been bombarded with so much heavy, heart-wrenching information in such a short time.

A brick wall served as a lean-to for Sheri as she handed out flyers to people visiting Job Force, a job training and career development organization that had a few locations scattered around the west side of the city. After a quick time check, Sheri continued passing out flyers and talking to whoever had an ear to listen, until it was time to pick up her musketeers.

At one point, Sheri was surrounded by a group of about six women who had just left one of the We Work! job training workshops. Under the shade of an awning, the women exchanged stories of either their children or other children in their family being harmed by lead exposure.

"We kind of just took it as a fact of life. Just one of those things," a woman with stylish, blonde-and-dark-brown freeze curls admitted to Sheri.

After the women moved on, Sheri patted her now empty tote bag and walked the few blocks to the children's school. She used that time to take a minute to affirm herself. She had truly been tried in the fire, and there she was—still intact. Titi's daughter was slowly coming around to having attention focused on her without wanting to fold herself into a corner. Being around bold, unafraid women had brought out the fearlessness within herself.

The spring air felt like a friendly embrace as she ran her finger along the metal fencing. Despite the turmoil, Baltimore would forever remain an absolutely breathtaking city to Sheri. She could sit in front of a picture window all day, just watching the city pulsate with its own rhythm. The ugliness that lurked just beneath the surface of such a brilliant place would never sit right with her.

CHAPTER 31

The sticky humidity of summer significantly annoyed Sheri that year. If she could have, she would've been on 95 South as soon as the final bell signaled that the 94-95 school year was over and done for at Mitchell Elementary. But Sheri knew she couldn't. She sat in her living room and stared out the window at a sparse patch of grass and a skinny, young tree that appeared to be getting its footing in the world. Three years. Three years come and gone. She sipped on a cup of chamomile tea.

Sheri had decided to take Mr. Matthews up on his recommendation to enroll her boys in the leadership classes that his fraternity sponsored. Champ and Popsee both really seemed to enjoy the weekly meetings. Champ had even gotten a chance to talk one-on-one with a gentleman who was a computer engineer. The young boy still cleaved tightly to his dream of being a "computer man," and now he had more words in his repertoire to fully articulate his dream.

Sheri would sometimes catch Champ speaking to himself in the bathroom. "I'm gonna be a computer engineer," Champ repeated over and over to his mirrored self. If Sheri could form some type of protective bubble over her babies to ward off the ugliness that was all around them, she would in a heartbeat. In the meantime, Sheri was on her last couple of drops of Aunt Myrtle's covering oil. For the entire school year, Sheri made sure to place a dot of the oil on the back of each child's neck before they left for the day.

Sheri continued enjoying her tea. Two lumps of sugar and a few drops of milk. Traffic steadily moved up and down Pennsylvania Avenue. The world continued to spin.

Earlier that week, Ms. Lou and the A Better Way family had thrown Sheri a Bon Voyage and Best Wishes cookout. Everyone wrote positive affirmations on pretty, flowery stationery paper for their departing friend as she moved on to the next part of her journey. Sheri would forever remain grateful for what A Better Way meant to her and her children. With all of the uncertainty and frustration surrounding the lawsuit, it was a true blessing to not have to deal with a workplace that would have rained down even more stress on her body. Sheri had made sure to take plenty of pictures and exchange contact information to keep in touch.

She was interrupted from her thoughts as the shrill ringing of the telephone cut through the silence in the two-bedroom apartment.

"Y'all ready? I'm on my way. Give me about twenty minutes." Yolanda sounded like she may have returned to her usual high-energy, full-steam-ahead self.

After the first ruling a few months ago, it was as if the wind had been knocked out of every member of the Parent Crew. The meetings went from weekly to twice a month. Attendance stayed consistent, but the energy was understandably low. During the summer, Sheri was sometimes accompanied by other Crew members when she distributed her lead awareness flyers.

Peach blew her breath in exasperation, trying to zip an aesthetically unnecessary zipper on the side of her neon-green dress. "I got it, Mama. We'll figure it out." Sheri could see her daughter growing increasingly upset, so she steered the little girl closer to her and leaned over to get a better look.

The family was already waiting at the top of the concrete steps when Yolanda pulled up in Ms. Millie. Everyone piled into the car and sat in the usual places.

"Umm, hey, Sis." Yolanda put a finger up to her lips in a half-hearted attempt to hide an extremely wide smile.

"Girl, you okay?" Sheri gave her friend a playful, furrowed brow.

"Here!" Yolanda thrust a piece of black fabric in front of Sheri. "Your blindfold."

The three siblings exchanged glances and just shook their heads. Who knew what Ms. Yolanda had up her sleeve?

Despite the blindfold, Yolanda and Sheri held a regular conversation like normal. Yolanda told Sheri she would be taking over the office manager job at A Better Way. She had grown tired of working under threat at the school. It was one worry removed from an ever-growing list. Yolanda pulled up a street, and the smell of something beyond this world entranced Sheri. They parked, and music filled the air. Suddenly, everything got quiet, and the only thing Sheri heard was Yolanda's instructions to guide her out of the car and up the stairs.

When the blindfold was finally pulled off, Sheri was greeted to cheers by the Parent Crew as well as other friends such as Delegate Alma and Ms. Brenda from Greater Gethsemane. Nishelle, ever radiant, stepped forward and took Sheri's hands. "Sheri, we love you and Kareem, Keyon and Maya. We are now always connected. You all are our family, and we wanted to celebrate you today."

Yolanda and Alex did a joint prayer of thanks and a prayer for traveling mercies for their sister and her family. Tears fell as Sheri pulled her babies closer to her. The music returned as Nishelle walked the guests of honor around to show off the spread that included fried whiting, oxtail, curry chicken, plantain, jerk mackerel, two different kinds of potato salad, rice and peas, along with steamed pepper cabbage.

It was truly the happiest everyone had been in months. The air felt good and easy. Cups were full of either fruit punch, ginger beer, iced tea or rum punch. The partygoers made conversation talking about everything from parenting anecdotes to traveling stories. Yolanda smiled and asked Sheri to come stand with her in the middle of the living room floor. Soon everyone got up to surround Sheri and gave her more personalized well wishes along with gifts and cards.

"Love ya, Sis." Nishelle hugged Sheri again as she gave her a quick peck on the cheek. "I saw these and thought about you." Nishelle handed Sheri a box wrapped in the prettiest white-and-silver wrapping paper. Inside was a dazzling pair of earrings made of coral beads and gold cowrie shells.

Happy tears continued to fall amongst the group as Yolanda waited last to speak her piece: "I'm so glad we connected on this journey, Sis. From the bottom of my heart, I mean this. You are a beautiful and genuine soul, and your presence was needed. You came to us when we needed you the most. This isn't a goodbye, not after all the hell this group has been through together. There will never be a goodbye between any of us. Always know that you are loved."

◆ ◆ ◆

Moving day found Sheri and the children in the middle of a Gloria and Skeeter bear hug, with neither cousin wanting to drop their arms. Gloria sniffed and gently wiped the tears from the corners of her perfectly lined eyes.

The parting kin did God knows how many rounds of goodbye hugs and kisses. Thankfully, Joyce was right there alongside Skeeter. After each round of goodbye hugs, Skeeter looked more and more undone. Eventually, Sheri, Champ, Popsee and Peach, along with Harold and Amir, made it inside the van and were finally on the road headed south.

Harold had known of Sheri's impending travel plans since April. How he felt about her leaving was a different matter. He and Sheri talked about it, and Harold knew he would need to process all of this at his own pace. Harold caught Sheri sneaking glances his way, and he reached to grab his co-pilot's hand and kissed it. The van with the storage container attached made its way down the highway. It was shaping up to be a quiet ride as everyone seemed lost in their own thoughts. Harold slipped in a tape, and the dramatic buildup of "Ai No Corrida" came out of the speakers.

"My dad got me on to him. I love all his stuff. He's my work ethic inspiration, too," Harold admitted with a quick laugh inside the quiet van. "The way I see it, if I can master my work the way Quincy can produce a song, then I'm on the right track." This revelation made Sheri chuckle, but she understood and appreciated Harold's thought process. Always continue to strive for your own personal best.

Quiet returned to the vehicle as everyone either ventured off to sleep or into their own thoughts. Harold sat ruminating about how he had wanted to meet the rest of Sheri's family, but not in this way. Harold cared for Sheri and the children, and his

admiration for how Sheri mothered ran deep. Harold's own mother had made sure the family never did without, but she was also rather detached. The fact that Sheri loved her children with her full self had captivated Harold early on. It had been his hope to make Sheri and the children a part of his life on a more permanent basis.

Harold and Sheri switched off at the Virginia and North Carolina state line. Sheri got behind the wheel to captain the final leg of the journey back home. The night air lapped Sheri's face as she drove over familiar roads. Harold was getting some much-needed rest, and Champ had nodded off in the backseat, so Sheri decided to keep her childhood memories and anecdotes to herself while she passed landmarks of her life. She turned off the radio and let the sounds of the night sing her the rest of the way.

◆ ◆ ◆

"All right now, it's gonna be a function at the junction ALL weekend. Our Sheri is back!" For the children, Eunice's unabashed happiness at the table that morning was contagious. Any questions and peripheral yearnings were long gone after a few minutes around their cousin. When she mentioned that their Mom- Mom was on her way to Greenville, cheers exploded in the house.

"Uncle Wayne is bringing up the ribs; they've been sitting in Aunt Donna's lil' marinade concoction, just so you all know! Uncle Syl and Aunt Catherine are bringing up their smoker. Mr. Harold, you didn't know you were gonna be in the middle of a Jeter reunion, now, did ya? I never really got a chance to have a housewarming for this place. So it's really a two-in-one occasion."

The August air was filled with the smells of fragrant rose bushes, burning cherry wood chips and grilled food. Laughter from frenetic children came courtesy of a bounce house brought up by Cousin Punchy. The party starters, Cousins Eunice and Janice, got an electric slide line moving, so now the fun could truly begin.

Eunice was exactly like her father, Sheri's Uncle Lucky. Both could get a party started and shut the whole thing down if they wanted to. While Eunice was one of Bethel's more religiously inclined grandchildren, she could cuss a man bald if she felt like it.

Sheri noticed Titi had managed to corner Harold to likely talk his ear off while Peach sat on her lap, twisting her freshly done braids between her fingers. Harold was growing out a goatee, and every so often, he would scratch it as if to mark time. Champ and Popsee had gone off to get into God knows what with their number-one best friend and cousin, Patrick.

Sheri decided to bail out her beloved and asked him to carry a few bags of wood chips to Uncle Syl. Once she'd safely freed her mother's captive, Sheri tickled Harold's beard and kissed his neck.

"Ms. Thomasina had her share of opinions about you packing up and moving to Baltimore. She's real glad you're back." Harold traced his fingers down Sheri's arm as the two found a quiet spot away from the celebration.

"One thing about Titi, she's gonna give you her two cents," Sheri shook her head with a laugh.

"I think Amir and I are gonna head out tomorrow afternoon. I should make it in later that night."

Sheri's heart sank. She'd never had intentions of jumping into a new romance; Harold made it easy to love him. She knew she had to make peace with the fact that their relationship would look different going forward.

The sun had long set as Champ, Popsee and Patrick trudged back up the hill toward Cousin Eunice's house. Patrick had so many questions about Baltimore. The two brothers put the battery in the young boy's back and made him promise to visit the city. As the boys rounded the hill, Champ spied his mother and Mr. Harold walking out of the house. Mr. Harold's arms were wrapped around his mother's waist.

"Is that Aunt Sheri's friend?" Patrick asked.

"Yeah, that's Mr. Harold. He's nice, and he really, really likes Mom. A lot," Popsee answered in a raspy voice, the end result of a full day of screaming and yelling.

Champ stayed quiet as they got closer to the house. He liked Mr. Harold, and he appreciated the fact that the man really seemed to care deeply about his mother. At nine years old, Kareem Champ Calloway was no one's relationship expert, but he'd noticed how much his mom and Mr. Harold were always grinning and smiling whenever they were around each other. In the furthest corner of his steadily developing mind, the boy made a note to get that for himself one day.

Frogs, lightning bugs and other critters began making their presence known to the revelers. Styrofoam plates and trays and Tupperware containers were passed around for to-go meals. Soon the smoker and the Spruce Junction family were loaded up and headed back up the road. Titi decided to stay the night over at Eunice's to spend more time with her grandbabies, whom she had missed more than words could say when they were in Baltimore. Harold and Amir retired to their room for bed. Titi had already designated that the living room would be the spot for the impromptu sleepover party.

For the first time in she didn't know how long, Sheri Calloway had a bed to herself. The sounds of the night and the scent of honeysuckle poured through the window screen. Three years come and gone. Sheri thought about Gloria and Skeeter and Jimmy Budd and Yolanda and Ms. Lou. Harold. What would Sheri ever be able to say about the unbelievable ride that had been her life in Baltimore City?

CHAPTER 32

2016

There was silence on the line for what seemed like an eternity. Alicia softly cleared her throat, likely at a loss for words after the journey she had just returned from courtesy of the single mother down in Greenville. "Umm... I just... I just wonder have you spoken to someone? Anyone? Like a counselor or a therapist?"

Sheri stretched her legs under the table and shifted her weight in the wooden chair. She stared out the kitchen window at darkening storm clouds. "Every once in a while, I catch the therapist talk shows. I really like to fish. That helps me clear my mind. I talk with Eunice every week. She's the minister and counselor for the family. I did yoga for a little at the community center. I was okay; I was more flexible than I gave myself credit for."

"What about your children?" Alicia asked, overwhelmed by the woman's matter-of-fact tone after the story she had just recounted.

"With all due respect Ms. Allen, they don't know what happened to them. They just know something happened to them. There's a difference."

Quiet returned to the line as the two women sat in their own thoughts.

"Well..." The reporter seemed to be at a loss for words once again. "Your story, your experience here in the city, it's all just so captivating. It had been my intention to inform our readers about the families of the lawsuit beyond the surface mentions, which I noticed when I read through older articles. We just want the people to know about the lives that were impacted. I can't begin to think of the toll all of this took on both yourself and your children. I know there was a settlement and ma—"

"That settlement was a drop in the bucket considering all the damage that was done. We take things one day at a time in this family, and we may be in a better place compared to others who were also impacted, but please know that the check those people cut will never compensate for what was stolen."

Another long pause came over the line as if Alicia expected Sheri to speak again. "Well, Ms. Calloway," Alicia's voice took an apologetic tone, "I didn't intend to take up so much of your day. Thank you again for taking the time to speak with me."

"Thank you for calling me. I look forward to reading your finished article," Sheri said quietly as she sipped her now cold tea.

"Yes, definitely. I'm crossing my fingers for a Thursday release. I will call you once it's live on our site," Alicia promised.

"That's good. I'm gonna sign off now. Try to get a little bit of rest in before I go in to work." Sheri slowly got up on her feet and made her way to the living room to place the phone back on the charger.

"Thank you again, Ms. Calloway. Please, be safe down there with the storm."

The two women said their telephone goodbyes, and Sheri rested the neon-purple cordless phone in its charging cradle.

Sheri sat down on her hunter-grey sofa and ran her fingers along the chenille fabric. She was so proud of her home. How clean it was, how inviting it was. The years of memories its walls contained. So much had gone into Sheri finally reaching a place in her life where she was at relative peace. The fact that she had found her peace in North Carolina and not in Baltimore brought to mind Titi's incessant reminders to Sheri that she didn't need to leave home. Everything you need is already here. Sheri, however, knew that the experience in Baltimore made her an entirely different person. She became more sure-footed. She became a leader. She became a fighter. She questioned what was put before her, and she pushed back.

Sheri got up and walked over to her curio cabinet, staring at the photos of smiling faces of family and friends. The bustle days were long over for Sheri. When Kayla and KJ came over, they usually busied themselves playing games on their tablets. Kayla even had to show her grandmother how some of those apps worked. Once she got home from work, it was Lady, the television and the pictures that kept Sheri company.

A bright, happy picture of Skeeter holding a bouncing baby boy watched over Sheri. Skeeter and the baby boy both had the same beaming smiles and round eyes as they wore matching striped button-up shirts. Skeeter's hair had a few grey strands peeking through her sleek bun, while the baby wore a little newsboy cap to accentuate his outfit.

Skeeter stuck around Baltimore for about five more years after Sheri left before she, too, returned to North Carolina. Ma Jackie's cancer had played a cruel game of back and forth. Periods of remission raised hopes only for them to get dashed again. When the cancer came back around for another visit, it buried itself at the base of her spine, and that's where it would stay. Skeeter knew it was time to return to her Ma Jackie, and she finally had to bid Gloria and Preston Street farewell. Coming back home also allowed Skeeter to be around Patrick more, who, by that point, was a teenager. Despite Jackie's fervent protests, she acquiesced to Skeeter's wishes and introduced the mother to her son as his cousin from Baltimore.

Jackie was determined to leave on her own terms and fought the disease like a true prizefighter. Every time Skeeter brought Jackie in for a doctor's visit, the front desk team could barely conceal their shocked faces. Ma Jackie would be wheeled in like a conquering empress, wearing her forest-green cape with the fox trim and a pair of glasses in vintage Gloria Vanderbilt frames. Jackie held on long enough to see her baby Patrick graduate from college and marry his college sweetheart, a pretty girl with a sweet spirit named Indigo.

About a year after Ma Jackie passed, the family learned that there would be a new addition. The arrival of baby David Patrick Jeter officially made Skeeter a grandmother.

"He's so small, Peanut. He has all this hair. He has very wise eyes. I just don't know what to do," Skeeter fretted on the call with Sheri shortly after David was born.

"Just be there for him. Be the help that you've always been to everyone else. Give him everything you can muster." Sheri already knew that this little boy was a special one, and he was going to get all of the love in the world with Skeeter as his grandmother. Much like with her cousin, the time in Baltimore had awakened something in Skeeter. She returned whole with no apologies. Skeeter was her own person, and if anyone had any issue, they were free to get the hell on.

Sheri traced her finger along the stained-glass panel of the cabinet. Three joyful smiles peeked over two little black baby angel figurines. Gloria had finally pulled herself out of the fog that hung over her after Jimmy Budd's death and decided to foster, then eventually adopt, a pair of twin siblings.

Gloria had confided in her cousin: "I'm seeing sides to myself that I didn't even know were there, Sheri. I'm genuinely happy. It's tough, and it takes you out of your comfort zone. I feel like I'm being forced to rise to the occasion every day, but I don't think I've ever truly been loved like the way I'm being loved now."

The picture in Sheri's cabinet was from the twins' lower-school graduation ceremony. Joy looked beautiful in her white gown while Jamar stood handsome in his three-piece suit. The twins were just about a hair shorter than their mother as all three beamed proudly in the photograph. Looking fashionable as always in a glorious peach straw hat and a cream suit, Gloria stood in the middle holding up both of the graduates' certificates of completion with a triumphant smile on her face.

Every summer, Gloria and the twins made a pilgrimage down to North Carolina for about two weeks to visit Carowinds and spend time with family. Gloria and Sheri would sit under the stars laughing the evenings away while they taught the twins how to play Spades. Every visit back home ended with a trip to Spruce Junction and up Jeter Hill, where Gloria and the twins spent time with Juniper. Joy and Jamar placed pebbles atop their grandmother's small headstone, while Gloria always left a handmade lei made of dogwood blossoms connected together by thin, gold wiring and twine.

Gloria confided to Sheri that the yearly visits to see family might become more infrequent now that the twins were getting older and looking to start work. She promised to keep up the tradition for as long as possible, but she couldn't make any guarantees. Sheri figured that was life for everyone now. Tomorrow wasn't guaranteed for anyone, so the key was to love hard and mean it right then, at that moment.

In a silver picture frame on the shelf below the twins' graduation picture was a photo of two square-jawed smiling faces. It was the same exact face on two different bodies, with a thirty-year age difference between them. Harold had gotten married about a year after Sheri left Baltimore. The couple were together long enough to have a little boy, then divorced about three years afterward. Harold and his ex-wife had joint custody of their son, Miles, with Harold keeping him during the school year while the boy stayed with his mother during the summer.

"Sheri, this guy is always doing something with his hands! You've gotta see him. He's always either building something or taking something apart only to turn around and put the thing right back together. I can barely keep up. Always running around here like that lil' Tasmanian cartoon thing." Young Miles appeared to have his father in total awe.

As Miles approached his teenage years, he began to gravitate toward engineering as a possible career path. Harold enrolled his son in different educational workshops and camps, with the approval of Miles's mother. The young man was already receiving awards and commendations for his work. Harold told Sheri that Miles planned to apply for an engineering program that would bring him to the North Carolina A&T campus for part of the summer. Although the two talked often during the week, it had been a good while since Harold had been down to North Carolina to see Sheri and the family, so he figured that would be the perfect time for a visit.

"Miles is trying to decide between Morgan and A&T for school," Harold had confided to Sheri. "If he chooses A&T, I've already decided that I'm moving down there."

"You're gonna be on campus with him like that, Harold?" Sheri asked incredulously. She didn't take him for the clingy parent type.

"No." He laughed, then quiet set in over the phone line. "Greenville. Even if Miles decides that Morgan is the better school for him, I'm still moving down. Business is going well, and North Carolina has been a commerce hub for some time. Sounds like a perfect opportunity to me."

"Oh." Now it was Sheri's turn to get quiet. "Well, Harold Dorsey, I wasn't expecting that at all. If you're able to come down here on a more permanent basis, it would make me happy. Very much so."

"We don't have time for 'ifs' anymore, Sheri—I am."

Sheri continued studying the faces that beamed back at her from her cabinet of memories made of glass and wood. She looked at a picture of Kelli, Yolanda's oldest daughter, smiling in her smiley face-covered scrubs on the day she became an occupational therapist. A picture of Tater standing proud and accomplished while wearing his cap and gown after graduating from high school. In another photo, Yolanda's youngest girl, Iesha, was surrounded by dozens of pink balloons to celebrate the opening of her beauty salon.

Greeting cards were arranged on the bottom shelf of the cabinet. Sheri and Ms. Lou continued to check in on each other and exchange cards during the holidays. Every year, Sheri sent a donation up to A Better Way. It definitely wasn't as much as they got from the people who wore the plain-looking, expensive clothes. More so, it was a token of appreciation for all that the organization had done for Sheri while she was fighting to keep her head above water.

The rain had started coming down stronger now, pelting Sheri's picture window. Lady yelped and jumped on the loveseat.

"Lady, we're tough old broads. You know that. What's a little rain to us?" Sheri playfully furrowed her brows at her concerned pooch.

She decided to turn on the TV to see what the weather people were talking about. After talking with the reporter, Sheri was looking forward to going into RightMart just to be distracted. Sheri knew she probably needed to talk with someone, a professional, about all she had been through. Outside of the occasional mention in conversations with Yolanda, Sheri had taken all of the madness that had taken place with the CEC and Sloane-Douglas and buried it deep down within her. Although she continued to fight and advocate for her children, the actual memory of being in the New Horizons Housing Program was locked away with the other traumas and bad memories.

Sheri thought long and hard about Alicia's question about whether or not she had ever talked with the children about what had happened to them. If there was one thing Sheri knew, it was that her children were extremely perceptive and quick on the draw. Once they moved back to North Carolina, rarely did any of them talk to their mother about the times when the lights would give them terrible headaches, the sudden irritability that seemed to overtake their little bodies or the struggles they had retaining the information they learned in school. Sheri suspected that they talked amongst themselves but were mindful to not do it around her.

"What you think about this storm, eh? Ya think it's really about to be something big, Ms. Lady?" Sheri whispered into her companion's ear while the pair watched Mother Nature powerfully twist and turn just outside the safety of the home's picture-covered walls.

The lights in the house flickered, which caused Lady to begin running in circles on the area rug in the living room. Sheri quickly slapped her thigh a few times, and the Pekingese jumped back into her lap. She gently scratched the fur on the back of Lady's neck as the two watched the rain come pouring down.

CHAPTER 33

Out of Sheri's three children, Peach had the highest levels of lead in her system. Peach seemed to have been born with an easygoing spirit, and Sheri prayed that the short fuses and irritation was a passing phase. In her heart of hearts, Sheri knew her daughter would be in for a lifetime of highs and lows that she wouldn't be able to make sense of. Sheri remembered the story Yolanda told of how her daughter seemed to turn into another person when she got angry, and how Yolanda couldn't believe that this was the child she had carried for nine full months.

Yolanda moved the Parent Crew meetings from Thursdays to Saturdays to accommodate Sheri, who would make the drive up from Greenville on Friday evenings, then turn around to make the return trip home on Sunday afternoons to make sure she'd be ready for work on Mondays. Eunice was gracious enough to watch the children when Sheri made the weekend treks up to Baltimore. This arrangement was in place for a little over two years, but ended once Peach's behavior started becoming more and more erratic.

"She's Dr. Jekyll and Mr. Hyde!" Titi would whisper in amazement to her daughter. "Sheri, what happened to her? What did you do to her?"

Titi and Peach had formed an immediate attachment when Peach was born. Even after Champ and Popsee had long stopped asking when they were going to go back to be with Mom-Mom, Peach still mentioned her grandmother almost daily when the family lived in Baltimore. As Peach got older, it got to the point where she was really only balanced and peaceful around her grandmother and no one else.

Peach was never outright nasty or rude, but she exploded when things triggered her, and Sheri realized the key was to find out what those triggers were. Like her brothers before her, she developed an aversion to bright, fluorescent lights. She also didn't like loud, sudden noises. Minor annoyances that others would possibly shrug off or roll their eyes at infuriated Peach.

When the settlement money came in, Sheri got to work allocating the money where the biggest needs were: weekend tutors for all three children and arrangements for Peach to see a behavioral specialist in Raleigh who ended up prescribing medicine that kept her contained but made her extremely sad and lethargic. Needless to say, the behavior swings impacted Peach significantly in the classroom, and school staff were quick to move the girl into an isolated study class.

Sheri tried her best to explain that her daughter had developmental complications brought on by being exposed to high levels of lead at such a young age. Sheri advocated for her child with a fury that always seemed to catch people off guard. She knew the truth, and she also understood that when people saw a black girl with difficulties, they wasted no time dismissing and pathologizing her.

Once she reached her teenage years, Peach's short fuse nearly caused a permanent rift between her and her brother. Champ had little patience for his sister's ups and downs, and he didn't appreciate the way Peach would talk to their mother. Sheri had to frequently remind her son that he wasn't Peach's daddy.

"I don't like the way she's always carrying on like that!" Champ would say, visibly irritated. "She needs to get it together!"

When Peach graduated from high school, Sheri breathed a sigh of relief and thanked God, Jesus and anyone else who had kept an eye on her daughter over the years. However, by that point, Peach had met up with a young man named Brandon, who'd moved up from Kinston. Brandon had a quick wit, silver tongue and a violent heart. Sheri rolled her eyes to the high heavens when she eventually learned of Brandon's nickname amongst his friends: Shot, short for Kill Shot. On one occasion, word got out that Peach had been hurt, and it was only by the grace of God that Popsee and his crew of friends missed Shot by a hairsbreadth.

On a foggy night, Shot and Peach stopped at a minimart along the highway headed back to Greenville. Peach had been dealing with nausea for about four weeks and her cycle was late. She knew she was probably pregnant, but didn't feel like having that conversation with Brandon. She didn't even know if she was going to keep it. Shot ran into the store and asked over his shoulder if Peach wanted anything. Peach said no as she reclined in the black Lincoln Navigator.

Peach had started meeting with a new counselor that Sheri arranged for her. The lady, Dr. Paul, was friendly enough and pretty no-nonsense. Dr. Paul and Peach had long conversations about what went through Peach's mind when she would black out in rage. Peach confided that when she got upset, it was an out-of-body experience. It was as if the real Peach stepped away as the other Peach came in and stalked around in anger.

The loud explosion of a gun blast snapped Peach out of her thoughts, then Shot came running back into the truck with an unhinged look in his eyes.

"Who you kill!" Peach screamed at her boyfriend.

"Girl, he ain't dead. I don't think he's dead, anyway." Shot shrugged as he drove off.

◆ ◆ ◆

It was quiet in the green Ford Explorer as Champ took the highway exit for the road that led to the Millbrook Women's Prison. Usually, Sheri made the trips to see Peach twice a month and talked with her daughter about once a week on the telephone. Champ made visits when he could, and Popsee tried his best to see his sister every couple of weeks. That day would make the first time in over two years that all three would visit Peach at the same time.

As with so many other things throughout the years, Yolanda would serve as a guide for her friend. When Peach was sent away, Sheri completely shut down and stayed in bed for five days. Yolanda couldn't stand to see her sister unravel, so early one Friday morning, Yolanda got into her minivan and headed to Greenville. She knew what Sheri was going through. It was the same thing she faced after Man got sentenced. A feeling of mourning what could have been and wondering what you had done to cause it all.

Although it was the hardest thing in the world to see her baby girl behind those bars, Sheri knew that there was a light at the end of tunnel. Peach would be getting out in less than a year and Sheri was excited for the possibilities. A chance for Peach to begin again, better her life and start a family of her own.

Popsee took a few last sips of his iced coffee as he scrolled through his phone in the backseat. Champ, eyes glued to the road, appeared to be lost in thought. Sheri rubbed her wrists as she gazed at the dazzling blue skies. Thankfully, Hurricane Donovan had taken a quick detour, and their part of the state managed to avoid any significant damage.

The blue-and-grey sign for Millbrook welcomed the Calloways as Champ pulled into the parking lot. The family quietly got out of the vehicle and shook themselves awake. Popsee let out a grunt as he walked around to where his mother and brother stood. All three slowly made their way to the visitor's entrance of the prison. After going through the processing center, Sheri, Champ and Popsee sat at a heavy-duty plastic table in the brightly lit visitation room to wait for their beloved Peach.

After a few minutes, a line of inmates walked up to the visitation room's doorway. A gruff officer with scraggly brown hair loudly called out each inmate's number before they were allowed to walk into the room.

"Four-nine-one-seven-eight CALLOWAY!" the officer yelled.

Maya Peach Calloway walked through the doorway to greet her mother and brothers. Everyone got up to quickly grip Peach's hands and blow her kisses, since there was a no-touching rule for visitors.

Silence sat with the family for about a minute, even though Peach had been inside four years. The experience was still very surreal for everyone—her brothers especially. Sheri remembered that they only had so much time. She asked Peach how things were coming along and whether Peach had thought more about what they had discussed the last time Sheri visited.

Peach stretched her long legs under the table. Sheri looked at her daughter and saw the most beautiful woman she had ever had a chance to see. As a little girl, Peach had Kenneth's mother's face and demeanor. As Peach got older, sometimes Sheri saw Titi.

Other times, she saw herself, but even still, Peach had a look that was all her own. Her cinnamon-brown skin radiated. Usually, Peach wore her thick hair in a bun at the top of her head. This time, though, her hair was cut in layers and swooped to the side.

The kicker for Sheri was, somehow, her daughter ended up coming in second in the sibling height race. For years, Peach and Popsee had kept up with each other gain-for-gain, but one day baby sister took the lead and didn't let it go. Although Sheri wrapped herself in the memories of their younger years, she always tried to remember and respect that her babies were grown now.

"I only have a few cosmetology credits left, and, once I wrap that up, my plan is to go straight to barbering school. I'm already learning about blade variations." Peach tucked her hair behind her ear.

"Barbering, huh? It's lucrative. Knowing how to do hair will always be a winning ticket," Sheri encouraged her daughter. "Ya know Cousin Tee still has her shop, I believe. You could help her out. You know she moved from Spruce a while back. I think they're up around Rocky Mount now."

"So you're about to be out here lining the people up? I'll let you get some customers under your belt first." Popsee gave his sister a mock inquisitorial glance.

"Better hope I have some availability. Looks like you could use a little three and a half to tighten up that line." Peach gave a coy smirk.

"Peach, don't play with me today." Popsee waved off his sister and her smart-ass ways. "My stuff still fresh."

Sheri realized she was on the clock, and it was obvious that they were all past the point of small talk. After fidgeting with her bracelets a little more, Sheri had a question. "What do you all remember about our time living in Baltimore?"

"Everything," Popsee chimed in without missing a beat.

"Everything like what, Keyon?" Sheri wanted to hear what her middle child had to say.

Popsee casually ran down memories of going to a center to get tested and having to talk to a doctor. He remembered the teacher who always seemed to single him out. Popsee recounted all of the friends they made at the church meetings with Ms. Yolanda. And Jimmy Budd.

Champ and Peach both shifted in their seats at the mention of their cousin's dearly departed boyfriend. It had been nearly twenty-two years since his passing, and from all appearances, the memory was still very much present. Although she suspected she already knew the answer, Sheri threw a question out to the table: "Were any of you aware of how Jimmy Budd died?"

"He was killed," Champ responded soberly. "We knew that back then."

Sheri could only shake her head at her naivety. All this time, she thought she had done a good enough job of protecting them from the truth.

When it was Champ's turn, he reminisced on memories about afterschool and summer camp and the time when everyone went skating at the rink. He also remembered when the parents would get together to talk in the church with Ms. Yo.

Sheri rubbed her arm and told her children about the interview she'd done a week ago. She told them there was a renewed interest in the Parent Crew and the lawsuit because of what was happening in Flint, Michigan.

The mention of Flint caused all three children to nod in recognition

"I've been following that on the news." Champ shook his head in disgust. "No clean water. Toxic pipes. And they expect for people to live like everything is normal."

"Because, at the end of the day, the people with the means to fix the problem straight up don't give a damn." Popsee folded his arms in his seat.

"So you and Ms. Yolanda and all of them were taking on some big names back in Baltimore, hug? Peach scratched her chin as she processed the information.

"Yup," Sheri said proudly.

Sheri talked about all the research she used to do at the library. She talked about how, among other things, lead exposure greatly impedes development. Sheri told Peach that all of those days when she was irritated beyond words and couldn't understand why was because of the months when the family lived in the house on Chase Street.

The emotions around the table weren't as high as Sheri had braced herself for. She was expecting tears, disappointed faces and narrowed eyes directed her way, which Sheri realized wasn't fair to her children at all. She had prepared for theatrics that never came. Sheri had come such a long way when it came to shaking off the mom guilt, but every so often, the thoughts did arise.

Sheri looked over at the clock, then quickly walked over to one of the guards to see if they still had time to get family pictures taken. Once she received the thumbs up, Sheri gathered her no-longer babies together and positioned them just like old times.

"Ma. We can pose now. We've got this." Popsee gently patted his overeager mother on the shoulder. The family took two pictures, one with the three siblings posing, Peach slightly out front with both brothers huddling around their little sis. The second was with all four Calloways staring at the camera with genuine, battle-tested smiles.

A guard shouted out the ten-minute warning, and everyone began wrapping up their conversations. Peach mentioned that Skeeter had mailed her a book of affirmations and a book about the history of gospel music that was currently getting her through the quiet times. Popsee told the table he would email out pictures from Kayla's dance recital from a few weeks back. Right when it looked as if Champ was geCing ready to say something, a loud timer sounded, and immediately, all of the inmates stood. Peach mouthed 'I love you' to her people and blew them air kisses as the guards came around to line everyone up. She ran her fingers through her hair one last time, then filed out of the meeting room.

Silence filled the SUV while everyone mulled over their own thoughts. Sheri lightly ran her fingers through her twist out which was now starting to get more silver strands amongst the reddish-brown tresses. She felt as if a weight had been lifted off of her. She understood that fear had been at the root of why it had taken so long for her to have a real sit-down about all that had taken place so long ago.

was now starting to get more silver stands amongst the sandy brown tresses. She felt as if a weight had been lifted off her. She understood that fear had been the root of why it had taken so long for her to have a real sit-down about all that had taken place so long ago.

"I bought a ring," Champ said softly to his mother, his eyes still glued to the highway.

"For Melinda?" Sheri put her hand over her heart. Just those few words alone were enough for the tears to start. "Who'd you go ring shopping with?"

"The fancy queen herself, Unique." Champ gave an exasperated eye-roll. "She had me running all around Raleigh and Durham going to all of those high-end little boutique jewelry stores. I bought a sapphire ring since Mel's favorite color is blue. I think I got it right."

Sheri smiled. Her son had definitely picked the perfect woman for the job. Unique was just like her mother Eunice; they both had an eye for the good, quality stuff. Sheri always knew the day was going to come. The thought of her little boy, her champion, being someone's husband and eventually someone's father made her heart flutter. Her three musketeers were adults now. Nothing can really ever prepare a parent for that moment.

"Maya's getting out soon, so I'll be able to have both of my siblings in the wedding," Champ said. "I'm going to invite Ms. Yolanda, Tater and 'em. I want to invite Mr. Harold, too."

Sheri gently rubbed her arm and stared out the window. "We talked the other day. He might be moving down here in a little bit. His son is thinking about going to A&T for school."

"Mr. Harold is tryin' to move down here? Permanently!" Popsee's mouth was wide open.

"Well, of course you know I'm walking you down the aisle." Champ nodded as if the matter had already been decided.

"Nah, playboy." Popsee leaned forward between the two front seats to make sure his point was clearly heard. "How do you get to be the one to walk her down the aisle? We're only a year apart, last time I checked. We're BOTH walking her down the aisle."

"When you get to be my age, marriage really isn't the end-all and be-all. I didn't think y'all were going to get like this. I said he might. Harold's got a cheering section in this car?" Sheri looked at her sons in amused shock.

"WHEN A MAN LOVES A WOMAN!" Popsee yelled from the backseat while continuing to scroll through his phone.

"Oh good grief." Sheri shook her head with a laugh. Her boys were still a trip after all these years.

The highway exit for Spruce Junction was coming up about a mile ahead. Champ glanced over at his mother to see if she wanted to make a quick pitstop, but Sheri quickly shook her head no. Then, after thinking it over, she lightly touched her son on his wrist. He flipped on his indicator to change lanes and turn off the highway.

Wrens sang songs in the distance as Champ snaked his truck through the byways of Spruce Junction. After driving through a thickly wooded area, which was become a rare sight since developers had come around to carve everything up, the SUV came to a clearing. Jeter Hill loomed in the distance. Sheri gripped her armrest as she looked out over some of the lushest and most fertile land in all of Eastern Carolina. The memories seized her and seemed to step right into the vehicle, same as a human passenger. As Champ switched over to four-wheel drive, the three Calloways came around the back side of Jeter Hill. Around front was where the main house stood, along with the infamous woodshed and a smaller wood-framed home that Uncle Syl and Cousin Fox built together for Fox's growing family.

Champ shut off the engine, and everyone gingerly stepped out onto the loamy ground. "I should have brought something," Sheri said to no one in particular as she walked further up the hill.

Although it was a fairly warm day, Sheri shuddered and rubbed her arms as she stopped at her intended destination. "Hey Titi, girl. We were just passing through. Wanted to say hey and wish you a good day, is all." Sheri dropped her arms to her sides as Champ and Popsee brought up the rear. Popsee slipped around his mother to kneel down and kiss Mom-Mom's headstone.

It wasn't until her mother passed that Sheri learned that Titi had had a minor heart attack while the family was still living in Baltimore. A part of Sheri always knew her mother wasn't going to be one of those octogenarian types. Bet had a sudden death, and her beloved daughter had followed suit. Titi's passing had been the proverbial straw that broke the back of whatever had held Peach's temperament at a relatively level place. It was as if losing her grandmother had given Peach the license to truly run wild.

"We saw your favorite girl today, Miss Peach Cheeks. She's talking about becoming a barber. Can you believe that? Gonna be out here cutting hair. I've got your fellas here with me. All big and tall. Just grown men, Titi. Ain't it something?" Sheri shook her head in amazement.

Everyone gave their love and said their goodbyes to the headstones of their departed loved ones resting on the hill. Popsee and Champ helped their mother get her footing as they made their way back to the SUV. Sheri felt hands on both of her shoulders as she was getting ready to get inside. She turned around to come face to neck with her eldest baby. Champ smiled at his mother as he lightly rubbed his forehead against hers, which made her giggle. Then he straightened up and looked his mother square in the eyes.

"Every day, I wake up grateful to be Sheri Calloway's son. I need you to know that. Thank you for everything. I love you."

Sheri nodded her head and patted her son on his shoulder while fighting hard to keep the tears contained. She kissed her two fingers and lovingly placed them on her son's right cheek. Champ helped his mother into the vehicle, and together, they took the winding, dusty trail back down Jeter's Hill.

Evening summer sunshine spilled onto the roads that led the three back home.

ACKNOWLEDGMENTS

On Saturdays, when I was a little girl, my mother and I would make the trek from our apartment on Pennsylvania and Preston to the main branch of the Enoch Pratt Free Library on Cathedral Street. In the children's section of the branch, there was a life-sized stuffed toy lion. I would pick out my books, sit cross-legged between the lion's paws and drift off to lands beyond space and time.

I will forever treasure those visits to the library with my mother. Books provided me with the keys to the universe and for that I am forever grateful.

Sincere love and thanks to the Joneses, the Fergusons, the Heath-Murrills, the Stanleys, the Calhouns, the Fosters, the Browns, the Collicks, the Stewarts, the Anthonys, the Harrisons/Burgesses, the Siler/Marriott/Thompson families and the Jones/Miller/Robinson families.

Big love to my North Carolina family that I've connected with while writing this novel.

Thank you to the angels along the way: the teachers and staff of the Greenspring Head Start center where my love for learning began, Dr. Matthews and the Park West staff, Dr. Zolicoffer, Maime Clark (forever), Mingo Watkins, Louise Simmons (rest in love), Wanda Coleman, Greg Holly, Barbara Erwin (rest in love), Vernon Rey, Victoria Stevenson, Diana Perpich, Kathryn Wickham, Theresa McNeil, the staff of the Reisterstown Road Branch of the Enoch Pratt Free Library – deepest appreciation to Ms. Gloria, Ms. Charlotte and Vincent Steadman, Jackie Fields, Carolina Rojas-Barr (rest in love), Teresa McCain, Dr. Earline Armstrong, the UMCP Black Explosion for giving me my first byline – Rah, Halima, Jasmine and Audre, Toby Jenkins-Henry, the University of Memphis Public Administration staff and alum – special thanks to Dr. Dorothy Norris-Terrill, Dr. Joy Clay, Dr. Charles Menifield, Dr. Laura Harris and the class of 2007.

Thank you to my DCPS students and colleagues – special thanks to Joyi Better-Rice, Rachelle Etienne-Robinson, Kristin Matthews, Shanita Burney, Brysant Carter, Jen Nelson, Sam Moore, Cynthia Lacey, Jocelyn Isom, Malika Harvey and everyone at C.W. Harris.

Big love and special thank you to the Women of Color Breast Cancer Support Project family! Isis Pickens and family, Carolyn Tapp and family, Lynn Fowler, Florence Britton (rest in love) and Debra Potter.

Sincere thanks to the youth of Covenant House – Los Angeles as well as Angela Citizen and the staff at the Inglewood Public Library.

Love and thanks to the brilliant writers and creatives of the Anansi Project. Your bravery set me on this journey.

Big love and thank you to my folks Geena Lee, Keith King (the first person I told about the book back in 2014), Clifton Lewis and Leneé Voss!

Thank you, thank you, thank you to my editors, Isis Pickens and Calee Allen, who saw a gem and polished it to a shine.

Books have been my comfort for as long as I can remember. Thank you to the writers who have inspired me: Mildred D. Taylor, Roald Dahl, Beverly Cleary, Alice Walker, Bernice McFadden, Dahlma Llanos-Figueroa, Bebe Moore Campbell, Terry McMillan, Connie Briscoe, Laura Lippman, John Berendt, E. Lynn Harris, Donald Goines, Nikki Giovanni, Eric Jerome Dickey, J. California Cooper, Amy Tan, Elie Wiesel, Randall Kenan, Angela Nissel, Alex Haley, James Baldwin, Isabel Wilkerson and Ta-Nehisi Coates.

Finally, love always to my ancestral literary godmothers – Ida B. Wells, Octavia Butler, Audre Lorde, Zora Neale Hurston, Ntozake Shange, Gwendolyn Brooks, Toni Morrison and Beah Richards.

-Jana